# Seven Sixes Are Forty-Three

**ALSO BY KIRAN NAGARKAR**

RAVAN & EDDIE

THE EXTRAS

REST IN PEACE

CUCKOLD

GOD'S LITTLE SOLDIER

BEDTIME STORY AND BLACK TULIP

# Seven Sixes Are Forty-Three

**Kiran Nagarkar**

Translated from the Marathi
by Shubha Slee

HARPERPERENNIAL
*An Imprint of* HarperCollins *Publishers*

HARPERPERENNIAL

First published in English in India by Harper Perennial 2017
An imprint of HarperCollins *Publishers*
4th Floor, Tower A, Building No. 10, DLF Cyber City,
DLF Phase II, Gurugram, Haryana – 122002
www.harpercollins.co.in

First published in Marathi as *Saat Sakkam Trechalis* by Mauj Prakashan, 1974

First published in English by University of Queensland Press, St Lucia, Queensland, 1980

This edition published in India by Harper Perennial 2024

2 4 6 8 10 9 7 5 3 1



P-ISBN: 978-93-5699-895-7
E-ISBN: 978-93-5264-427-8



Typeset in 12/15.2 Adobe Garamond
Saanvi Graphics Noida

Printed and bound at
Thomson Press (India) Ltd

MIX
Paper from responsible sources
FSC® C010615
FSC www.fsc.org

This book is produced from independently certified FSC® paper to ensure responsible forest management.

He came home drunk again. Like every other day. Pratibha shut the door quickly after him. Whatever happened, however angry, terrified and hopeless she felt, she would always shut the neighbours out of it all. The shame of it must be contained within these four walls, always.

She cowered in a corner of the room while he swayed unsteadily in the centre, lurching out and slamming into her whenever he could make contact. At first it had been his mother. A stinging slap across her face. Pratibha had liked that. Then it was Pratibha's turn. He'd hit her whenever he flew into a rage, with whatever came to hand, wherever he could lay his blows. Aai wasn't a patch on Pratibha. Pratibha was plump, as if she hadn't lost her puppy fat. He felt great working on a body like that. Really great. Not stopping to check whether she had the time or the inclination. Never restraining his open-handedness. Mounting her pulpy body after the thrashing would really thrill him. Spasm on spasm of dripping satisfaction. She, limply reluctant and tired, and he, worn out with all that effort. He felt like a king. Like the lord of the whole world. He could even feel pity. His hands would itch, his ineffectual lower lip tremble, and his eyes turn a glazed red. He had had a really hard day.

Her voice came to him from her corner of the room, squeaky and high-pitched. 'You hit me once more and I'll set fire to myself. I'm fed up. I've had enough. I don't want to live any more. You can look after Anil and Jyotsna. I don't care what you do. I just don't care any more.' And so on.

He burst out laughing. A hideous, besotted laugh. 'Why, you whore! Are you trying to threaten me?' The words dribbled out of his mouth like spittle. 'So who's stopping you, you stupid bitch? Go on and do it if you have the fucking guts. What are you waiting for?' he sneered.

He stared vaguely at her. She poured a bottle of kerosene over herself, muttering, 'I'll teach you a lesson, just wait, you'll be sorry.'

She shuddered as the cold kerosene seeped through the folds of cloth and touched her skin. She lit a match and held it to a corner of her sari. Yellow flames sprang up. Some red, some orange, blue at the edges.

Jesus, what fucking guts! He squeezed his eyes into narrow slits and looked. She had grown small. 'Pratibha, you've become teeny-weeny! How did that happen?' Then he opened his eyes wide. 'And now little Pratibha is big again. And now she's teeny. And now she's big. Teeny-big. Teeny-big.'

She had begun to scream. At the top of her voice. Scream and run from wall to wall. Round the room. And the flames went round and round too, like a whirlwind. She tried to embrace him. Then he moved. Ran. 'Get off me, you bitch.

Don't come near me. You said you didn't care, right? I'm fed up. I've had enough. That's what you said. Well don't touch me now. Keep your bloody flames to yourself. Damn it, I don't want to bloody die.'

Someone started to bang on the door. A lot of people were banging and crashing at the door. And her screams were getting louder too. Shit, she might really die, the stupid cunt. He opened the door.

~

Before she lost consciousness. Before they took her to the hospital. Before the police arrived. She hung on to the doctor's arm with all her strength. And asked him, again and again. Over and over. The same questions. 'I want to live, Doctor. I want to live. You will save me, won't you? They need me – my children. And my husband. He needs me too. You don't know, do you, that he'd lost his mind and I made him all right again? He said so himself. I'm going to live, aren't I? I'm not going to die? I don't want to die. Never, ever. Why do you keep nodding your head? Can't you tell me I'm going to live? I'm going to live – all the time – mornings, evenings, when Anil comes home from school, when Jyotsna wets her bed, I will be here. Always.'

I was sent to bring his mother home. She had been staying with her brother for the past few days. She always divined her son's angry fits coming on and made for her brother's house. Leaving her poor husband with her son and his wife.

I was out of breath as I climbed the six flights of stairs to give the woman the message. She was a little hard of hearing.

'Run away?'

I repeated the message slowly and solemnly. In case she might faint at the sudden bad news.

'Who do you think I am, your girlfriend? Stop whispering and mumbling. I can't hear you.'

'She burnt herself.'

'Run away? Was nobody at home? What did she take with her?'

The old hag was impossible.

'Not run away, burnt herself,' I yelled into her ear. 'Poured kerosene over herself.'

'Good lord! And if the house had caught fire?'

I didn't know the answer to that, so I kept quiet.

'Why couldn't she have burnt her own house? She had to choose ours. And only last week I gave her one of my old saris, torn only in a couple of places, too.'

There was something wrong here. The old hag wasn't talking about Pratibha at all. But who could stop her now? She was off to a good start and she sailed full speed ahead.

'Pestered me for months, she did. Ah well, even the poor need clothes, I said to myself, don't they? But there is no gratitude in this world. You can't expect it from these people. You go back and tell Pratibha to sack her. Never did much work anyway. I was the one who mopped the floors, did the cooking. They might as well let me be the servant. I might earn some money, eh?'

My head started to reel.

'What are you shaking your head for, you dolt? The way they treat me – worse than any servant.'

And then, as she paused for breath, I said quickly, 'Not Radha. *Pratibha*.'

'Pratibha? Don't you tell me anything about that one. My Ajit was such a sweet boy until she arrived. He was even scared of mice when he was a child. Still is. Then she came. And turned his head, told him nasty stories about me. That old witch will die soon, she told him, don't pay her any attention. Old witch, am I? I'll outlive her, see if I don't.'

'Aai. Pratibha burnt herself. Set fire to her sari. Do you understand? She poured kerosene over her head and lit a match.' Once again I repeated, slowly and clearly.

That silenced her. But not for long. Emotions flitted across her lined face. Was she going to cry? But she changed her mind.

'So be it. Tormenting an old woman, and what did she get out of it? It's like a judgement from heaven. God is always fair, that's what I say. You can't get away with it, not forever. It comes to all of us.'

'Are you coming home?'

'Me? What for? I couldn't bear to look at her. I can't stand that sort of thing. I dropped some hot oil on my hand once. Raised a big blister, it did. And then it burst and water ran out of it, for two whole days. Her body will be one big blister now. It will swell and burst. I don't want to see that. What does she look like? Has her skin turned black? I can't come.'

'Appa has asked you to come. They are all waiting for you.'

'I'm not coming. Leave me alone, you've given me a headache. Go away.'

She didn't come. I had to return alone.

Three days later Pratibha died. Her husband wept. Real tears. People were watching him. That bitch is really dead. Before she went into a coma, she made a statement that she had tried to commit suicide, because of an incurable illness.

I will never die again. I'm going to live, always. She'd said that.

And then died. That's patent nonsense. It's not right. It's just not done. Damn it, it won't do. I won't have it.

She was short. And round. Layer upon layer of fat. A fat, round body and short, fat fingers. I had only to think of her and I was done for. Not done for in a poignant way. Simply done for. I had to do it. That's all. I was as determined as she was fat. If I ever asked myself why, there was always the ready retort, why not? I don't have conversations like that with myself any more. I just make up my mind to do a thing and go hell-bent after it.

'Sugar, my pretty sugar, every pound that makes you round, I idolize,' I sang as I entered the arena. But to venture is not necessarily to win. Certainly not against her.

She demurred and I grew devious. That's the way it always was. She was in no hurry. I might stumble and lose my way, but I would finally get there. She was sure of that. So she held off, letting me muddle along without interference. How was she to know that I was panting to get on and get it over with?

Finally I took her butter-soft hand in my two hard, bony ones and fondled it. Stared at it soulfully. How fat. How soft. I raised it to my lips and kissed it. Made love to it with my lips. Softly, tenderly. She began to sigh. Long, breathless sighs. How much longer are you going to draw this one out, you damned woman? I forced my attention back to her short fat fingers. Her nails were bitten to the quick.

'You have beautiful hands.' I had to say it in English. Couldn't bear to say it in Marathi. After all, it was my mother tongue. I opened and closed her hand. 'Really exquisite fingers. So delicate. Positively artistic,' I lied. Her breathing became heavier.

'Really?' She sighed. She didn't believe me, of course. Neither did I. I looked deep into her eyes and nodded my head. She measured my lower lip with one short finger and breathed, 'No one has ever said that to me before.'

That super wide body. That unending expanse. Those limitless thighs. I could have fitted into them several times over, with room to spare. I. Long, thin lines and angles, I had to bend over to talk to her. This business is always a struggle at the best of times. Clumsy. Bits and pieces of bodies intertwined and indistinguishable. But this one was going to be impossible. This disparity of length and breadth. I couldn't cope with it. I knew I couldn't.

Then she took to visiting me at home. Occasionally. For days I would not hear from her. For months, even. Then one day she'd be at my doorstep. Smiling. 'How are you?' If I'd had a haircut recently, she would say, 'You've become thinner,' and if my hair had grown, 'My, you have put on weight, haven't you?'

~

The first slap on your bottom as you come into the world tells you that your days of mollycoddling are over. The sooner you understand that, the better you are prepared for the pain and the unhappiness. The world doesn't mind your indulging yourself. You are welcome to starve yourself to death if you want to. There is just one life for us. This one. BEST buses don't have a third floor. Shanta, who lives next door, ignores me and goes and sleeps with Nirad who lives at Mahim. Vilas's parachute failed to open. That crazy Sanjay talks too much. Talks and talks, even about things best forgotten. It's an unreliable world. Full of faults. Not worth living in for human beings. True. But we don't run this world. The Big Boss around here is someone else. We take what is given to us and give what is taken away. If you keep up the illusion of words, you don't feel the pain so much. Whether we accept it or reject it, this is the only world we have. When Shah gave money to Chintya, he did it without a word. When pressed, he said, 'Chintya may be a liar, but he has to eat.' Shah put his finger on the Big Boss's pulse when he said that. The Big Boss remains inscrutable except for this pulse. And that's all there is to him, I'm sure. But that's his problem. And he's always looked after his problems well. It's we who don't know what to do with ours.

Believers, non-believers, we all require an audience. The believer has someone up there who will listen to him. The non-believer flings a passionate glance at the sky and says, 'I'm a stoic.' But for a human being, stoicism is only an aspiration. He struggles hard to achieve it. He'll never succeed. The only true stoic is the Big Boss. And he doesn't know what stoicism is. A stoic is a mindless idiot. Shall I eat? Yes. Shall I not eat? Yes. Do you exist? Yes. Do you not exist? Yes. Nod, nod. And that's not quite right, either. He doesn't have a head to nod with. And even if he did, he isn't interested. He doesn't give a damn.

~

Why spurn Opportunity when she comes knocking at your door? I've never done it. Never could. So she always had me. She had a lover in Bombay, for whom she brought along her aching and lonely-for-you night and her folds of fat. Poor chap. Wife, kids, and mistress. You cannot fit a triangle into a square. But he managed somehow. He had to.

She called herself an artist, and artists survive on a special diet. I am not an artist, so I don't know what it means. When she finished with me, she went to him. She took great care not to hurt me. She never spoke to me about him.

We met in a restaurant once. I had my nose in my plate. I hadn't eaten for two days. Out of the corner of my eye I saw a sari and was instantly distracted. I can't help looking at a woman, regardless of her age, whether she's seven or seventy. She smiled. The man with her began talking to the man at my table. I looked up at the photograph of the late owner of the restaurant hanging on the wall and sent him a silent message of sympathy. Why don't we leave the dead in peace? We frame their photographs, garland them, burn incense for them. May they leave your soul in peace, fat man, I sent another silent message. And went back to my meal. It was amusing, really. If she introduces him to me, shall I greet him as my mate? My mate who shares this woman with me? I prayed she would not introduce me to him. Him to me. Then me to the man across from me. And so on. Right up to the man in the photograph. 'This is Kushank,' she said. I smiled a sweet smile and put my nose back where it belonged – in my plate. He was a gentleman, he did not introduce me to anyone else. Then I forgot all about them and did not say goodbye when I left. She has never forgiven me for that. She had relied on my sensitivity, and I had let her down. Hopeless bastard that I was.

~

There were times when I wasn't in the mood. After a long, sleepless night, my body ached, my mouth felt stale, and she would turn up. First thing in the morning. Not at the crack of dawn. But at nine or ten. Early enough. And then what had to happen would happen. If I shilly-shallied, she would grip my hand firmly. She cooed my name with love, breathed shallow sighs. To the accompaniment of this mood music, she'd take my hand on a conducted tour of her body.

License my roving hands, and let them go
Before, behind, between, above, below…

Her eyes being closed, there wasn't much use my looking piteously at her. I prayed for release. Cut it out, you bitch. Haven't you had enough? You've got to replay this scene with him very shortly, let me go. I would just watch, like an impartial observer from the United Nations. She would not let go. Who would, with a lamb ready for slaughter? 'Let's do it,' I'd say finally and plunge in. After all, who knew when the next fuck would come around.

I had never tasted such ashen lips before. They reminded me of my aunt. How she had shrunken in death. Laid out on the bier, amidst a profusion of white flowers. Her mouth hadn't quite shut, so they had filled the gap with a wad of cotton wool. Her family kissed that shrunken mouth goodbye. I tried, but could not. If my lips strayed, she would bring them back into line.

I suddenly thought of Rashid. Rashid and his beautiful girlfriend. The first time she asked him he was startled out of his lovemaking and sat up in bed abruptly, right in the middle of it.

'Rashid,' she whispered.

'Umm-m?' he half-answered and ignored the danger signals.

'Rashid,' she said again. Women like to whisper a lover's name, he thought, and ignored her again.

'What is sin?' she murmured softly.

He sat up at that, and mopped the beads of sweat on his forehead. His pulse was still racing. He cupped her beautiful face in his hands.

'Begum.' His voice was barely audible. Her beautiful eyes grew wide and even more beautiful with anxiety. 'Begum,' he said, deeply disturbed. 'Are you angry with me?'

'Of course not,' she answered, mystified.

'Then, my princess, for the love of God, don't ever do that to me again.'

'Do what, my lord?' Her eyes searched his for her mistake.

'That question, Begum, that deadly question, at a moment like this? You can't be so heartless!'

She did not understand. Why was he so upset? What did he mean? But she promised never to ask him again. Not at a moment like that. Rashid forgot the incident the next time around, but he doesn't forget things like that any more. And she, what can she do, poor thing? She is a slave to her own questions. So he shuts her mouth with his lips or his hands.

When I looked as if I was losing interest, she got furious. I learnt to play the scene at two levels. I thought my thoughts while my body did what was required of it. What is the word for a male whore? Gigolo? Aaroti once said, anyone who sleeps around indiscriminately is a whore.

'You were born lucky, weren't you?' said Jitendra as he removed the needle from my vein. 'They brought you straight to the emergency ward. If they hadn't, you'd have had it.' He unwrapped the adhesive tapes from my wrist and wrapped the long tubes round the saline bottle. Then he left, saying he would be back in the evening. Sometimes he did come back. In the evening, or late at night, or the day after.

Sometimes bringing food with him, sometimes not. Maybe he was busy working out a diagnosis for the honorary surgeon. Or maybe he had gone out of the hospital. He doesn't need permission to go out. There were people like that. They can go anywhere. Any time. There are two kinds of people in the world – the sick and the not-sick. The sick person lives in a world of his own. The not-sick have a collective world of their own too. I was very curious about that other world. I wanted to ask a thousand questions about it. When a nurse finished her duty in the ward and prepared to go out, I wanted to hold on to her tightly for five minutes and ask her a thousand questions. What is it like out there? Are there people? What do they do? Is there a sky? Just like the one I can see through that window? Blue? No difference? Do they call it 'blue' too? Do they eat? Speak? They don't sleep at night, do they? And don't ever forget? Always remember that they are alive? And breathing? In. Out. Never breathing the same breath again. Will they surround you when you go out? Hug you? Hey, you still alive? Won't they be surprised? But they must believe it as soon as they see you. They don't waste their time on useless speculation. What will you do with that sky? Out there? Blue. And the breeze? Do you walk on the street? On your feet? Anywhere you like? And nobody stops you? Are there trees? Tall, with green leaves? Some leaves that have turned yellow in the sun? Do you see the sun? I wanted to jump up and down in my bed. Throw my arms about. I wanted to hold that smooth dark hand in mine. Will you take me there? To see your sun?

I have been here three days. Whenever visitors come into the ward, I try to attract their attention. But you can't do that. They are a different breed. They had come in from the outside, and they can go out again. You must be polite to them. They might get angry if you ask them too many questions. I try to eavesdrop on their conversations. They speak a different language, and if I listen carefully I might pick up some words. When they come to see someone, I pretend to ignore them, my ears pricked up like a dog's. But they never say anything special. How are you today? No, we didn't bring any oranges, they're too expensive. Get well soon. The doctor says you are being deliberately slow recovering. Then, silence. Half an hour. Three quarters of an hour. Like visiting a grave. Can't really blame them. They come from another world, a world where people are alive as long as they live. Then they leave. So long. See you tomorrow. Or the day after.

In the ward we are not at all sympathetic towards one another. Everybody else in the ward is a damned nuisance. Getting sick, sometimes very sick. We have no time to waste on each other.

'What a dramatic entrance you made.' I stretched my lips in a smile suggesting modesty. He lingered by my bed. 'You came in the day before, didn't you?' His bed was across from mine. 'I liked your sense of timing. What an hour to arrive. Four a.m., when we had awakened but weren't yet awake. And there you were. What's your name?'

'Purandare,' I muttered, making room for him on my bed.

'Ajwani.' And then seeing my questioning face, he added, 'My name, that is. There is a rule against sitting on other people's beds.'

I didn't want to talk to him. But he borrowed a stool from the prisoner at the end of the fourth row, and sat down. They were good friends. 'There were three nurses with you,' he went on, a little awed. 'You couldn't walk on your own. And that friend who came to see you just now. Injections. Oxygen. And that tube that refused to stay in your nose. In ten minutes they had a doctor here for you, just like in a film!' He had obviously not liked my performance. Thank God he hadn't been present when they brought me into the hospital. They poured me into a gurney and I promptly fell out of it, four feet to the floor. They could not find the RMO, so they could not officially admit me. And so on. 'But you recovered in half an hour and started to joke with the doctor and your friend. Your friend – a medical student, isn't he? I know everything that goes on in this hospital. I've been here three times. I am a diabetic, where do you come from?'

'Bombay.'

'What are you doing here then?'

'I was on my way to somewhere else when I fell ill,' I mumbled.

'Ah, well, now that you are here…'

I could not bear to look at his face when he talked. Those horrible insecure teeth in his horrible skeletal face scared me, they would drop on me one by one, keep dropping even when there weren't any teeth left in his mouth. His spit sprayed out of his mouth when he talked. A drop fell on my hand and he brushed it off with his finger. He was used to it. And a man must talk. Even if he has nothing to say. What can't be helped had best be ignored. He went on talking.

I couldn't bear his being so close to me. Please, please, get up and go. Don't stay here. Don't talk. Can't you hear me? I'll hit you. I'll smash your bloody face and scatter all your damned teeth all over the ward. Shut up. *Shut up*.

He must have heard my thoughts.

'You seem uneasy. I get tired too. They gave me a transfusion three days before you came in. I can't eat properly. My teeth are too weak to chew. When one of them falls out, they have to give me a transfusion.'

He began to scratch. I used to scratch too. First under the sheet, then openly. He had lost his self-consciousness a long time ago. He never stopped scratching simply because a nurse was around. When he itched, he scratched, regardless of who was with him. We all scratched. Arms, legs, head, back, everywhere. Scratch scratch. There wasn't much else to do all day. Our bodies were sponged only at the extremities. From the tips of the fingers to the elbows. From toes to knees. Few of us were allowed baths.

'Today is the doctor's visiting day. But I doubt if he'll come now, it's so late. And he hasn't even looked at you for a few days. You can't be discharged without his orders. You'll just have to rot here till then. We have the same doctor. He is quite a nice man. I have a bet with him. He says I won't last long enough to get my BCom degree.'

The wife of the heart patient on my right called out to me. Anything to escape Ajwani. I turned round eagerly, gratefully.

'He wants to tell you something.'

He wasn't allowed to turn over yet. This was his second attack.

'Don't let that man discourage you. Your doctor will come. It's never too late.' His voice was very faint, as if it came from somewhere beyond his throat.

Ajwani stumped off to his bed.

'Rest now. Even a few words tire you so,' the heart patient's wife said to him. What difference does it make?

Why try so hard to live? Don't move. Don't eat. Don't scratch. Don't cry. Just one more attack and he'll be dead anyway. Nobody says to him, 'Don't die.' He smiled at me sadly, pathetically. His widowed mother and his sister looked at me with respect, awe even. They had witnessed my arrival and my quick recovery and my jokes with the RMO and Jitendra. As soon as they came to visit him, they would start praising me. Holding me up as an example to him. I was so brave, so courageous. I had faith in life. They sought my help to assure him of his recovery. Now he was throwing my own words back at me. But he meant what he said. Unlike me.

There were some private rooms to the right of our ward. Also for emergencies. Most were empty. One was occupied by a retired police inspector. He had recovered a month ago. At least as much as one recovers when one is old. But he stayed on. He said they didn't feed him at home.

Trying to get him to leave the hospital was one of the routine acts of the day. Nobody took it very seriously. After the RMO's daily round in the morning, two nurses took him his breakfast, and the fun began.

'Here, old man, this is your last breakfast. The head doctor is coming today to throw you out.'

'What, what's this about the last breakfast? What son of a bitch is going to have the guts to throw me out?' he would thunder, hopping on one leg and letting off a stream of obscenities. 'I'll stay here and eat here till the day my heart stops beating, do you hear? No bloody doctor is going to throw me out. Just let him try. Let him come forward and I'll break his fucking arms for him. And his legs. And his jaw...'

'Oh-ohh, you shameless old man. How dare you use such language in front of a woman? You will be sent home. I will not stand here one more minute and listen to your filth,' the dark nurse from the south would scream back in her falsetto. Her starched blouse and bra had by now given up the pretence of being a bosom and lay flat on her chest. Her yellow eyes anticipated the next lines in the well-worn dialogue.

'I won't let you have your crutch back. You'll have to leave without it. You can apologize as much as you like. I won't give it to you.'

'I? Apologize to you?' he roared. 'You little chit, how dare you talk to me like that? Give me back my crutch at once or I'll beat the daylights out of you.'

Sometimes he became violent. That's why there were no bottles or jars in his room. He had used his crutch on a nurse once, and they had confiscated it. The nurses were forbidden to enter his room alone. His wife and mistress came to visit him every evening. Together. The wife wrapped in a nine-yard sari and the mistress in a long skirt. Hardly talked to him. He didn't speak either. Some mornings, when he was really unwell, he would bleat to the nurses, 'Don't send me home, I beg you. Those two witches will starve me to death. They will put my bed out in the street and watch me die. All they want is my money, those whores.'

'How is it you never open your big mouth when they are here? It's your money, isn't it? But you're scared of them, aren't you? You are scared of your women,' the nurse would taunt him.

'I'm not scared,' he would scream. 'Why should I talk to them? They don't want a husband, they want a pimp.'

'Yet you can't appreciate a decent woman when you see one.' And then she would recite to him an abbreviated list of her virtues.

One afternoon he had to leave. They returned his crutch to him. We were looking forward to a final grand scene. But he left, just like that. By himself. Without saying anything. You can't rely on anybody, can you?

~

The prisoner died last night. In a diabetic coma. Hale and hearty and in good form when he went to bed. He died wearing his prison uniform. White shirt with black stripes and shorts. Last night, like every other night, he had had his little joke with the policeman who stood guard over him.

'Hello, how are you? Going to get some sleep tonight?' And then laughing mightily, he added, 'No? Well, I am going to bed. Who's being punished, you or I? Well, good night!' The night nurse scolded him and tried to shush him, because some of us would already be asleep. But his kind only ever talk in a bellow. He ignored her. Some nights when he was bad-tempered, he would shout at her in his coarse country accent. 'Look at that old bastard there, he has been unconscious for two months. He wouldn't know it if I screamed in his ears or pulled off his eyelashes. But when you stick a needle into him, he yells loud enough to wake God himself. There isn't enough flesh on him to stick a needle into anyway, stick it in and it comes out the other side. But that's never prevented you or your doctor from giving him injections. His screams don't bother you. But my voice gets on your nerves, does it?' The nurse from Kerala could not understand a word he said, but that did not stop them from having a conversation.

I took a long time to fall asleep. A neon light at the end of the corridor kept me awake. The prisoner turned over and stumbled out of bed. Before his hands could reach out and hold on to anything, his guts started to spew out of him, spraying a nearby wall blood-red. Everything he was stuffed with poured out in an endless stream. The vomit had taken over, making him dance in it. Roll in it. In great gasping breaths. He stood up, trying to stuff his hands into his mouth. There was no end to his regurgitations. He had nothing left in him. Yet he went on. He must have vomited at least two or three more people from within himself.

Suddenly he spun around. I was one bed away from him. He threw his red soul at me. It clung to my left arm and my chest. A layer crept under my skin. I would have to peel my skin off to get rid of it. Ajwani fixed his glazed, insane look on me. His jaw had got locked. A thin trickle of blood dripped from his dilapidated mouth and appeared blue in the neon light. A decayed tooth, yellowish, gently slipped out. I spent the night trying to strip the prisoner off me. As soon as I tore a bit off, a wormy yellow tree grew in its place. And a million overripe teeth hung on it, waiting to drop. For three days I tried to rid myself of the prisoner. But the teeth kept falling like unending rain. I came to on the fourth day. Ajwani and the heart attack man had died.

I am not going home today. I will stay here, leaning against this parapet. If I feel sleepy, I have a raincoat. Can't remember how I came by it. I think someone left it behind. But he forgot to leave his rain hat. When it rains very hard, I cover my head with a plastic bag. The clouds are low tonight. If I reach out and touch them, the sky will rest its weight on my hand. It has been threatening to rain for an hour or so now, but it hasn't started yet. Maybe it won't. Just the dark sky above and the dark sea below, the faint blue lights, and me.

The sea is so eerily calm. Six feet below me, licking the wall. Holding itself in perfect control, like a vast black Moby Dick. Showing off its mastery in every muscle. Handling its power effortlessly, a magnificent, universal Moby Dick travelling the world.

You love this bit of salt water, don't you? The sea here and the ocean over there, where you are. You wrote to me about it, talked to me about it when you came back for a holiday. The setting sun and the orphaned sea with its twilight memories. And then, not even those. But why am I talking about it? Shall I show you the slides? You asked. And I said no. You or the sea? You. And yet, that evening at Marine Drive before you went away. I wasn't going home that night. We came out of the Parisian Dairy. It must have been about half past eight. I will stay till ten, you said, shall I? And then go home. Why don't you say something? All right. So we've been over all this before. I'm not to meddle in this part of your life. Your secretiveness about your lonely nights is none of my business. Keep them to yourself. In fact, none of it is my business. I won't say a word. Shall I wait, till ten? Half past ten? Okay, no more wisecracks. Nine thirty. Shall I? So I can share some of your sleepless hours with you? And then you left, but not in anger.

You? You are very special to me, among all people, among all things. That was a bad night. Like so many other nights. It clung on. The same night and the same sea. From Cuffe Parade to Marine Drive to Breach Candy. If you had been with me, your sea would not have been so monotonous. I have never understood the sea. It makes me despair. The sea, your sea, going back and forth, endlessly. Like me. Sometimes I don't like this sea of yours. I dislike it with clenched-teeth loathing. That night at Nariman Point when the policeman looked at me suspiciously and said 'No pimping around here', I felt revolted and I spat into your sea with disgust. I wouldn't have reacted that way if you had been there. I could have borne myself. But I am lying. And one can never lie to one's suffering. Even when you're making love there's always an island called I.

If you toss around enough, a third being may come to life. But two people can never become one. In suffering, even less so. All you've got is you.

~

The light is still on in the Parsi woman's room. What is she doing at two in the morning? She has lived by herself for fifteen years and will probably continue to do so for the next fifteen. She will never marry. Made of twigs, wrapped in a sari. Her white sadra peeping out of the neck of her choli. Like a plucked chicken with only its cockscomb. Probably writing. I guess I'll have to read it the next time I see her. She is addicted to her loneliness. She won't let go of it, not even in a crowd. They can't do without each other. If she ever had the ability to respond to others, it's lost now, rusted through lack of use. She is drunk on loneliness. Like people who rub tobacco on their gums, Shireen rubs her loneliness over herself till she is intoxicated by it. And then she writes poetry. Poems about her childhood in Aligarh, neat poems about young soldiers at the beginning of the war. Mistaking her inability to fall in love for a touch of lesbianism in herself. Enlarges on her eleven years in Paris. Short stanzas about the neighbours' late lamented cat. A page. At the most a page and a half. Picking with one finger on the foreign typewriter in her office. Stunted poems about stunted feelings. A collected edition in a yellow file. Bloodless, like herself. Colourless. Measured irony. In the past occasionally and with great effort, but now with monotonous regularity, a poem every fortnight. Things will really get out of hand once she owns her own flat. She has been saving up for it for a year and a half. Soon she will have the whole place to herself: living room, bedroom, kitchen, bathroom, the works. All to herself. No one will be able to sober her up then.

She has started writing short stories now. About incest against a background of violins. About Roman Catholic nuns in a convent school, trying not to feel contempt for ragged girls with wrong accents, who will never progress beyond 'What, man'. About an outrage on a prostitute's modesty. Slight, facile, symbolic.

She loves India. That's why she came back from France. After eleven years. Besides, she couldn't stand the cold winters. She plays the harp. Loves music. You should hear her talking about music and books. For years we kept bumping into each other. Saying hello, how are you, what's new. One day, without warning, she held up a sheet of paper in front of my eyes and said, 'Read it. Now.' Then it got to be a habit. After the preliminaries, out came the yellow file. Poems, short stories, she was convinced I was ignorant of the lot. She pitied me for being a graduate. Was contemptuous even. But it was a controlled contempt, well disguised.

'Why don't you have your poems published?' I often asked her.

'Oh, they are nothing special, just my little hobby,' she would answer. And simper. Someone should take this woman to bed soon.

She invited me to her flat once. She hadn't a chance of

a promotion till her boss died, and he would live another twenty years. He was bald, but there wasn't a wrinkle on his smooth cheeks. They were very good friends, she and her boss. She was very good at her job, too. A thirty-five rupee raise every year. She walked home from work on those long legs, oblivious of the street, of the world around her. Her window looked out over the sea. The harp shrouded in blue plastic in a corner. Her dressing gown on a hanger, the pink and white bedcover smoothed over the hurriedly made bed.

'Pardon the messy room, won't you?'

I grunted.

She looked surprised. 'You find it untidy? Well, sit down.'

'No...'

'Okay, stand if you want to.'

I sat on the bed. 'No, I don't think the room is untidy.'

She smiled. 'Take off your shoes and relax. Welcome to the palace.' Waving towards the sea, expansively, 'The sea is yours. I'm going to have a quick shower. Sit and listen to the Master.' She put on Bach and left the room.

It was very still. For a while I could hear the water running in the bathroom and then that too stopped. The sky a deep blue with pink and orange scarves flung across it. The sadness of twilight, a sadness without words. A deaf mute sadness, consoling itself. You could get addicted to it.

I don't understand music. I like it. Bach is beautiful. He must have been a great man. Creating a sombre god out of brass tubes. I remembered you. Ali Akbar's Sindhu Bhairavi.

Saigal. Kesarbai. Satyajit's *Devi.* Kishore's voice. And Camus. Thank you. Thank you. Thank who? Hence, God.

She came and sat down in the chair. I was afraid she was going to talk. But she didn't. When the record came to an end, she pulled the harp towards her. Peeled off the cover and caressed it. Plucking at a string occasionally. And waiting till its echo died down. The sun fell on her quick fingers and made them appear boneless. Her face had remained still for five thousand years. Gradually she was flowing out of the harp. The notes issuing from her fingers made patterns of lines behind my closed eyelids. She had left the original melody behind. She had become the harp and was now playing herself. Hollow lines, twisted lines, delicate lines, wild unruly lines, lines that blossomed, swayed, became clear, intertwined, burst into colour, red, purple, orange, came together, separated, ran around in circles, dizzied, turned blue, threw back their heads, lost balance and were green.

The sounds of the day are different from those of the night. It is quiet here today. The caged sea like a black dog lapping water. A bit scary. When I lived in Poona, the nights belonged to the street dogs. One dog started off with a mangy little bark and the next instant, all the dogs in the world were in Poona. Like children rushing in to answer a roll call. The Portuguese one saying hello to his friend from Shivadi, the Thai arguing with the Liverpudlian. And when that lot tired, their place was immediately taken by the ones from Mars and Saturn and Venus. All arriving right outside my window, not at all tired at the end of their journey. Their feelings bubbled over, could not be contained. Such fools, dogs. Incapable of keeping anything to themselves. Broadcasting to the world not only their own thoughts, but the thoughts in every other dog's mind too. Never waiting for an answer. If one asks 'What are you doing?', the other never says I'm frying bhajji, or enjoying the breeze, or making time to cool that bitch-on-heat out there. All these answers will come repetitively from a third dog who was never asked, while the dog who was asked turns on his questioner and growls over and over: 'Why aren't you answering my questions?' When I lived in Poona, I strangled thirty-eight million, five thousand and twenty-four dogs, slit the tongues of four times that many. But it was no good. If you cut off a dog's tongue, he barks with his paws. If you cut off his tail, he barks with the short end of it. If cats have nine lives, then dogs have five million and eighty-four. I did all I could. Then I left Poona. But those bloody dogs follow me wherever I go.

The first time I realized that human beings are capable of being noisy even after midnight was when the Madrasi on the floor above died. You never saw our house in Bombay. I didn't know then that you existed. We got that house very soon after I was born. There was an explosion in Bombay harbour and a lot of people decided to leave the city. So we got our flat. Front room, kitchen and bathroom.

When we disagreed about the date of a particular day, my parents sent me across to the Pradhans' to check.

'When was that? Yesterday evening? Ah yes, now let me see. Your aunt Sunita came to visit you on Sunday, didn't she? No, not the day before. That was when Ankush's two girlfriends came to see him and then he went out with them...'

A couple of years ago, when Don and Ursula were staying with us, Arvind, who lives in the next block of flats, accosted me. Ursula and I were walking to the corner Irani shop for a cup of tea. Arvind had never spoken to me before. I had lived the last twelve years outside of Bombay and anyway I never felt like getting to know him or his people. Arvind crossed the street to talk to me. Jerking his shoulder in his peculiar way, he squeaked, 'Hey, has Ankush sent his wife home from the States?' I stared at him. Ursula, taking him for a friend of mine, said a low-voiced hello and turned away.

'Or is she yours?'

'Belongs to both of us actually, we take turns,' I said and I followed Ursula. I thought that would shut him up. But even now when I pass him in the street, he jerks his shoulder and hitches up his trousers and says, 'Where is that white woman of yours? Haven't seen her around.' And so on.

My mother tried to pat me to sleep at ten, but noise till midnight was inescapable. By ten, everybody had finished their dinner. Nine thirty to ten was devoted to the same heart-rending, tear-jerking Marathi play that had been regularly broadcast ever since Independence. 'Baba! Baba! Don't, oh don't! We are ruined! O Lord, we are doomed! This is the end. Who can save us poor souls now, except you, dada?' some ancient or modern-day Shivaji or Sambhaji would invariably ask over twenty-odd wireless sets in the block.

And then the beggars started. 'Give, for the love of God. Feed my children so yours never go hungry. Give, and all your sins will be forgiven, you will be blessed eternally.' The women of Hindu Colony expiated their and their families' sins every night. With one ear cocked to the radio play, they reached for leftovers, yesterday's soured dal, the dried rice from the husband's lunch box, the pickle Sarla mami had sent over and which had gone slightly off. 'Here, spread your cloth out a bit more, or do you want me to throw the chapatis into the same pan?' The ladies of Hindu Colony, not wasting an opportunity to demonstrate their piety. Never mind about the famine in Bihar. They fed the starving populace of Bombay every night.

The beggars in India are a race apart. They will digest anything. If the intestines of beggars all over the world were to be dissected, the Indian beggar's insides would emerge as the toughest. They eat everything. Good, bad, poisonous, they assimilate it all. A beggar is like God – with an infinite capacity to absorb.

Mr Kathavte, on the second floor, always felt the itch to beat his daughters at night. After ten. And he had many daughters. The youngest was in the fifth standard. First he had three sons. Then he started on the daughters. He had white hair at forty and was sixty-two when his youngest daughter was born. A tough old man.

Even now, when his married daughters come to visit, the bastard has beating sessions. To make them feel at home. At night. Only between ten and twelve. The youngest has quite a nice voice. The two middle ones have terrible voices. Rekha sounds like a vulture being dragged along the ground. Meena is hoarse and scratchy. Her voice has stayed broken for twenty years. She started wailing in a little boy's voice, and then it somersaulted and changed, flattened as though it had been through a sugarcane juice wringer. All of them were beaten quite impartially. But these two were his favourites. Mr Kathavte was called Bhau by his family.

'Bhau, don't,' Meena would move from A to F-sharp. From the kitchen to the front room. Then a pause, a little argument in raised voices. And then, 'Have you no shame, you little hussy?' Without waiting for an answer, 'You stupid, worthless girl, you bitch.' Slaps and kicks accompanied the words. A stick or a leather belt. On to the little balcony. 'Don't, Bhau, don't beat me, please.' With every slap Meena enhanced her father's sense of high drama.

When I was ten, she introduced a new line in her daily performance. After that I could not sleep. Mother would scold me if I tried to get out of bed, so I pulled the sheet over my head and shut my eyes, but that didn't help. I saw her smashed into a million red pieces in front of Mr Pradhan's door. 'Bhau, if you hit me once more, I'll jump off the balcony. I'll kill myself, Bhau.'

Bhau's answer changed the world for me. He kicked her threats aside. 'Kill yourself? Jump off? Are you threatening your father, you little slut? Go ahead and jump then, go on. You don't scare me, you little chit.'

Rekha didn't get away either. Everybody got beaten equally. Occasionally, Mrs Kathavte intervened, dragging her dangling breasts with her. And then she got her share. 'Get out of the way, you stupid woman. It's all your fault. You let these girls go too far. Now stay out of it and let me deal with them. Get out. Not another word from you, Meena.' He was an expert at changing tracks without warning. 'One more peep out of you, Rekha, and I'll beat the daylights out of you. Just you, I won't touch anyone else. So shut up.' Then a blow across the face.

When Rekha was ten, Bhau stopped beating his sons. Only the girls were privileged from now on. The eldest son, Kishore, had warned his father, 'You raise your hand against me and I'll smash you to a pulp. You won't be able to move for days.'

Bhau stopped beating him.

Bhau seemed to enjoy beating the girls more and more as they grew older. The girls had a highly developed sense of drama. Specially Meena. Little Meena, who never got beyond the eighth standard at school. She would call on God for help. 'O Lord!' she screamed. And then she called on Anna Pradhan, who lived below them. 'Anna, save me, you're the only one who can help me now. Anna, have you no humanity, no compassion for me? Listen to the cries of a poor lonely girl, Anna.'

Anna, who had fathered his last child thirty-two years ago, would be too embarrassed to show his face. If the yelling and screaming grew unbearably loud, he would finally appear. 'Kathavte, that's enough for now, Kathavte. Give it a rest, and let us all get some sleep. She is getting too old for this, she's a big girl now.'

Bhau would lean way out of the second-floor balcony and look down at Anna, his eyes flaring under his halo of wild white hair. Pradhan would withdraw. Bhau would pull his head in and resume with Meena. I could never understand why those girls did not die from their beatings. One of them fainted once, but Bhau says she was shamming. I could not get used to the beatings. I told myself that Bhau and his daughters enjoyed the performance and their roles in it. I knew that. But every time it happened, I wanted to throw up. I wanted to run away. I prayed for those girls to die. I still do. I didn't pray for Bhau to die. I knew he wouldn't.

I used to be convinced in those days that after Bhau, nobody would produce any more children, ever. Children were forbidden. Bhau's youngest daughter was the last child in the world. Having watched Bhau in action, what man would dare to produce a child? All the prime ministers in the world, the Pope and Franco came to our flats one day and passed a law making children illegal, to save them from their fathers.

Bhau did not lose any sleep just because I lost mine. There have been nine marriages and thirty-four babies in our colony in the last ten years. Now that Bhau's daughters are married, they are often away. So Chandavarkar locks up his son in the lavatory. If his wife lets the boy out, Mr Chandavarkar beats her up. There are always new children and new fathers. Children get beaten in the evenings. It gets dark. Men and women sleep with each other. And make babies. When I get married, I will do the same. After all, I am Bhau's heir, his nocturnal disciple.

We all have our own darknesses. Every darkness with its own shape. Who lives in your locked-up darkness? You talked of it only once. Very briefly. They used to lock you up in the dark to cure you of your fear of it. Even now, when you shut your eyes, the hateful memory presses on you like a swarm of bees. The darknesses change with age. Vijay now goes up those stairs by himself.

'E aaye-e,' he used to call out from the bottom step. Then his mother or the servant came down to walk him up. His father installed lights in the stairway for him. When his father died, the lights stopped working too. And then the servant left. Now Vijay takes a deep breath and tries to negotiate the two sets of stairs. The fears of childhood are left behind. But there are always echoes in the hollow darkness. If we listen carefully, we realize how closely we are bound to them. All our future is in the dark.

When I was five, the Madrasi was about fifty. His hair combed back, he was three times as tall as I. He used to spit and blow his nose from upstairs, and the spit and the snot landed in front of our door. It infuriated my father. It was my father's opinion that spit belonged in the washbasin and snot in the handkerchief. So they had many arguments. The neighbours watched and listened through open doors and windows and balconies. If I went out to play, the boys asked me, 'Why is your father so quarrelsome?' Then I stayed at home for a few days. Mother never asked me why I didn't go out. One day, we stepped out of our front door and the Madrasi spat. On my mother's head. My father called him down. He came, spluttering, 'What? What? So what?' My father, at least a foot shorter than him, slapped him across the face. His face turned livid. We went back inside.

I brought back snippets of what the neighbours were saying. There would be a court case, the police would come to investigate. My mother pulled my hair affectionately and said, 'There's nothing to be afraid of, you know. Nobody is going to take Baba away.'

If my father was late coming home from work, I was convinced they had got him. I harangued my mother. 'I told you. They must have taken him away from his office.' And when she started to shake her head, I continued, 'Why don't you go and bring him home then? Where have you hidden him?' That scared Ankush too. The three of us sat on the front steps and waited for my father. If I persisted, she would get up and say, 'All right, I'll go and look for him. Ankush, you mind your brother, and don't fight.' This was worse. 'No, I don't want Ankush, I want you. Take me with you.' And back we would go to waiting on the steps. Ten months later, I still had not lost this fear. Maybe not today, not tomorrow, but one day they would take my father away, I was convinced. I did not confide my fear to my mother in case it made her unhappy. I had recently learned to call people bastard, son of a bitch and so on, but I never called my father names, not even when he was angry with me.

I heard a scream in the middle of the night. A terrifying, unintelligible scream. Not in Marathi. I bet my aunt in Delhi heard it too. My throat was dry and I hugged Baba tight. But the scream went on and on. It was never going to stop. It came from upstairs. There was a deep wound and it ran with red blood. It hurt, it would always hurt. It sounded like the Madrasi's wife. Lights came on in every flat, at the Pradhans', the Kathavtes', the Bhonsles'. But I was never going to open my eyes again. People were running up and down the stairs. There was a crowd at the Madrasi's door.

His wife did not lose her voice all night. She howled and cried for hours. After the first five minutes, she screamed in Hindi. After all, nobody in the colony understood Tamil. 'What will happen to me now? O Lord, what have you done to me? Why don't you take me too?' The women tried to console her. Collectively and individually. But the old woman did not want to be consoled. This was her one big moment and she was not going to have it spoilt. Her husband could only die once. He had died and she was determined to make the most of the opportunity. She had finally found a purpose in life. Most people live aimless lives. But she had discovered a reason for it. Slowly she warmed up to her role. In a flash, her life had changed. She now played her new role like a consummate artist. A whole new world, a whole new universe was open to her. Her husband had died and she had the whole colony as her audience. She would cherish the moment of his death forever.

They brought him down at nine o'clock in the morning, with difficulty. The staircase was narrow and his wife would not let go. They put the stretcher down outside our window.

'I'm going too,' she insisted.

Poor innocent Mr Pradhan. 'Where to?' he asked.

'Cremate me too,' she said. 'Take us both. I cannot live without him.' She banged her head against the stretcher, again and again, as though she would never stop. They picked up the old man and she returned to her flat and her wailing.

In the confusion, they brought two urns to collect his ashes. One was enough for the Madrasi. The second was left, along with a few sticks from the bier, outside our window. It stayed there for two days. The sweeper would not touch it. Finally, my father threw it into the garbage bin.

The sun doesn't rise out of this sea. It only sets here, to emerge on the other side. The night is beginning to crack open. Tuesday. What are you doing now, this moment, seven and a half hours behind in time? Time has infiltrated the whole world. Every corner of the world, every little corner. God has a sack, as big as the universe, and God is in a hurry. He is stuffing the sack with every second he can find, frantically, desperately. From the moment he created the universe, he has been asphyxiating the present into the past. He has gone berserk and he is driving us mad. His work is never finished. He drips with sweat, yet all over the world, the future stretches to infinity. As I write this, as you exist seven and a half hours from now, as Mr Russell pours his anger out on the Americans in Vietnam, as fifty thousand women produce new babies, as Don chews hash in the Globe Hotel in Kathmandu, as Kombiamma washes the steps of the Mahalaxmi temple, and as Raghu explains to his girlfriend, 'Look, I like you, honest to God, I do. And I like it too. But for Christ's sake, I can't be doing it all thirty-two hours of the day, not even if I wanted to.'

At Kothrud, Tai said to me, 'Bow and touch it, Kushank. I'm older than you and I tell you God is in every stone.' Maybe. If God is in every stone, then there is a saffron-painted stone in the heart of God.

Nothing escapes God. Nothing slips out of his sack. He has no eyelids. He had them once, but they fell off from disuse. They had no purpose, since he never closes his eyes. He is obsessively greedy, incurably so. But he can't cure me of my obsession either. I don't care about this moment, here and now. Only one moment concerns me. It might take days, years to die, but death will occur only at that one moment. That is the moment I have set my whole being against, all my life. The moments of your death, my death, my mother's death. I can't understand God and his affairs. I don't want to. You said once that we had been given a choice. And you were right. He has made up his mind to keep his eyes wide open, always. I, to keep mine shut tight. He has stomached a million sins. He will stomach mine too. One day, today or tomorrow, he will swallow us whole. He has set my limits for me. But I can always scream. Granted, I have no voice to scream with. So much the better. Less trouble for others. War. Total war.

I wish I could see you today. If I walk across the sea in a straight line towards you, I will reach you in six months, won't I? Six months of longing? When I confront you, I'll have to fake it. And when I get to you, I'll turn back and look at India. You said things look different from afar. Maybe they do. The country where I was born, where I grew up, went to school, that I often abuse, that I cannot talk about without reservations, that country will become the Indian subcontinent. A subcontinent among the underdeveloped nations. But I could never look at the world, at life, at others, at myself, through your eyes.

When we talked of this, you thought I was accusing you of having become a foreigner. Perhaps I was, for you were certainly different. You would have to be a block of wood not to have changed at all. But distance didn't make you a stranger. Some people change, some assimilate change. I don't know which of these happened to you. I try to understand myself and assimilate the world around me, with a persistence verging on the pig-headed. Maybe that's what you try too, in some other way, in some other words. The point is not whose way is better, it's just that our modes of perception are different.

You see people. In groups, in countries, in societies. Indians, Englishmen, Spaniards, Germans, Chinese. And then Caucasians, Semites, Mongolians. And then others. Second-generation Americans are more naively and dogmatically patriotic, you observed. Perhaps your training as a sociologist has something to do with that. I see only human beings. As individuals. Isolated, occasionally in groups. Stretching themselves, dreaming their dreams, engaged in love, surviving like animals, human, without compassion, shameless, unhappy, generous, inflicting sorrow, mindless, tied to each other. At best, I am a practising human being. Nothing else. I don't understand the Indian subcontinent, it doesn't exist for me, it doesn't worry me.

All I see, understand, do not understand, all that hurts me, is Prachinti.

'I'm off, Kushank,' she said, and left forever. And I couldn't stop her. For ten months, I saw her grow fainter and fainter and diminish before my eyes, but I couldn't block the doorway and stop her from leaving.

Five feet tall, hair down to her knees, delicate, frail, Prachinti – Shatlaj's wife, and the mother of little Arshad. When she and Shatlaj and I couldn't bear it any more, we took her to the municipal hospital. She stayed there for twenty-seven days. I waited for her to say something, but she was silent. Shatlaj took Arshad out for a drink of water and Prachinti reached out one pale hand and took mine. 'You'd said you'd never bring me to a hospital again.' Yes, I had. So what? Don't you know me? I say what is convenient. She said, 'I want to go home. Will you take me home?'

The same hospital, nine years ago. Her family did not believe that she was dying. For ten months she died. Slowly, as I watched her. They had never believed in an illness with a face, two arms, two legs, eyes and ears, nostrils. And if it did not exist, they were not going to waste money on it. Her doctor too, such a clever doctor. Economical. Everything in small doses, even the antibiotics, so that soon she didn't respond to any at all.

If Prachinti had been taken to hospital ten months earlier, she might have lived another couple of years. But we mustn't cry over the past, must we? No, of course not.

Shatlaj tried to sell his paintings. Tutored others in painting. And then sold his paints and easel too. To buy Prachinti's medicines. Sometimes, I tried begging, but begging doesn't necessarily get you anything. Certainly not money. My friends were happy to take me to the movies, the theatre, concerts. But they didn't offer me the money for the tickets. So my wallet stayed empty and Prachinti went without medicine for days.

Two years ago she had come to our house. Waited till my father had left and then said, 'I need money. Four hundred rupees.' I laughed. Me? Money? If I had money I wouldn't come and eat at your house every other day. 'There's no one else I can ask. I've already borrowed from other friends. And they ask me why I always need money. To survive. To eat. Why don't they understand? Don't they ever get hungry? Morning, noon and night? Why not just eat once? For a lifetime? Why do we eat so often? Even people who have never lent me money ask the same questions.'

'And what happens if you don't get it?' I asked, to gain time.

She shook her head. 'I will get it. You will find it for me. We have to pay the rent so we can live in the house.'

We went to a friend's house. Made small talk. 'You know I'd give it to you if I had it. If only you'd come a month earlier,' my friend apologized, glancing at this tiny, unknown woman. Why should he give it to us anyway,

I told myself, maybe he's hard up. And then to another friend. Finally to Rashid. 'You have to give it to me, even if you don't have it,' I said to him. When he left the room to get it, Prachinti nudged me and whispered, 'Ask for another twenty-five. Shatlaj needs paints. Please, Kushank.'

But I didn't ask for the extra twenty-five rupees.

And what if you came again and shook your head and said, 'I need it. You're going to get it for me.' And if I don't have it, nobody has it, nobody wants to give it to me, then I'm going to get mad at you, I'm going to wipe you off the face of the earth, why do you ask me to do things that I can't, go away, don't bother me, why can't you look after yourself, go take yourself, your Arshad, your Shatlaj, go wherever you want, so long as you're out of my sight, live, cry, be happy, be sick, live on the pavement, in a bungalow, why don't you go away from here, can't you understand when you've been told a thing once and what if I can't give you the money next time?

She didn't ask me for money again. She only died, slowly. Through ten months, ten times thirty days. Days and weeks and all the hours of the day. You are overdoing it, Prachinti. You have no sense of balance. No sense of proportion. Every time I left your room I didn't turn back to look at your oxygen cylinders, temperature charts, jars of saline, bottles and bottles of medicine. What was the point? There's a limit to everything. Don't you know? You had become so pale and small that if I had turned around to look at you, you'd have vanished. The name of the hospital stamped in red on the sheets. That's all. But you were still there. Why do you insist on doing things you can't afford? I want to talk to you. I want my money back. Every paisa, right now. Listen to me, Prachinti.

Three days before she died, she turned to me and said, 'I can't bear it any more, Kushank. I can't.' She shook her head from side to side, violently. The nurse held her head firmly, to stop all those needles from falling out of her arms, her nose, her head. Stop lying, I muttered. When I was in seventh standard, the teacher said to me, 'For heaven's sake, how can you write such blatant lies? Aren't you ashamed of yourself? Seven sixes are forty-three? What are you staring at the floor for? The answer's not written there, you know. Now rub out that nonsense and write the truth.' If you can't bear it, you will pass out, die. As long as you are conscious, you can't say I can't bear it.

It was the last time I saw Aaroti. When we were together, I was always aware of the parting to come, every moment. When I wasn't with her too. I could never have said goodbye to her. I never had a chance to. Her friends – the woman in trousers and her two sons – came to see her as I was leaving. They had chosen their moment well, unknowingly. Aaroti's husband had already left, to avoid having to say goodbye to me. I suppose I was grateful to him. I really infuriated him. He was a gentleman, and magnanimous. I had stayed with them for nine days. He could have thrown me out any time he wanted to. He must have been paralysed by my utter lack of shame. His friendly face was harassed by my continued presence in his house.

'Is he worried that I might be in love with you?' I asked Aaroti.

'Are you?'

'I don't know.'

'Maybe he doesn't either.'

Our relationship – his and mine – was acted out with the ultimate-in-twentieth-century sophistication. We were never less than polite to each other. I made tea for him every morning. There were nineteen brass tumblers on the shelf in the kitchen, all in one shining row. 'Brass doesn't break,' said Aaroti, as she demonstrated by banging one on the floor. I would give him his tumbler of hot tea, wrapped in my handkerchief. The first couple of days, we tried to make conversation about the war in Vietnam. He answered my questions. We aired our opinions. Then we stopped talking. Aaroti would break under the strain and scream at me. 'Why don't you talk to him? Damn it, you don't have to make it so awkward.' I stared back dumbly. 'Oh, stop being so bloody perverse, so opaque.'

'I have nothing to say to him.'

'I know, you fool, I know,' she hissed. She spoke in English. Only when her husband was absent, and so that Sunheria and the children wouldn't understand. 'But you don't have to shut up. You could try and make some sort of conversation.'

~

I put on my shoes and went out. Aaroti was caught between us, between our silences. She was being suffocated. But she was never 'poor Aaroti'. You could never pity Aaroti. She could be hurt, terribly hurt, and I could hurt myself over her. But pity was out of the question.

'Why don't you let me go?'

We had already spoken about this. She smiled, faintly, mischievously.

'Go tomorrow.' She'd said that three times before. I had finished my money. She was going to lend me the fare, and I would return the money later.

'Why don't you understand that I've already been here much too long?'

'How can I understand? You're the only one who understands, the only comprehending one.' We both laughed. 'You know you can never come back here.'

'I'm perfectly aware of that.' I was beginning to growl. She ignored me.

'Two or three days more, that's all. Then, never again.' I understood her words, knew she felt them. I had met her sister, Koshinda, a couple of years ago. Out of the blue she'd said, 'Aaroti is not one of us any more. She says she feels alive every moment. Morning, noon and night.'

Her daughter, Prutha, was real enough. But Aaroti's sister's words had gone over my head then. Now I was beginning to understand, just a little.

It was almost impossible to sleep in her house at night. All four rooms were taken over by rats. They'd scamper over my legs, my head, my body. My room was a special favourite of theirs on account of a large jar of sugar kept there. When I switched on the lights, they'd scurry behind whatever offered shelter. The moment the lights went off, they'd be back at work like creatures possessed. Nibble, nibble, crunch, crunch. They had already built luxurious palaces within those walls, but there seemed to be no end to their digging. All through the night, lumps of plaster and peelings from the tarpaulin stretched across the ceiling would come hurtling down. As soon as I made the mistake of dozing off, a piece would crash into my back or face. I'd spring awake without giving the rats sufficient warning, causing much commotion among those who had settled on me. They'd jump off me then, in helter-skelter haste. If ever Aaroti caught sight of one of them in the day, she would fix it with a cold eye and say in the sombre tones of an oracle, 'This house has been eaten away by rats. One day it's going to collapse on our heads.'

'Not on mine, it isn't. Not if I can help it. I'm leaving.'

'Really? Are you? Oh well, if you are so determined, I'm not going to try and stop you.'

Which reminded me, I couldn't leave unless she lent me the money.

'Beautiful, kind, generous lady, all I ask for is a hundred rupees.'

'You idiot, I was beautiful yesterday,' she said, measuring every word for me, tersely.

Yesterday, early in the morning, she came to my room, and said in a strangely resigned tone, 'Really, Kushank, I can't help it if I happen to be the most beautiful woman in the world.'

It stuck in my throat, that sentence. I couldn't believe it was Aaroti talking about herself.

'What are you staring at? I can't help the truth, can I?' And then she laughed aloud, and I laughed with her. As she turned to go out of the room, she repeated, 'Truly, the most beautiful woman in the world. Me.' Today her tone had changed. 'You haven't learnt anything from being with me. Not even the difference between today and tomorrow. Today is now, tomorrow is another day. And today I am ugly. Yes,' she went on, 'it grieves me to say this. I'm the world's ugliest woman. What can I do? It's a fact of nature. And this – my hopeless hair, to match my ugly face. Whatever I do to it, and I have tried everything, it will not behave. It sticks up all round my face, as if I had seen the Holy Ghost. So help me, God.'

Just once in a while, the strain of the forced humour would show through, but that was all. Prutha was a private battle, and she planned to fight it alone.

And the rats continued to devour the house. At first, that house of hers used to get me down terribly. It used to sit me down, head in hands. It made me gibber. I would try and hold it together with words, but it had long escaped all human restraints. Aaroti's house was plunged in chaos. A divine chaos. It was as if God held a giant churn in his hands, and Aaroti was its handle. Her husband, Prutha, Guddu, and Sunheria and her daughters were the blades. Sixteen hours a day God churned that house. In the remaining eight, Sunheria and Aaroti rushed around straightening the mess. Reshuffling the mess at the bottom to cover up the one at the top.

Guddu used handfuls of dal to draw an unending line round the house like an unsteady stream of piss. Prutha, in frustration, banged her head on the metal bars of her chair. She had only two ways of expressing her anger – she either drummed her head on the bar or hung it way down, tucking her pupils into the corners of her eyes. In the meantime, if she forgot to hold her saliva in, she'd dribble all over the front of her dress or sweater.

When her banging failed to attract attention, she dragged her triangular contraption of a chair to the far corner of the kitchen. Sitting still for a moment or two, staring into the valley. You could see the long, winding, climbing road from there. She loved to watch the cars driving up the road. Suddenly she kicked at the big brass pitcher left on the ledge to dry in the sun. It rolled down the slope, crashing loudly against the rocks as it plunged. Prutha tried to jump up and down in her chair with excitement, elated at the sensation she had caused.

'Why, you little horror!' screamed Aaroti, exasperated. 'What's eating you? What's your trouble, eh? Who the hell do you think is going to fetch that pitcher now?'

I leaned over the railing and scanned the valley through Aaroti's husband's binoculars. I could just see the pot, about eighty feet below, battered and twisted. Flattened on one side and bumpy on the other.

'Aaroti,' her husband called in irritation, 'can't you hear me? I've been calling you. Where are my trousers? My polyester ones, not my woollen ones.' Aaroti ran around, looking through the clothes, rummaging through the cupboard, scrambling in the pile that lay on the bed, throwing saris, blouses, shirts all over the place, in an attempt to find her husband's trousers. A laudable effort and utterly hopeless. No one doubted for a minute that the trousers would not be found today. But Aaroti was not to be deterred by such flimsy reasons. 'Forget it,' he cried in despair, 'you are not one of those who seeks and finds, are you?'

'Polyester trousers?' I ragged Aaroti when he had left. 'Are you sure he ever had them?'

She threw a wet rag at me. It stayed where it fell all day.

Her saris were always beautifully ironed, so I knew how to get her really mad. 'You shameless wretch, you don't give a damn what he wears, do you, just so long as your clothes are beautifully laundered and pressed?'

The trousers were not going to be found, not today, not tomorrow. And her choli would be lost too. One day her husband would probably go to work without his trousers and Aaroti would go without her choli.

When I teased her, Aaroti would sometimes feel remorse. She'd try to defend herself. 'No, really, Kushank, didn't I iron his shirt last night?' And when I looked disbelieving, she was irritated.

'Well, why doesn't he look after his clothes himself? He has always worn the first thing that comes to hand.'

She would frown. 'Do I really seem so useless to you?'

Prutha could never be left alone, not for a moment. Aaroti looked after all of us – Prutha, Guddu, her husband, me, and herself. We never missed a meal and her husband never went without his trousers.

'I was only joking. What the hell does it matter if your husband gets fed on time or not, your house looks neat or not? I don't give a damn. All I want is for you to wear beautiful saris and look ravishing.'

'Kushank, stop it.' She pretended to restrain me. Then softly, 'What if someone hears you!'

On the first of every month, Aaroti bought a giant box of Surf for washing her own, her children's, and her husband's clothes and Sunheria and her family's, as well as for all the pots and pans and everything else that needed washing.

The box would be finished by about the fifteenth of the month, and then we had to make do with the hideous yellow cake of soap, the cheap, local kind. I was forever washing clothes, since I had only a few. It was the second week of the month and I was having a great time with the Surf. Aaroti called me a dhobi. 'Go on, wash away. After all, when will you see so much detergent again? Why don't you send for the rest of your clothes from Bombay?'

Sunheria could not restrain herself. 'Bibiji, he is a guest in our house, you mustn't be rude to him.'

And then Aaroti laughed at me. 'Gathering support, aren't you?'

Sometimes, I wanted to read her a poem. Then we would start a giant hunt for the book we needed. They were everywhere, lying in piles. Finally, when we couldn't find it, not even on the bathroom shelf, Aaroti quoted in a small voice, 'Forgive me, o Goddess, for he was so strong and I was half-asleep.'

Our arguments over books and over my writing drove that social scientist husband of hers into a silent rage. He had a beautiful nose, straight and righteous. He tried to ignore us, but failed to hide the contempt in his eyes. Aaroti wondered why he never boiled over, why he never lost his temper, and forgetting his innate goodness, why he never screamed at her. But he couldn't. Sometimes he was rude to her. At times, when he could stand it no more, he'd aim a stinging kick at the puppy that Guddu used to torture innocently. He was deeply hurt somewhere, but it was in a remote place. And he would tolerate me with the same resignation with which one tolerates an injury that has no visible marks. He could so easily, so rightly, have said, 'This is my house. I don't want you here, please leave.' But he never did.

When we three sat down to dinner, he pretended I didn't exist. He'd talk to Aaroti. They would squabble over burning problems like national integration, Kashmir, regional languages, and suchlike. His opinions had attained the sublimity of truths that had withstood the test of a hundred years. Yet when these truths were propounded at the table, Aaroti invariably felt obliged to raise conscientious doubts. He hated my presence. When he couldn't take it any longer, he held a book on political geography in front of his face. Turning the pages regularly every two minutes. I'd finish my meal calmly, staring at the girl in the red dress on the wall. The girl showed off her virgin armpits and thrust her fingers into her hair as she advertised a brand of radio-set. Her breasts were always about to bounce out of her dress. There were many such maidens hanging on the walls of the house. In the bedroom, a nubile female reclined on a rock. The water only came up to her toes, but her entire white sari was soaked through and through. She would remain drenched the whole year. She looked rather pleased at having forgotten to wear her blouse and bra. Her pink body strained heavily against the white sari. But one is never allowed to see a woman whole. Her nipples had vanished behind clever folds. I'd asked Aaroti the first day about these voluptuous, simpering ladies.

'God, what are these terrible women doing in your house? I thought you preferred straight pornography to this coy prurience?'

'He likes them,' she said coolly. You could never patronize Aaroti.

Every morning and evening Prutha had to do her exercises. Exercises that one day would hopefully release her limbs from the constraints she had been born with. She hated them, screamed when she had to do them, went rigid in protest. But Aaroti would not give in. She had blinded herself to the success or otherwise of the exercises. 'God, but I see sometimes and then I can't carry on, I can't,' she cried out, clenching her fists.

She cajoled Prutha, sang to her, abused her, threatened her, but she got her on the floor to do the exercises. To amuse Prutha, I joined her sometimes and waved my legs and arms about. Guddu hardly ever played with me. I never knew if he resented my friendship with his mother or my spoiling of Prutha. He accepted sweets from me, but that was all. He preferred to ignore me.

'This one is going to hate you when he grows up,' said Aaroti.

'I know, I'm glad he's only three.'

She pulled Guddu to her and kissed him. 'But you'll be around when he's grown up, won't you?'

I sat mute.

'I feel as though I've been writing to you for six years. I start in my mind with Dear Kushank, and then the letter becomes a conversation. I don't even know if I should be saying this to you. We're all going to die anyway, and it is good to tell when one likes and good to know one is liked. You see, I don't need you desperately or longingly or anything like that. Or maybe this is a kind of longing and desperation, needing someone in this way – how do I know? But you're there, and it's frustrating and not right when you're not. I'm not unhappy or dissatisfied – I'm not. And I don't think of you in particular moods, but it seems natural that when I feel deeply about something, you're the one I want to talk to.'

Guddu had climbed out of her lap long ago and disappeared. Prutha slept, and the house was peaceful. I sat on the plinth and stared at the floor. Unable to talk.

'Damn it. Why can't I have two men?' she said, and suddenly everything turned upside down.

I hated her. The books I had read, the films I had seen, my periodical phoney self-respect, all came to the surface. 'I'll be damned if I'm going to play the other man. And anyway, I hate playing platonic fiddles to anyone.'

I hurt her then. Why did she bring out the worst in me? I used words like sharp nails to tear at her. And when I had drawn blood, I grew calm.

'Why, Kushank, you don't even know if you love me.'

She had pricked my balloon with the tiniest pin, so gently. There are some things I don't understand. I see things happening before my eyes, I take notes, of details, irrelevancies. I remember it all, just as it happened. Then suddenly an incident breaks loose, an incident that has no beginning, no end, that has been lost in memory, an incident that suddenly avalanches on top of me, engulfs me and changes the course of my life, unknowingly, independently of me. Aaroti said to me once, 'Won't you ever understand, Kushank? The trick is in seeing the obvious.' But when it's happening right there in front of my eyes, how the hell do I miss it? And then months later, sometimes years, it catches up with me like a slap in my face. And I sit down with a thump. Having to settle the debts of years and years without warning. When I've forgotten to wear my dentures. I try to get a grip on myself and even tell the truth in the confusion. And once you tell the truth, everything is locked up and put away. The keys too. No bars on the windows, no windows, no doors. The whole world is open to you. The retreating horizon, your prison. The timeless horizon pursuing you in all directions. And then you have to apportion the blame. Let us close our eyes. Tight. Quickly. Else somebody might lay the blame at God's doorstep.

It was thirteen days before I realized that my mother was dead. I was there when she breathed her last. 'Come home when you finish your exams,' she had written. Why the hurry? I had been working hard and I deserved a bit of a rest, I muttered to myself. I want to catch up on my reading.

I'll come as soon as I can, I wrote back. Two days after the exams, I got my father's cable saying 'come home'.

I lived alone in Poona and had got into the habit of talking to myself. Won't leave a man alone, I mumbled away as I packed my case. Other fathers would be only too happy to have their sons stay away as long as possible. Actually, my father had not given me much cause for complaint. But you can't rely on anybody, the elderly are always so inconsistent. I was even more furious when I got home and found the front door locked. They are at the hospital, the neighbours informed me.

When I saw my mother, she had been unconscious for fifteen hours. The doctor said she might live if she came round within forty-eight hours. But mother carried her sense of humour with her to the end. She got past the fifty-first hour and then while Ankush and I kept a close watch over her, she quickly gave us the slip. My father sent me to get my aunt.

'Is your mother worse?' she asked me on the way.

'No, just peaceful,' I replied.

At six the next morning, my father left to collect her ashes. Someone knocked at the door. It was my cousin Shailesh, on holiday from medical school, with his huge trunk and massive holdall. He hadn't seen Ankush for eight years, there was much slapping of backs.

'I want some tea. And my favourite vegetable for lunch, with lots of onions. I'm sick of hostel food,' he shouted as he walked into the kitchen. 'Where's Mavshi? Where's that cup of tea?'

'She's just gone out,' said Ankush, putting the kettle on. Shailesh washed and sat down at the table. Suddenly he noticed the time.

'Where did she go so early in the morning? It's only half past six!'

'She wasn't feeling too well, so Baba took her to the doctor's.'

'You bastard, all those years in Paris haven't cured you of your secretiveness, have they? Where is she? And what are you doing here anyway? What about that job in Delhi?'

'Aai wasn't well, so I came over for a day or two,' muttered Ankush.

The medical student in Shailesh was aroused. 'What's wrong with her? How long has she been sick? Who's treating her?'

'Nothing much. Come on. Have your shower now. We'll chat later.'

My father walked in with a paper parcel in his hand.

'Oh, hello, Shailesh. What a pleasant surprise. Why didn't you let us know you were coming?'

'Well, I just felt like seeing you people, so here I am. Now, what's that you've got for me, so early in the morning?' asked my cousin from Gwalior.

Two o'clock in the afternoon and they still kept coming. All these people wanting a share of our sorrow. My father made tea for everybody. They all drained their cups obediently. We had to get extra milk from the corner shop. I was tired of serving tea. My father, my brother and I had no tears to shed. But that did not stop our callers from shedding them for us. Wiping their eyes. How did she die? When? Who was the doctor? Why didn't you let us know earlier? Who was with her at the end? Didn't open her eyes to see Ankush even when he came all the way from Delhi? The same questions, throbbing with sympathy.

And the doses of philosophy and courage for me and Ankush to swallow. 'This happens, we all have to go one day. Today, tomorrow … it's God's will.' And so on. Stroking my back with their hands. 'She's happy, she's with God. We are all but pilgrims in this world.' There was no end to their consolations. They had no intention of leaving us alone. I told my father I was going to the movies and left.

On the thirteenth day, we had a prayer meeting for the dead. A few friends and the family. After the second hymn, Surve spoke about my mother. I wondered how long he would go on. After a couple of minutes I stopped listening. As I pulled at the thread in the carpet, I heard Surve say, 'We all called her Mai…' I tried to hide behind Ankush. Clutched my forehead, clenched my jaw. But the sentence stuck in my throat like a sob and my tears would not stop.

However late in the day, at least I did understand that my mother was dead. But some things I don't understand at all. Why did I scream my head off at that Alsatian who was merely trying to be friendly? My school friends and I went to Kashmir in the summer holidays. We got as far as Gulmarg, and Rakesh came down with pneumonia. It had been snowing for three days, and we were stuck in the hotel with him. The snow was beautiful on the first day. It was an unseasonal snowstorm, and we were delighted with it. Just for us, we wrote home in long letters. It was the first time any of us had seen snow. The letters remained with us, unposted. It was too cold, and one pneumonia case was enough. God's white, fluffy ashes fluttered down from the sky all day and all night, and the wind chased them, whistling shrilly. Rakesh shivered and trembled despite the layers of blankets. The doctor had instructed us to keep the fire going, and we took turns tending it. On the second day, the enforced isolation began to tell on our nerves. We snapped at each other and lost our tempers. Bickered. Heated arguments about nothing ended in blows. Tearing at each other's clothes, flinging shoes, scratching, slamming. We grouped and regrouped against one another every few minutes. On the fourth day, the sun came out and suddenly we were in heaven, at peace, surprised at the first sunrise in the world. We loved each other. We stood on the veranda, stunned with amazement. Then hugged each other. 'The sun, it's the sun, here comes the sun. Can't you see it? What son of a bitch could take him away from us now? Hurray!'

Groups of people in bright clothes spilled out of the hotel. We followed them. And then we paused. Rakesh. Alone.

Someone had to stay with him. Eenie, meenie, minie, mo, and I was it. I turned back. Soon everyone disappeared in a flurry of snow. I leaned my head against the veranda railing and listened to the silence. I only had to move my head a fraction and the sun's rays streaked into my eyes. The cold of the railing went right through my cheeks, in, in, to where I was. I felt alone. Those disappearing figures, were they figments of my imagination? But it didn't worry me, nothing worried me. Just a bit of loneliness. If I lay down on the snow, I thought, I wouldn't even feel that.

Without warning, a huge Alsatian suddenly hurled himself at me, his front paws on my shoulders. I lost my balance. His wet nose touched my right eye and I leaped over the veranda. He sprang after me, but before he could jump over me again, I found my voice and began to scream, 'Get him off me! Take him away! Leave me alone!' The dog rolled me over in the snow and bounded all over me. My face was covered in his saliva. I was still screaming when the hotel manager pulled him away.

'It's all right. Nothing is going to happen. He's harmless. He was lonely, just wanted to make friends with you,' his owner was saying. 'Come on, Apollo, shake hands with this young man. He didn't realize you were trying to be friends.'

I stared up into the dog's face and shook my head with mistrust. I was frozen and it took me a few seconds to pick myself up. But the moment I was on my feet, I took off like a frightened rabbit, screaming, 'I hate him, I hate him! Take the bastard away! Don't you dare let him get near me!'

How long had I known Aaroti? Eight years? Nine? I can't remember. And anyhow, what binds me to her isn't going to become clearer just because I remember the number of years. The links between us will probably continue to guard their secret, like a silent symbol, long after Aaroti and I and her husband have gone. Secrets are for two things. For blurting out or for keeping. These bonds are never going to understand that the people they were meant to hold and torture have slipped away, leaving them fluttering idly in the breeze.

The day Aaroti got married, whether I loved her or not became irrelevant. I happened to meet her soon after that. In Delhi. She was having a cup of coffee with her sister Koshinda at Kwality's. I made polite conversation for a few minutes and left. Later, when that incident cropped up in a conversation, Koshinda said, 'Even an idiot could have told you that you were in love with her.' I didn't argue. Maybe yes, and maybe no, and pushed it out of my mind. But today I was angry with myself. There are limits to how stupid one can be. At least about one's own affairs.

It has always been like this, ever since I first met Aaroti. When we were together, we never wondered when we would see each other again. What is going on? What are we to each other? What of the future? – these wise and practical questions never came up. The possibility of self-analysis arose because of Koshinda's words. Till then I had never needed to keep a close watch over myself and what I did.

I counted the number of shelves. Ninth from the bottom, third from the top. I'd just make it if I stood on my toes. This was my third trip to that row of books. I'd better get it this time. My look of studied indifference lacked conviction. Sneaking a look at the proprietor writing accounts at his table, I noticed uneasy suspicion in his eyes. To get up, or not to get up, that was the question perplexing him. What is yon lean and hungry Cassius up to behind those books? Dear lens-eyed proprietor, yours truly has a humble request to make. Hold on to your curiosity for just two more minutes and I'll be through. Then you may rise. Thanking you. Yours truly.

One deep breath and the book was in my hands. His stealthy footsteps behind me, his hand on my shoulder, and I turned round, startled. She plucked the book out of my hand, dropped it into her handbag and snapped it shut.

'What right do you have to spend my money? Doesn't Pitaji give you an allowance too? All those films you go to, how can you afford books? I'm going to call Pitaji today. I'm not going to put up with it any more. You're always trying to squeeze money out of me. But you're not getting it today.' She did not stop as we walked up to the manager. 'If you need more money, why don't you ask Pitaji for it? Wretched coward, imposing on your poor sister, I'm ashamed of you.' I stood rooted, speechless. 'Shut up!' she continued. 'I don't want to hear another word from you. Keep your words for Pitaji. Ma is quite right, you have absolutely no idea of the worth of your sister. Wait till I get married and go away, see how you'll pine for me then.' And she pushed me out of the shop.

Slinging her bag over the handlebars, she directed her bicycle on to the road. Who the hell was this woman? Girl? Black Bengali sari with yellow stripes. Atrocious combination. But looking good despite that. Weird hair. She was not fazed by my careful inspection. Thick plait. Full fringe over her forehead.

'Thanks,' I said.

'You're welcome.' She put her foot on the pedal and started to move away.

'My book,' I yelled and ran after her. She braked with one foot on the ground. 'You forgot my book.'

She smiled, a devastating smile. Infinitely sweet. The wind blew her fringe. 'I think you're making some mistake.' Then the same smile and she was gone.

A fortnight later, in the college library, I stretched and yawned and looked up from my book, only to look down at it again, hurriedly. But there was no escaping her. She walked up to me and stood by my chair. My neck ached from the strain, but she didn't move away. Finally I had to look up. She stood there, smiling her sweet smile. Rotten sod, what was she doing at my college? She closed my book and asked, 'What are you reading?' Then, seeing the cover, 'Like O'Neill, do you?'

I kept quiet.

'Lost your tongue?' she continued. 'Never mind, happens sometimes. A fortnight ago, you seemed eager to talk.' She paused, then added, 'I'd love a cup of tea.'

I gave up. 'What do you want?' I asked angrily. 'Who are you?'

'Shush, you don't know how to talk, remember? Maybe you'll find your tongue again when you buy me a cup of tea.'

I made her bear the brunt of my six months of silence, my loneliness. Since I had come to Poona, there had been my room, the library, and me. Sometimes, for days on end I didn't feel like touching a book. Those cool green walls. I was almost driven to bash my head against them. Occasionally I did. From the window I could see the top of the hill, and from April to June, the pink and white blossoms of the cassia tree. As I walked up and down the stone floor, thoughts ricocheted in my head. I turned up the volume of the transistor radio to drown them, but it disturbed the people on the floor below. 'Turn that bloody thing down. If you're so fond of music, shove your radio into your navel.'

So many people at the university. Boys. Girls. You're so pretty. May I talk to you? I want to talk. Talk and talk and talk. What shall we talk about? The college spread over miles. The hill was within the grounds too. And the trees. With their brittle yellow leaves, like crisp crackers. Naked trees waiting for new leaves. Shivering in the cold wind and the early morning mist. Just like me. All bones. All arms. Arms with so many hands. Hands with long fingers ready to plunge into eyes. Pointing to each other. To the blue sky. Not a soft blue, but a dark, cruel blue, a careless blue blue. And in the middle of that blue, the sun – colourless. Aloof. On its own. Belonging to each one of us. Your sun, my sun. White hot, so white that it hurts to look at it. But it's there, hiding behind the hill, burning the blue sky a darker blue, scorching the yellow leaves yellower. Leaves that float to the ground like so many thoughts. A leaf was blown by the wind and started to fly away. Up it went. A crazy leaf. Where's it off to? Who knows? Just one direction, three hundred and sixty degrees of directions. Whichever way a thought points to is its destination. Look, there's a hole in the air, and all the wind's rushing out of it. Leaf from the branch. Leaf on the road. Leaf within a thought. A thought at the core of a leaf. Come along, breeze. Let's blow away.

I couldn't stop talking. She was studying physics. She stared at me, her chin propped up on her right fist. How is it you read so much literature then? And how she read! Books I hadn't even heard of. I have reading sickness, she said. Always at the top of her class. What do you do with your scholarship money? My father puts it into a bank account. Can you imagine it, my money and I can't lay my hands on it?

'I'm off now. Do you realize you've been talking for four hours? Aren't you tired? I'll never drag you off for a cup of tea again!'

'I paid for the tea, remember?'

'Oh? You mean you wouldn't have talked if I had paid? I like that. I'll never buy you a cup of tea then!' She didn't turn back to look at me. Just cycled away, very fast.

Every time I saw her, she looked different. Even if she wore the same sari. When she forgot her bike, she sauntered up the street. If we met outside the university, she didn't speak to me. Tossed her fringe and shook her head in silent warning. She lived with her elder brother and his wife in Poona. They were her guardians. Religious, righteous, very proper. She never opposed them openly, because life was easier that way. Her square-faced sister-in-law recited to Aaroti her husband's bedroom frolics. 'I'm telling you all this for your own good. Maybe you'll be married one day, your brother and I will certainly keep trying for you.' Her generosity would overwhelm Aaroti. She would mimic her sister-in-law for me. 'When you are married, you will sleep with your husband. Then you'll remember what I'm telling you now. Men are very strange. The man you see as your brother during the day is a different man in bed at night. Absolutely different. You should see him. He's insatiable. When he wants something, there's no stopping him. The things he does, how he forces me, the tantrums he throws inside me…' If I looked embarrassed, Aaroti would tease me, 'Don't you want to know more?'

I never had enough time. As soon as Aaroti gave me a new book, I went straight to my room and plunged into it. My landlady cautioned me. 'Electricity costs money and money doesn't grow on trees. Don't forget to switch off the lights when you go to sleep.' She wore old-fashioned nine-yard saris and walked into my room without knocking. One morning she came in at a quarter past six. I had just stepped out of the shower and was stark naked. I had an early lecture that day. She looked me up and down. Slowly. Surveying every nook and cranny of my body. I reached for a towel to wrap my nakedness. She came very close and poked me in the ribs. 'I began my menopause five years ago. Are you afraid I'll rape you?' She ran her fingers through my hair, found it wet and rubbed it dry. It felt good. 'What an ungrateful wretch you must seem to your parents. How old are you? Seventeen? Eighteen? And they brought you up to look like this? Even a vulture wouldn't descend on you. Why don't you look after yourself? I know you read a lot, your room is full of books. Why don't you spend a bit of time living? Instead of living through books. Fool, that's what you are, a fool. That Canetti of yours, Halldór Laxness, Pär Lagerkvist, I've read them all. When you're not here, I borrow your books. Some of them write beautifully, some are just a load of rubbish. However, they can look after themselves. Take books in your stride. You're here to live, not to worship books. Drink milk. And switch off the lights at eleven. Going to lectures at seven thirty and reading till four in the morning – does that make sense? I've never seen a man abuse his body like this. Get dressed or you'll run a temperature just to spite me.' I was stunned out of my wits to hear her speak English. I couldn't move. 'Go on, put on a shirt,' she said and left.

I had lived there for six months, but all I knew was that she had three children who did not live in Poona, and that she had pale grey-green eyes. I don't get on with people who have pale grey-green eyes, I'd protested to my mother. 'You're not marrying her, are you? Stay for a few weeks and see how you get along,' she said.

She and my mother had been at school together. She had agreed to let me stay there because I was 'Sulu's boy'. They had never been very close friends. 'She was always quiet,' my mother reminisced, 'even at school. We used to call her snooty then. The only reason we were friendly was because I used to ignore her. Her family married her off immediately after the matric exams. Didn't even invite me. Just a quick goodbye and she was gone. Wrote to me once a year, regularly, just to say she was still alive. The year I didn't get that card, I'd know she was dead!' And the annual card still arrives, even though mother's gone. Sometimes my landlady used to disappear, to see her children. They never came to see her, at least not while I was there. 'Make sure the door is locked when you go out, don't just turn the key and hope it is.' And she would drive away in a cab.

She came into my room once again, briefly, just before the exams. 'You had better look for another place for the next term.' She paused, half expecting me to say something. 'I'm leaving Poona,' she said, and went out.

I knocked at her door as I was going for my examinations. 'Come in, Kushank.' And before I knew what I was doing, I had bent down and touched her feet. As I straightened up I saw her face, her fair face had turned red and her eyes were like coals of fire. Her teeth were clenched.

'Where will you go?' I said.

'What business is it of yours?' Her voice was still very low.

I smiled. Of course it was none of my business. 'None, of course.' And then I fumbled to say goodbye.

'Just because I spoke to you in English and knew the names of a couple of writers – is that why I get all this respect all of a sudden? I suppose you wrote to your mother too – Aai, your friend in the nine-yard sari reads books. Did it make a good story for your friends?'

'Of course I haven't told anyone.' I was angry. 'Only Aaroti.'

She didn't ask me who that was.

'And what did she say?'

'She said you sounded crazy. Makes you think, she said.'

'She obviously has more sense than you. Go now, you'll be late.'

Aaroti had always wanted to meet her, but we never managed it. The idea of seeing them together appealed to me enormously. One day Aaroti said casually, 'I'm coming to your room, to see that woman of yours.'

'To my room? Really? Come on then, before you change your mind. Let's go.' And I started to pull her away. It wasn't till she had gently tugged her hand free that I came to my senses. Then I stopped.

'When shall I come?' she asked.

'I don't know. I'll have to check with her when it is convenient. I don't even know if she wants to see you.' This last was true. But you couldn't fool Aaroti so easily.

'You're angry, aren't you?'

I had nothing to say. The last month had been hopeless. It was almost impossible to meet Aaroti. There were a thousand places that were taboo to us. My brother's friend lives down this street. There, someone will see us. Her sister-in-law's sister sometimes walks down that street. So many hurdles. Our imaginations worked overtime. The more obstacles we conjured up, the more exciting life was. We imagined the most impossible problems. The library was the only safe place. But even that, not too often, in case someone noticed. We put on such a good act – Fancy meeting you here! I could not understand whom we were trying to fool. I sometimes accused Aaroti of trying to overdramatize things. She was impatient with me then.

Once, when I was going to the movies, Aaroti said, 'I want to see that film too.'

'Let's see it together then. Tomorrow afternoon? Okay?'

'No, you go today, and I'll see it tomorrow.'

'What the hell is this nonsense? We both want to see it, so we'll go together, simple.'

'You won't understand, will you, Kushank? You're such a fool.'

I avoided seeing her for a fortnight after that. If it seemed inevitable that our lectures should coincide, I skipped them. I longed to see her at times, just to look at her. I was obsessed with her fringe and the way it moved in the breeze. But I could be stubborn.

Finally she caught up with me. I suppose I had wanted her to. I was waiting outside the lecture room when she passed behind me, muttering, 'In the catacombs, in the catacombs.' That's what she had named the archives under the library. There we had spent many hours, talking, breathing the stale dusty air of thousands of books.

She was there before me. Sitting in the left corner, behind a pile of German tomes. Leaning against the window bars, gazing straight at me. I wasn't ready to look at her yet. The sunlight through the ground glass window fell onto her face, making it look timeless. I was afraid she'd disappear into the sunlight if I breathed hard. Her eyes had dark rings round them. How still her eyes were. I saw them for the first time then. And beyond them. Right at the other end, there was a place called Aaroti. Shall I come there? And forget the last fifteen days? Tell you all about them without saying a word? But you know it all already. That's where I've been these long days. Kushank wants to lose himself in you. He wants a place called Aaroti.

'Kushank, Kushank, Kushank. You are Kushank, aren't you? For fifteen days, there has been nothing but Kushank in my mind, in my eyes, obstinate Kushank. Kushank … I'm going to Delhi, after the exams. Not to return.'

'What's this? Why didn't you tell me before?'

'Because I only found out this morning. When I woke up, my brother announced that if I wanted to continue studying, I must do so in Delhi.'

'But why? What's the problem?'

'Me. I am.' She smiled bitterly. 'I was writing to you in my diary. A letter, to try and explain to you. About that wretched film. Three hours – we'd have sat together, yes, but not talked to each other. We could have spent that time here, talking. And if not talking, at least looking at each other, me looking at you, Kushank. I tried to tell you. If anyone had seen us together at the movies and told my brother, we could never have met again. But you didn't listen. Then I was angry with my brother. Hadn't he made a simple movie into a criminal act? I wrote K for Kushank and let myself go. I told you in my letter that I had had my fill of other people dictating to me and telling me how to live my life. I really let myself go. I said, there didn't seem any point in living in this world with a brother and a sister-in-law. I said what I've wanted to say for so long, that there must be a way of doing away with them.' She laughed loudly.

'How dare your brother read your diary?'

'What's the point of getting angry about that? There are centuries between us, dividing them from us. Last year, my brother told my father that he should take me away as he could not cope with the responsibility of looking after a young girl.'

She sighed as though she saw the scene repeated before her eyes.

'God, did he hit the ceiling when he read that last bit about him and his wife! The police station, that's where he wanted to lock me up. Told me I was a blot on the family name, that I had homicidal intentions towards them both. How can I face your sister-in-law? he asked me. Me? You wanted to kill me, your elder brother? I, who have devoted my life to looking after you? And your sister-in-law, just about to be a mother for the fourth time? He had the grace to blush at that, the bloody hypocrite.'

And then she laughed louder, surprised at herself.

'But he couldn't get the police station out of his mind. What were you going to kill me with? A knife? A gun? And now Bhabhi searches me every morning – for hidden weapons! Blouse, petticoat, bra – everything.' She shuddered in disgust. 'You know, I really think she has a hidden passion for me or something. She never unbuttons my blouse, just thrusts her hand in and has a feel. She's getting so fat – and those fat fingers linger, ugh. But if I object, she has a ready excuse: Why the great rush? Your brother has instructed me to search you thoroughly. You're a devil, he says, a cunning devil. All he is obsessed with is this K! Who is this K? What is this K? What sort of a name is that? It's quite unnatural for anyone to be called just K. If he doesn't have a name, he can't be real, can he? Tell me who he is, he says. Anyway, you're off to Delhi, where you cannot carry on like this.'

In the split second before I could take it all in, she drew a fingernail down my cheek, and laughed. 'Want to take me to the movies?' And left.

Was Gone. To Delhi.

~

She had said she wouldn't write, and she sent a tiny card, with 'a letter, a letter, my kingdom for a letter'. Told me to write to her care of her sister. When I first met her sister Koshinda, I found it impossible to talk to her. I concentrated on my Coke and answered in monosyllables. She called me Lover Boy when she talked to Aaroti about me. Because I wrote such long letters! 'What a lover, writes epics, not letters! Oh God, don't ever let me fall in love with one of these literary types,' she ribbed Aaroti. Aaroti read her bits out of my letters. My parents, and Ankush in Paris, were upset with me for not writing to them. 'Don't write long letters if you don't want to, just answer three questions,' they wrote. 'How are you? Are you taking all your medicines? When are you coming home?' Ankush threatened, 'If you don't answer my questions this time, I swear I will fly these five thousand miles and break your neck. Don't be smart and tell me I can't afford it. I'll steal the airfare.' Aaroti didn't ask questions. And if she did and I didn't answer, she never got mad with me. I mailed her a letter whenever I passed the mailbox. No beginning, no end. About the man across the street standing on his head, the undertaker coming to take me away, my anger at people who cut the trees in the campus, about my aunt whom I wasn't going to see any more, because she asks too many questions, about why I don't use my brains and why I always get a third class. 'Does it bother you, Aaroti, my not getting a better grade? Seriously, does it? I'll write and tell you the outline of a story before I forget it. But I must mail this now.' Aaroti's letters always ended with, 'And then, what happened then?'

Suddenly, one day, 'I'm going to be married'. But not for a couple of months yet, and she filled up those months with more letters. She hardly ever wrote to me about her fiancé. I was sure she wouldn't invite me to her wedding, but the card arrived. I should have known it would. There was only one adjective for Aaroti – normal. She never reached out for herself; she was herself. I didn't go. And I don't think she expected me to. Then the wedding. And a letter or two. Like before. Then no more. I can't remember who stopped first. We both did.

Aaroti's husband's friends were coming to tea at four and she was in her usual flutter. Should guests be served tea in brass tumblers? Decisions, decisions. Finally she decided to borrow a teapot and cups and saucers from the Kapoors next door. 'We'll have to put thirty rupees aside,' she said, laughing. 'The Kapoors will have to be bought a new set, I guess!'

Prutha and Guddu couldn't take their eyes off the new toys. They wanted to touch the teacups, play with them. 'Get your hands off them at once,' Aaroti warned. 'They don't belong to us. And for Christ's sake, let them stay in one piece, at least till the guests have left.' Guddu blinked and allowed a sweet, single-toothed smile to spread all over his face. 'Oh, my darling,' Aaroti was bowled over, 'what an understanding child you are.' She moved forward to pick him up. With his radiant smile still stretching from ear to ear. Guddu flung the brass tumbler in his hand on the teapot. Aaroti took a very long second to follow what had happened. Prutha began to jump up and down with unbearable joy. Guddu stared at his mother's stillness, stunned at what he had done. A soft, thin-sharp 'swine' escaped Aaroti, and Guddu turned tail. Suddenly, at the scene of the crime stood Aaroti's husband. He gradually turned a deep red, his lips trembled and his body shuddered. He was trying, through sheer concentration of vision, to draw the shattered pieces of the teapot together. His body began to sway in that breathless stillness. The effort he made to bring his various faculties under control forced all the colour to drain out of the neck visible above his Lucknow kurta. His face still looked delicate with that rather exaggerated fineness of nose and lips. His shoulders started to droop and his legs seemed to give way. I pushed a chair under him. He didn't sit, only rested himself on its arms.

I was transfixed by his eyes. They would either bind the teapot together or shatter into smithereens themselves. They looked at Aaroti, piercingly, till they disintegrated. They were empty now.

Really, there is no end to it while you are living. No end for him, for Prachinti, for me, for anybody. For Aaroti.

That day Prachinti said something, and I thought I'd hit rock bottom. It was as if she had put her finger on a raw nerve. I winced, because it had found its mark, but I was also relieved that she had finally said it. A false relief.

Shatlaj had been gone an hour. I was just beginning to worry about him. Prachinti had closed her eyes as he was leaving the room. After nine months of illness, she had not much strength left for pretence. We were all too tired to pretend to be brave at the end. If crying would have helped, we'd have cried. But tears weren't going to solve any problems, give any relief. Tears weren't going to help little Arshad. What would happen to him? Tears would only have confirmed the doctor's verdict, the hopelessness of it all.

We play-acted sometimes, of course, when there was no alternative. There are not too many options open to the dying. And so the occasional pretence smacked of last rites. A man can only live while he is alive. After death, he stays dead. There is no in-between, no no man's land.

I was suddenly aware that Prachinti's eyes were open and that she had been looking at me. She breathed hard and moved her right hand towards me to take mine. 'Give me the other one too,' she said. But she didn't have the strength to hold them and rested them on her stomach.

'How many times have you given me your hand? Especially in the last few months? No. Even before that. Ever since we have known each other, remember? I used to be furious with you, because you always talked only to Shatlaj. I made you a cup of tea and you said thank you. You still say it.' She laughed and I laughed with her. 'It's months since I made you a cup of tea and heard you say that.' Have you ever seen Prachinti's eyes? Shall I tell you of Prachinti's eyes? Once upon a time, there was Prachinti...

'Such rough hands you have, like a labourer's. I like your hands.' She turned over on her side. 'The number of times you've recited your law of sheet proximity. Again and again, to warn yourself. You said to me that the day you felt sexually attracted to me, you'd stop seeing me. I was never afraid of that.' And she went to sleep. With my hands in hers. I was worried about Shatlaj now. Why wasn't he back? I'm lonely. I want the sound of Shatlaj's teasing voice. I don't like these dim nightlights tonight. I don't want light. I want a voice that rubs itself against my body.

'Prachinti, why hasn't Shatlaj come back?'

Her eyes opened slowly. 'How like Arshad you talk sometimes. He'll come, maybe he's having trouble finding the medicine.'

The nurse felt her pulse and went off to find the doctor.

How much weaker could the pulse get? 'What are we going to do, Kushank?' Prachinti asked, and I didn't know.

I didn't know, and I said, 'I don't know. I don't know. God, why do you ask? Don't you understand, I don't know?' I didn't cry, but she didn't hold me close to her.

'Did my question hurt you so much? Really? ... And yet, you will use me, won't you? When I am dead?' Her question had the certainty of a full stop. There was no bitterness in it. 'You write, don't you? You'll write about me, changing my name, to protect my identity. You might not even get paid for it. But you'll publish it anyway – because of some compulsive urge for expression or communication or something of the sort.'

~

Pimping, using others, comes naturally from the moment of birth to all of us. Not always as a form of necrophilia. If not someone else, then ourselves. If not for money, then for literature, patriotism, art, or what have you.

For as long as you live you can't hit bottom. Once in a while you think you've crashed down to it. But even after the bruised buttocks and broken spine, the bottom continues falling away from you.

That's it. The end. Fini. The end of all the unhappiness in the world, in life. The pain, the evil, the disease, the mental cruelty, the loneliness, the sadness, the lot. You have finished with it all. Experienced it all. Passed on your debts to your children, cheated people, slept with Sulabha, your traditionally chaste Indian sister-in-law, given real ten-paise bits to the blind beggar instead of plastic buttons when no one was looking, pretended not to have seen your daughter being fondled by her uncle, told the truth all your life, peeped through the hole in the bathroom window, not only at Mrs Chitale, but at Mr Chitale and Master Chitale too, worshipped your god every day, but that bastard paanwala across the street has a seven-hundred-rupee transistor radio, and you have none, not even a medium wave one, suffered it all, thought about it, about man, about the universe, deeply … you are great, you've written books, been unhappy in love, happy in love, lived in a shed, fought for principles you didn't believe in, been kicked and shoved and pushed. Rock bottom, man, the absolute rock bottom. You have taken it all, the whole jingbang lot. Everything that this world, and every other, has to offer. There's nothing that's ever going to shock you, jolt you, make you wince.

But there is never an end. It's no good fooling yourself about that. When you think you've reached the bottom, you throw your head back and allow your weight to rest on your hand. But before you've taken one deep breath, the bottom shrinks away, as bashful as the receding horizon. There is no bottom where you are. Just one non-stop, hair-on-end, down, down and down.

Don't you believe them, or yourself. If you've taken the worst, there's worse to come. The Black Hole of Calcutta is full to the brim. There's no room to breathe. The walls almost rip at the seams. But there's always room for one more. And then another. Like those people who run round in circles.

Or straight miles. Breaking world records. Half a second, a quarter of a second, point six seven of a quarter of a second.

Look at that bugger there. His lower lip is no longer working its way round his mouth. Just limp. God, I could take him to my breast and let him weep till he had washed me clean of a heart. What's happened? What's the matter? Tell me. The teapot broke. The Kapoors' teapot broke. The china teapot broke. Was it Guddu? Prutha? Some such? All such? Aaroti? I?

Aaroti could not stop wiping her hands on her sari. Her eyes had gone dry searching for her Shatlaj. She seemed so alone. Licking and comforting her lips. She still couldn't believe what had happened. She shook her head because it couldn't happen. She swallowed and started towards him. Cutting her bare feet on the blossoming crockery on the floor, she went to him, five steps away from her. A trickle of blood started making its way towards me. I could contain my helplessness no longer. I went out of the kitchen.

A couple of hours, that's as long as I could stay away today. I tried to stay longer. I was used to being on my own for days. Without seeing faces around me. But today, I couldn't hold my own amongst those hill station crowds. Those men, women and children, I tried to hold them in my hands, but they fell away like sawdust. Lifeless. I had come to know them pretty well by now. I used to sit and watch them for hours. But they had nothing to offer me today. I used to lose myself among them every day, but today it was as though I was seeing them from the wrong end of a telescope. The old man, under his two sweaters, cap, thick wool coat, his socks just visible through his dhoti, was trying to console his little granddaughter who had grazed her knees. A man in a red tie, green shirt and dark glasses leant against the rocks and smiled fixedly at his gold-encrusted wife. She seemed to have got the box camera stuck to her right eye. After two minutes of 'freezing' his pose, his smile soured and he screamed at her, 'I've been standing here for two hours and you can't even take a picture of me. Just press the button, for Christ's sake, that's all you have to do!' His words reached me through layers of cotton wool. I was once again convinced that my surroundings and I were nothing but a mirage. I remembered the first time my parents, Ankush and I reached the cinema before the previous show was over. I could hear the dialogue between a man and a woman. 'It's not too late, Marina, you can still repent,' the invisible man advised. And then the woman's voice, helpless, 'But how can I repent, Padre, when I don't feel guilty?' How completely those two had bypassed the existence of people outside the cinema. I shrank further within myself at the renewed thought that my world was all illusion.

I couldn't lose myself in this melee, though I had absorbed every detail about these people. Stranger. Me. They were conscious of my gaze today. My arms and legs slowly came to a stop. Any act is an offensive against death. But if one can't catch someone's eye, what's the point in keeping one's head above water?

I'd have liked to have gone to the movies. To a Hindi movie. They go on for almost three hours. Plus a ten-minute interval, marvellous. But I didn't have any money, not even fifty paise.

And I didn't want to go back. What would I do there? I'd be just as bored. Maybe worse. I didn't even want to think about what might be happening at Aaroti's. I knew I was sunk, that's all. If Aaroti's husband's friends had lingered, I'd have found it easier to slink in. But I didn't want to meet them. At least the atmosphere outside was free of tension. Just me and the other tourists. Leaving their familiar burdens at home for a week or two. Seven thousand feet above the sea. Strangers to each other. I could have spent the entire evening anywhere, doing anything. At the tourist office, on the bench at the bus stop, leaning against a taxi, and if someone had said, 'You think that cab belongs to your father?' I could have gone and sat on the swings in the park. There was just one problem, the lack of will to do any of these things. Or anything else. I wanted to sit down. Even better, to lie down. To sink into a deep sleep, silent, wordless, thoughtless. Sleep.

The bitumen road near Aaroti's house seemed quiet. The cars had probably not yet left the traffic post down the hill. For the next five minutes at least there would be no traffic on the road. I laid my head on that smooth black bitumen and lost consciousness. Every little bit of me turned to bitumen. And then from within me – a lorry, a Fiat, a bus, some bitumen and then a lorry. And more. And suppose her friends had finished their tea? Damn. Again that thought. Even when I don't exist, that thought scratches at the sole of my foot and enters every pore of my body. Then Aaroti and her husband, and I the bolster between them. Three's a crowd, two's company, double trouble by the Zuider Zee. Stop the world, I want to get off.

When I was ten, my father sent me to my second aunt's house, with a message. Her son opened the door, and I stumbled as I heard the raised voices.

'Sit, Mummy will be here in a minute,' and he left me on the veranda. I tried to make myself as small as possible in the large green cane chair. My aunt and her husband were in full swing.

'I won't tolerate any interference.'

And he, furiously interjecting, 'Don't you tell me what to do.'

'You're always sticking your nose into every damn thing.'

'Me, or you? You always get into a mess and I have to clean up.

'You're the bloody limit.'

I couldn't sit in the chair. I started to walk up and down. The son reappeared – 'Hey, what are you standing for? Sit down' – and disappeared again.

'Watch your tongue. I may be your wife, but I'm not going to stand any more nonsense from you.'

'Oh, aren't you? What are you going to do about it?'

'Don't you scream at me,' she yelled. 'I can't stand people shouting at me.'

I turned the door knob noiselessly and crept down the stairs, gently pulling the door behind me. I went home.

'What did Aunt say?' my mother asked me.

'Nothing.'

'But your father asked you to wait for an answer.'

'She didn't give me one.'

My aunt knocked on the door that evening as I sat eating my dinner. I could hardly swallow. Her husband was with her. It wasn't possible. Was it some other man with my uncle's voice? I could still hear them so clearly, no longer fighting, loud, angry, and screaming, as I had heard him ask again quietly, menacingly, 'So what are you going to do about it?' She had replied equally quietly, viciously, 'I'll leave you. Alone.' And then once again, shrilly, 'Did you hear me? You want to know what I'm going to do? I'm going to leave you.'

My aunt held my father's hand and was pointing at me. 'Really, Rushand, your son takes the cake. Don't you ever have scrapes in your family? You won't believe this, but your son is a mouse, a real scaredy-cat. He just slipped out of the house, without telling anyone. Just because we were having a shouting match inside…'

Aaroti and her husband could not even have a full-blooded free-for-all. I was tired, exhausted by uncertain sympathies and loyalties. If these two had stood up like a Greek chorus and ordered me out of the house, I might even have shaken hands with her husband.

Sunheria's little girl was playing with Prutha in the front yard. Prutha put her arms out when she saw me. I wanted to pick her up, to rub my nose against her fat pink cheeks and to forget it all. Sometimes she was so affectionate. And then became tiresome within five minutes. She expected so much of others because of her own immobility. I ignored her and went inside.

Used teacups and plates, Aaroti's housecoat. There was no one in the room. Not even the ubiquitous rats. I went over to my favourite spot, the tiled balcony beside the kitchen. I swung my feet over the railing and dangled my legs over the valley below. I loved that place. Mountains on either side of me. I could stretch out a hand and draw a line across their peaks. Rows of mountains, one behind the other. And through them, like someone playing hide-and-seek, the winding road, visible, invisible, swinging, climbing. The sky turned grey and clouds gathered. Still. Totally still. The stillness before the beginning of the world. God must surely have created the world at a hill station. Each separate thing. So still and quiet that the sounds moving at the base of the silence never came out crushed or crumpled. The lorries straining up the hill. Guddu's sudden laughter from next door, Prutha's whining, Bismillah playing Darbari Kanada on the radio at the Palace Hotel. Sunheria's daughter gathering the teacups and sucking back the snot into her throat. I could hear all these sounds, could see the mountains looking at me. Everything seemed close, clear.

An unbroken stillness. And solitude. An awareness of existence, an unbroken circle. A completeness. A complete aloneness. Alone at the tip of the world. The aloneness of going to meet God and not finding oneself.

Then the hail came. It came with a vengeance. Clattering on the tin roof of Aaroti's house. Crashing against my head, bringing up bumps where it hit me, battering me. I wasn't going to get up and give in. I'll stay right here. Let the hail bludgeon me, I'll not move.

Sunheria's little hunchbacked girl ran out of the kitchen door to get the clothes off the balcony railing. The house rumbled. The decrepit, rat-eaten balcony slowly started to crumble. My stomach heaved, lurched, fell over. Fell over with Sunheria's little girl, down, down, down, she went, rolling over and over and then suddenly her neck jerked free and down she went, to join the smashed pitcher in the valley. I did not run to get the binoculars.

Sunheria came in the evening. She did not look at me through her yellow eyes, eyes turned yellow from years of blowing at the smoky stove. Should I have taken the clothes off the railing? The police had come, Sunheria. The Kapoors sent for them. I sat there watching the mountains. The part of the railing against which I leaned did not give way. The rats hadn't got to it yet. I'm still here, in my bed. Why don't you look at me, Sunheria, and why is Aaroti crying? The doctor gave me some pills to take, so I'll be better tomorrow. I want to sleep, Sunheria, sleep with my head in your lap.

~

I'm leaving the day after tomorrow. At four. We went and booked my ticket yesterday. I loved going out with her. To forget, momentarily, the tensions in the house. She was still beautiful. Especially yesterday. Her figure was trim, even after two children.

Something went wrong on that walk, for no reason at all. The last week was reason enough. We didn't say a word to each other. My discontent seemed to be in the way. Got the ticket and started to walk back.

'Come, let's have a cup of coffee.'

'No, I don't feel like it.'

'Why not? You wanted one before, you nagged me for one.'

'But not now.'

'Stop being childish. Come on.'

But I did not stop being cussed. Not till the next day. I was suddenly tickled by an idea and laughed out loud. Since I had stopped talking to her, I felt as if those two were guests in my house.

'Aren't you going to talk?'

I was quiet.

'You're off tomorrow. Are you planning to spend the rest of your time here without a word?'

I shook my head.

She wanted to go and buy a new tea set for the Kapoors. We planned to escape without being noticed by the children. Prutha was playing her favourite game in the backyard. Whenever the sun shone, Prutha's chair was put out in it, so she could soak in as much sunshine as possible.

Her helpless fingers were engaged in scooping water out of a bucket.

We breathed a sigh of relief as we shot around the corner. The short cut to the bitumen road and we were there. But we hadn't escaped. 'Amma,' yelled Guddu as he spotted us and ran towards Aaroti. Behind him, Sunheria, trying to grab him by his pants, and then Prutha, with her twisted limbs screaming wordlessly. I stood there and watched quietly. I thanked God for Prutha's intractable limbs. If she could have run, Sunheria would have had to chase wildly in two directions simultaneously, and Aaroti and I would have gone back home.

On the way back, we stopped at the solitary Madrasi café for a cup of coffee. I pointed out Shiva's blue nipples on the wall calendar. Sitting on Mount Kailash, with his eyes closed. Ganapati on the calendar next to him. Same coloured nipples. At that, Aaroti could not help herself. She burst out laughing and had to leave her dosa unfinished. She used her one and only Marathi cuss word. 'Gandu, you're absolutely shameless.'

On the train, I could not stop thinking of Aaroti. Just before I left. In the glass-enclosed veranda. Before her friend arrived. Her eyes swimming with tears and the memory of her pregnancy. When Prutha was born. At home. It was a tradition in her husband's family. They had a Punjabi doctor. When Prutha refused to budge after six hours of labour, Aaroti's father-in-law said again and again, let's go to the hospital. Her mother-in-law and the doctor said it was quite unnecessary. The baby would come out in good time. It had to. It didn't. It remained jammed. They held up her legs and used forceps to drag Prutha into this world. Aaroti's insides cracked, her thighs spilled over, her vagina split. The dazzling pain. The pain of birth, kaleidoscopic pain. As if the man was bringing forth the earth from her thighs. Her legs stopped hurting. Only one pain at a time. The pain of the whole world. Then the doctor was breathing air into Prutha's lungs. There were two wounds on her head. Deep blue wounds from the forceps. She was indifferent to the world, to the doctor. For an hour and a half he breathed life into her.

'Everybody says she'll be okay one day. When she is five, you won't even remember she'd been so ill once. Oh, is she already five? Really? Doesn't look it. Don't worry. Another year or two and she will be fine. Who are they trying to fool, the bastards? You think she will? She'll talk? It's the mind. I want her to have a mind. To decide if she wants to go on with this world. Tell me, Kushank.'

Raghu came back from Geneva a month or so after you left. Thumping loudly at the front door at half past three in the morning. It was barely twenty minutes since I had closed my book and dozed off. Who the hell is banging at the door in the middle of the night? I reached for my glasses and switched on the light and half opened the door. It was too dark to see, and whoever it was seemed in no hurry to come in. I called out, 'Who is it?', but no one appeared in the doorway. I opened the door wide and saw a movement in the light that spilled out. There he was, swaying and rocking on his heels. The only creature I know who is totally in tune with dried-up trees and dead leaves, water and sunlight, dew and shade, with the pulse that beats in the heart of the earth itself. Raghu. Animal, child, completely natural. His joy, his unhappiness, his awareness of the body and its pleasurable sensations, his anger and his hatred, his infinite capacity to involve himself. The sun was setting one day in Nandadhela. Raghu's head in its centre. A strange light came into his eyes as he ran his fingers through the soil heaped on either side of the pit. Stillness and solitude all round. His dilated gaze slipped off me and entered the sky. His body began to sway ever so softly. I had the awkward feeling that I had walked into something intensely intimate and personal. I turned away.

A suitcase in his hand and a broad smile on his lips. Then his deep, strong voice. 'Hi, Shank. How's it going, man?' He enunciated each word in a soft cadence. We had known each other since we were both ten. He was twenty-nine today, but he looked ageless.

'Happy birthday, Raghu.'

'So you remembered. You always do.' And he dropped his case on the floor and gave me a bear hug.

Raghu had been in and out of India for eight years. He graduated as an engineer from Poona and went to Aden as a deck passenger. From there to Greece, France, England. Doing whatever job came his way, making do with sleep when he could not get any food, he finally reached the United States. He specialized in mining and got himself a highly paid desk job. Three days later, someone asked him if he would go to Africa for relief work. And since then he had been with MORE. Like CARE and Oxfam, this international organization with its headquarters in Geneva collected money from where it could and sent its experts to disaster-struck areas across the world. The experts, with the help of volunteers, rehabilitated and rebuilt.

Raghu had no time for altruism and noble motives. He earned less than he would have in that first job, but he still made a lot of money. 'In the last six years, I've been to wherever there has been a famine, an earthquake, a flood. But I've never lost sleep or gone without a meal because others were starving. I do a job not because I'm a do-gooder, but to earn a living. And if I manage to derive some emotional satisfaction from it, well, that's fine.'

For the past six years, I have always seen him in that outfit, khaki or grey. His bush shirt unbuttoned all the way down, or tied carelessly with a belt. For field work, either a pair of shorts with a hundred pockets or trousers with a thousand. Great, big desert boots or Kolhapuri chappals. Shorter than me, but always managing to look at least four inches taller. His was not a powerful body but, standing or moving, it had a natural balance and grace. An animal grace. The compact and complete Raghu. There was a quality about his wrist and neck that suggested a subtle sinuousness. Like a cheetah. And when he shook hands, his touch reached out to the muscles of your neck.

There were three things in which not many people could hold their own with Raghu – concentration, an almost inhuman capacity for work and women. No one, least of all Raghu, understood what made him so attractive to women. The lower left-hand pocket of his safari jacket always carried an address book that opened with a spring action. Within its covers were the addresses and telephone numbers of millions of women all over the world.

'The MORE-man always arrives on the heels of disaster. I wouldn't be surprised if people confuse MORE with the disasters themselves.' Raghu laughed. To a lot of husbands, Raghu must have appeared to be the personification of disaster. But no one had thought of asking the women their opinion in the matter.

This time, Raghu was here on a job. As he was leaving Bombay, he said, 'Shank, want to come with me?'

'What am I going to do there? You don't even know if there's going to be enough to feed you.'

'Don't worry about that. Maybe MORE will take you on as an observer and pay you too. We might even do a brochure or a book if you take photographs like you did for that hospital job. MORE is always short of money, and this could be good advertising. I have to call Geneva tonight – shall I ask them about it?'

I had been jobless since that hospital project. Six months of fruitless searching for a publisher. A couple of Indian publishers had shown some interest, but the bad printing would have ruined the photographs. So I looked for a publisher overseas. Two of them held out promises, but even after a year, there was little progress. A whole year of despondency and hopelessness. No doubt they had good reason for the delays, but I had almost run out of money. I applied for a number of jobs. The replies were predictable. Why did you give up your last job? How do we know you won't do it again? I tried to get a job with my old employers. They were sympathetic, but the managing director said, 'What did I tell you?'

I woke up one morning and decided to give up the book. If they publish it, well, that's fine. I started to tutor schoolchildren. Bought myself a book to brush up on my grammar. Sometimes I got bored and told them stories. One of the parents warned me against this a couple of times, but the boy and I got on well, so I hadn't been sacked yet.

We started off late in the evening. Most of the journey was to be through parched, famine-ridden areas, so we could travel only at night. Raghu had a BSA. I had a hundred rolls of film, and if Geneva passed my first lot of pictures, they would pay me a retainer.

We were going to Nandadhela. For a month, three MORE experts and their Indian helpers had been trying to dig wells there. Something seemed to go wrong every time they started to bore or dig. The three experts almost died from food poisoning, and the whole project was about to be abandoned. Then MORE sent for Raghu, with his special knowledge of the terrain. The BSA Bullet was a beautiful bike. Doing at least fifty miles an hour, we covered about five hundred in a night. We took turns driving. The road ahead wound and disappeared into the pupils of my eyes. Every few miles we stopped to consult a map. Then Raghu found a track that finally took us to within a hundred miles of Nandadhela. The sun was coming up.

I wish the day had not dawned. Raghu was determined to start work that morning, but I was doubtful if we'd find anyone alive. Man and nature, both had changed unrecognizably here. As the motorbike passed, flocks of kites and vultures rose lumbering, then slowly settled down to work again. Sporadically we saw human beings sitting, lying, dying by the roadside. Skeletons. On the move.

'Where are they going?' I asked Raghu.

'To the city,' he said. 'Half of them will get there. By any reckoning, the other half ought to die. They'll probably live. But don't ask me how or why. Half of those that reach the city will die of cholera or dysentery or typhoid or plain starvation. Ten per cent will go mad. But still forty to fifty per cent will return home to wait for the rain clouds next monsoon. I know all the figures by heart. What I can't understand is their extraordinary capacity for survival.'

Humans and animals. And their faint shadows in the early morning sun. It wasn't eight o'clock yet, but the earth was a smouldering cinder. The same endless landscape and the same endless sky. Not a bird in sight apart from the carnivores. No green or yellow leaves. No dry leaves. Just the scorched and crumbly earth and an occasional eye-stinging whirlwind. The scared, shrunken trees. I wished I had a Sten gun with which I could rat-a-tat-tat all the animals in sight. And the humans? I put my head on Raghu's back and shut my eyes. There was a gigantic female spider inside my head. If I kept my eyes shut, she might go away. I shut them very tight. The spider put one foot forward, between my eyelids and the eyeball. I picked up my chappal and brought it down hard on her. Smashed her. Her stomach burst and millions of skinny little spiders spilled out like ants out of an anthill. Into my nose, my mouth, my ears. I opened my mouth to spit and a thousand others swarmed in. Some crept up to my brain and some down my throat to my stomach. My nose was blocked and I couldn't breathe. If only I could sneeze.

They were crawling down my windpipe, each one on his eight hairy legs. If only I could vomit before they reached my stomach. Then all the pores of my body were blocked and my stomach, full of millions of spiders, started to swell. More and more spiders forced their way in and my bloated stomach touched the blue sky. And then it burst. And the spiders were flung all over the place.

'Jai Ram ji ki.' Raghu stopped the bike. A bullock, his bones sticking out, gave up pulling the cart and slumped down in the middle of the road. The family in the cart were thrown forward and the baby landed at the front wheel of the bike. Its mother gazed expressionlessly at the sky. Her left tit, dry and puckered, pointed at the sky too. I jumped off and picked up the baby. It must have been dead a couple of hours. Its rickety stomach was stretched and swollen tight over its ribs. In a minute it would touch the sky and burst.

'Where are you going?' asked Raghu.

'Don't know, sahab,' sighed the father.

His wife looked at the dead baby and turned away. Her four other children formed a frightened little group by the roadside.

'Then why did you leave?'

'What's the point of staying? Everybody's gone.'

'There must be some people there,' Raghu persisted.

'Yes, there are some. More cursed than me … There's a curse on Nandadhela that not even the white men could lift. I might have died too, if Sardar Bhishander hadn't been kind enough to buy my land from me.'

Raghu stared at him, incredulous. 'You sold your land?'

'Yes, sahab. Not just me. A lot of people in the village sold theirs too.'

'What price?'

'Price?' he smiled feebly. 'How can I bargain at a time like this? It was God's gift, my piece of land. But I took what they gave me.'

'Did you put your thumb on the deed?'

'Of course. To receive money and not put my thumb on the deed – it'd be as bad as masturbating in a whore's bed.'

'Will you come back with us?'

'No, sahab. It's no use.'

Raghu started the bike and we went on. 'I thought for a moment back there you were going to burst into tears or something, Shank,' he said after a time. 'I won't mention this again, but you and I have no time for tears. I think that guy will return. His wife won't last long and God knows what will happen to the children. Now multiply that incident a thousand times and if you want to have hysterics, let's get them over with. Obviously Nandadhela has its stock villain. We need cool heads to deal with him and getting emotional won't help.'

Nandadhela's first hut.

The Bhangi colony. Three mongrel dogs. And one mother kicking her child out of her way. A thin abrasive haze of dust softened the outlines of everything around. Then the village. A kid started to chase the bike. The women at the well pulled their saris over their faces. The old man at the door of his hut spat a greenish-yellow gob at our wheels. It spattered our legs as the bike went over it. The tailor, the peanut vendor, the doctor with the potions against old age and impotence, the grocer, the Ram temple, the blacksmith and his son working the patched bellows and hammering a red-hot wheel. Then a few scattered houses. On the left, far away, a high brick wall surrounding a two-storey house. A few minutes later, the MORE van stamped with its insignia. I felt as though I had come home.

All four tyres of the van had been slashed with a sharp knife or a scythe.

Raghu went into the MORE tent. He stood still for a minute. 'People who get food poisoning suddenly don't leave their tents looking so tidy,' he muttered.

I threw myself on the bed, but Raghu had other ideas.

'Shank, I'm going to the site. You take the Bullet to the Nehlapur hospital. See Rizzoli and bring back the keys to the van, and news. And a letter of authority so we can get our parcels out of the post office.' He dropped three one-thousand-rupee notes into my hand.

'Rent a truck. Bribe them if you have to. Get six new or second-hand tyres. Pick up all the stuff at the post office and hurry back. Oh yes, and a giant-sized drum for petrol and another for water.' He repeated the list for me, scrawled a note for Rizzoli and before I knew it, I was on my way.

'What did Rizzoli say?' Raghu was surrounded by geological maps of the area around Nandadhela.

'Leave at once if you want to stay alive.'

'And?'

'The water truck comes every other day. Give the dog a drink before you have one. There's enough tinned food in the truck to last us for a week and there's grain and medicine at the post office for anybody who wants to work on the well to last a fortnight. No grain for anybody who doesn't work, and that goes for women and children too. If you relax that particular rule, every digger will acquire twenty dependants. Don't eat food cooked by anybody else. Don't accept any invitations to meals.' Personally, I thought Rizzoli was overdoing the ten commandments. But I was a fool. 'Look out for Bhishander, and even more so for his son Kartar. Here are the keys. Here's the water. I've had a drink.'

'Did you test it on the dog first?' Raghu rapped sharply at me.

'No. I'll have to adopt one.'

'Don't be a bloody ass. Rizzoli knows what he's talking about. Don't underestimate his advice. Next time you ignore a rule, you can piss off back to Bombay.'

Raghu and the truck driver unloaded the truck and had

six tyres changed within an hour. I'd had the sense to hire a battery. The driver took the old one away for recharging. Raghu test drove the van and I went to sleep.

It was seven in the evening when I woke. I unlocked the van and got some tins of food.

'Keys?' Raghu put out his hand. I gave them to him and he hooked them to the chain around his neck. I didn't like this new Raghu.

When we were walking to the site later, Raghu said, 'Shank, things are bad, really bad. The shaft for boring the well is broken. Since Rizzoli didn't say anything about it, I guess I'm right – it was broken deliberately. I'll cable to Geneva and Bombay tonight from Nehlapur, but it will be at least six weeks before the new shaft arrives. I plan to dig two wells by then.'

'What with? Our hands?' I joked.

'Yes, with our hands. It'll be good for morale even if we don't strike water. And another thing. If you find an intruder in the tent, pick up anything that comes to hand – knife, dagger, whatever – and strike. But do it swiftly and hard enough to stop him from coming back at you.'

Raghu and about ten others were digging with spades and hoes, a large hole about six feet by six. Raghu jumped in and came up again looking thoughtful. He pulled me away from the well and said, 'Something stinks. I've bored a lot of wells, dug a few too. I've almost developed a sixth sense about them. No matter where the water level is, I can feel its presence in my bones. There's no water here. I'm sure of it.'

By the next evening, the well was fifteen feet deep. Raghu was either in there digging with them or encouraging and supervising. When I started to take pictures, the diggers stopped and stared. But they got used to me. The villagers, too. Now and then one of them would step out of the crowd and ask me to take a picture of him. The women would cover their faces and disappear, but sometimes, when they thought I wasn't looking, they would watch me, half expecting me to photograph them. I attached a mirror lens to my camera. Now I could point it in the opposite direction and catch them unawares.

That left the three ancients in the village, two men and one woman. When I first saw them, they were squatting under the large fig tree, their heads between their knees. Mouths slightly open. God alone knew if they were alive. Some lungless forms of respiration seemed to be keeping the life going in those burnt black, transparently fragile bodies. Occasionally an eye blinked. Then maybe the other one too. If not, the whole world looked lopsided. At first you thought you were seeing them through a very fine mesh screen. Then gradually you looked closer and discovered the landscape of their faces. Millions of lines, infinitely finer than hair, held those faces together. Only the long snow-white lashes indicated that the old woman had a pair of eyes. The eyes of the old man on her right were petrified with watching the goings-on in the world for so many years. The seven spaced hairs on the other old man's bald head were like periscopes, observing the movements in the village from a distance.

They had seen, suffered and experienced all. They had blessed the birth of the sun and the moon. I had an overwhelming desire that they should survive this famine.

Each morning, enough water would collect in the one well in Nandadhela to fill three or four buckets. When that was gone, the women started to fight. But there was no spirit in their fights. They were too starved, too desperate, too weary to utter any more than half-hearted abuse. Then that too died down and the village relapsed into a hot stillness.

After going without a bath for four days, Raghu and I should have been stinking. But even the smells of the body did not last long in that infernal heat. I stuffed my nostrils and plastered my lips with cold cream to stop them from cracking open.

Every evening we had three chores. First, pay the diggers. Then, sell them grain. I asked Raghu why we couldn't skip the farce of the daily wages and simply give them the grain. Raghu frowned. 'Idiot. You, of all people, ought to know the value of earning a living. Give them money and leave the choice of spending it to them. That's self-respect. If they want to spend it on booze, that's their decision. Try giving them nutritious food instead of money and they won't work half as well.' For an idiot, I was learning fast.

After the food shop, the surgery. Raghu said, 'Shank, you will make a fine quack.' I nodded acceptance of the compliment and shoved another anti-typhoid and cholera needle into another emaciated buttock. I gave all the diggers allergy tests for penicillin, sulfa and streptomycin, and noted their reactions. We never lost an emergency case through an anaphylactic shock. The patients were divided down the middle. The women preferred Raghu.

One evening, as we were finishing at the well, a Packard stopped a short distance away. The team foreman, Amar, ran to salute the figure in the sherwani. Raghu looked up and said, 'Bhishander.'

'Have you met him yet?'

'No, but I will.'

The next day, a group of young men arrived at the site, standing well away from it. Watching. Words like helplessness, humanity and poverty had no meaning in Nandadhela. But even in that famine-ravaged place, I had not seen people quite as broken, crushed and barely human as these. They just stood. For a couple of hours. The diggers ignored them completely. I had already asked them a few times whether they wanted to work. But they only shrank further into themselves. I couldn't stand it any longer, so I asked Raghu, 'Who are they?'

'The village untouchables,' replied Raghu without looking up.

'Shouldn't we give them work too?'

'You just asked them, didn't you?'

'Maybe they're embarrassed.'

'They'll have to get disembarrassed, won't they?'

I lost my head in the heat and yelled at him.

'You blasted smug-face. I could puke at you and your indifference.'

'Save it, Shank. You're making an ass of yourself. We're only here while wells need digging. Then they're on their own. Which son of a bitch in Nandadhela do you think is going to let the untouchables drink from this well? They'll have to fight and force their way if they want the water. If things have to explode, let them explode while the well's being dug. Then they'll have earned their right to drink the water.'

'And if they don't dare, we'll leave them without a well, I suppose?'

'One well at a time, my sweet social reformer.'

~

On the fourth morning, Raghu said, 'They say there used to be a river here, about fifteen miles away. It disappeared a couple of years ago. Let's go and have a look.'

He had almost torn the geological map to pieces by now, studying and restudying it.

'There's something queer about these maps, but I can't work out what it is, yet. They've been fixed all right, but by someone who knew what he was doing. If I could only get a clue.'

It was seven o'clock when we reached the river. Its one-time existence was confirmed by smoothly rounded pebbles. Otherwise the land lay flat, arid, baked and crumbly. Raghu touched a pebble and shot up five feet in the air. 'Jesus Christ!' I thought a scorpion had bitten him. 'Was that stone hot!' He was licking his hand.

While Raghu worked, I took a few pictures and looked around for shade. I found only Raghu's shadow and mine. I plucked the crash-helmet off my head to fan myself. Raghu was busy digging up soil samples from different places. I joined him, preferring to die of work rather than of heat. As the soil came up more and more moist, we worked faster. We were a couple of feet down by eleven o'clock. Suddenly Raghu dropped his spade and said, 'Come on.'

'Not me. You go,' I said in dead earnest and collapsed in the heat.

'Shank, you bastard … If you die of sunstroke, I'll bury you in that hole. Come on, let's go.'

He picked me up, dragged me to the Bullet, loaded me on the pillion seat and sped away.

It was two days since we had abandoned the first well and started to dig at a new spot. After many calculations, Raghu had settled on this place a few yards away from our tent.

Once again the Packard drove up. Right up to us this time. He was an impressive man, Bhishander. Face like an eagle's and mock sleepy eyes. He might pounce suddenly and leave no trace of you.

'Who gave you this piece of land to dig on?' he asked through clouds of smoke, puffing on his pipe.

'Never mind that. I know it doesn't belong to you,' replied Raghu coolly. 'You'd better tape this conversation, Shank.'

I pressed the button on the little recorder.

'Are you threatening me?' growled the thakur.

'We didn't come to see you. You're the one taking the trouble to do that.'

'Haven't you heard what happened to...?' He stopped himself. 'There is no water in this village. You're wasting my people's time. Giving them false hopes. You'll up and leave one day, but they'll stay on and die of hunger. These are my people. I won't stand by to see them suffer.'

'Fine, then give them jobs and two meals a day.'

'Watch your tongue. You might regret what you say.'

Sparks flew as Raghu struck a stone with his spade.

And then things started to go wrong. We were woken by Amar's shouts. A cow had fallen into the half-dug well. Her throat was cut almost through, but she still breathed. After a lot of threats and cajoling, Raghu got Amar and a couple of other men to help lift her out. But the ill-omen had worked. No work was done that day. Nor the next. Raghu's temper rose with the heat. The water truck arrived that evening. As usual, the first drink was given to the dog tied to the tree. He vomited all night.

Then Mr Mistri arrived. He looked after the MORE staff in India.

'Well, Raghu, how are you?'

'Very well, thanks to you.'

'I dropped in at the Sardar's house on my way here. He said you chaps were rather upset with him.' He smirked. 'Didn't you get my report before you left? There is no water in Nandadhela.'

'What would you advise me to do?' asked Raghu innocently.

'Stop wasting MORE's money.'

'And what about my cut?'

Mistri hesitated. Raghu and I looked expressionlessly at him. Mistri raised a questioning eyebrow in my direction. Raghu winked. 'A good friend and corrupt as they come.' Mistri smiled. 'We'll talk to the Sardar.'

'No tape recorder this time?' Bhishander's son laughed.

'No.' Raghu laughed back.

'And camera?'

I held out my hands and smiled.

'Good,' said Kartar. 'Now you are behaving like grown men. How much?'

'Forty thousand for me and ten for him,' said Raghu.

'Too much.'

'You bought half the village for practically nothing. What's fifty thousand to you?'

'We'll talk tomorrow. Come to my house.'

We found Bhishander, Kartar, Mistri, a huge Alsatian dog and a stranger waiting for us at the bungalow. After some polite conversation, Bhishander's daughter-in-law brought food and sherbet. A little sherbet spilled as she handed it to me, and she bit her lip. Wide forehead and the tika on it as big as the sun.

'Sorry,' she said softly.

'We are very forward-looking. We don't have purdah in our family, unlike the rest of the village,' bragged Bhishander.

'I'm forward too,' rejoined Raghu.

I barely controlled my laughter. Finally, the Sardar produced the money.

'That's forty thousand. Count it.'

'Yes, I will. But where's my friend's ten?'

'Here it is, take it.'

I counted my share, and Raghu and I got up to leave.

'Stop,' said the stranger with Bhishander. He produced

a pair of handcuffs. Mistri and Kartar blocked our way. 'You're under arrest for bribery,' he said, and showed us his CID badge.

Raghu and I must have paled. Kartar laughed aloud.

'Seen the morning paper yet?' I asked nonchalantly.

'Shut up and don't waste time,' shouted Bhishander.

I pulled out the Nehlapur daily. We had spent the whole of the previous night at the newspaper's office. In the lower right-hand corner of the front page, it said in bold type, 'Sardar Bhishander's Generous Gift to Famine-stricken Nandadhela – Rs 50,000'.

I thought I heard Bhishander's daughter-in-law giggle at an upstairs window.

We rode to Nehlapur and credited the money to the 'MORE Relief Fund for Nandadhela'.

That night I went to the Bhangi colony.

'I've met people like you before, many times,' said Kanhaiyalal calmly, self-assured with the wisdom of his seventy years. 'You come and get us when you need us. Leave us scratching our armpits when the job is done. Sure, you get help. But who helps us?'

'Why don't you help yourselves?' I egged him on.

'I'm sick of this argument. All I know is this – every time we're offered jobs, houses, land, all that happens is that we lose yet another privilege.'

'You allow them to, so they take away.'

'No one bothers to ask us. They take away as if everything belongs to them.'

'Why don't you do the same then?'

'What are you, a reformer?' He smiled and handed me a chillum. I took a few deep drags and choked till my eyes filled with tears. I liked the old guy's sense of humour.

'Give the sahab a drink of water,' he said, over his shoulder.

'No.' I coughed.

'No water?'

'Yes to water, but no to the reformer accusation.'

'You must be desperate for help, then. Or you wouldn't be here!'

'It is not my well, you know.'

'But you'll get the credit, won't you?'

I stood up to leave.

'Angry?'

'No.'

'Then you agree?'

'Sure I agree. But you and I can't really talk.'

'Whose well is it?'

'Whoever fights for the right to use it. Just because you dig the well it doesn't necessarily mean that you will be allowed to use it.'

'And you still expect us to come and help you?'

I had no answer.

The next morning Kanhaiyalal and his seven companions stopped outside the tent. They wouldn't come in.

'Don't misunderstand me,' he said. 'I'm not fooled by your talk. We will work because it is the only way to get food. But let's not have any false notions about who that well belongs to.'

Work proceeded at a good speed. We had rope ladders to go up and down the well. Raghu and Kanhaiyalal's men dug all day. The women took away the soil in baskets on their heads and soon there was a mound of earth next to the well.

Raghu would disappear on and off. God knows how many of the women shared in his largesse.

When I had finished developing some films in the temporary darkroom we had set up in the van, I found the door locked from the outside. I hammered and kicked and yelled, but Raghu must have died or something. It was suffocating in that small space.

Finally he opened the door, brushing his hair into place. 'You lock me in there again and I'll leave, you bastard.'

'Hey, where's your sense of humour? I was just having a bit of fun.'

'A bit of a fuck, you mean.'

He shut up.

I didn't understand why he was being so unusually secretive about this bird. Not till a few days later.

I was sleeping outside the tent, when I was woken by faint sounds of laughter. Laughter like the bubbling of a hookah. I turned over and tried to go back to sleep. But that strange, echoing murmur persisted. I got up to look in the tent. Raghu wasn't there. Not even in the van. I walked towards the well. It was so deep now that it made me dizzy to look into it. I lay on my stomach and looked over the edge. Deep down, there in the bright moonlight, I could see two bodies moving, and then Raghu's trousers thrown over a bright yellow sari, like inanimate objects locked in lovemaking.

She tickled Raghu and laughed louder than him. Her long hair swung round as she threw her head back. Like the still wings of a bird hanging in space. Raghu raised himself on his elbow to kiss her breasts. I remembered her hidden laughter at Bhishander's house. I lay there for a full minute in sheer amazement at Raghu's audacity. Then the bark of a dog in the distance jolted me wide awake. A hurricane lantern bobbed towards us. I could see the vague outlines of a man and a dog. I cupped my hands and whispered hoarsely down the well. 'Raghu!' He heard me the second time. I saw her look up at me, startled. She hid herself under Raghu.

'Here comes Kartar.'

'Good God.' He jumped. She brought her hands up to hide her breasts and then quickly down between her thighs. Raghu hooted, 'You aren't the first naked woman he's seen, you know,' and then to me, 'Where is he?' I suddenly realized why I could hear only in half-tones. I had plugged my ears with cotton balls to shut out the noise of crickets. I pulled them out now.

'Almost here. He's got his dog with him.'

'What will I do?' She began to cry.

I ran to the tent, got my brown sheet, threw it at them and pulled up the heavy rope ladder. The dog, that bloody dog, what was I going to do with him? I remembered those old 78 RPM records from my childhood and yearned for that docile, lovable creature listening attentively to his dead master's voice grinding out of the phonograph horn. I was back in the van, staring stupidly at the tinned stuff on the shelves. I tried to read the contents of the cans, but I invariably turn illiterate when in a panic. After a superhuman effort, I pieced together the various letters and symbols on one of the tins. 'Candice – instant, irresistible chicken soup. Heat and serve.' Sorry dog, you'll have to drink it cold. I peeled off the lid with the tin opener above the sink, poured it into a dish, got four sleeping pills and mashed them into the soup. As I was leaving the van, I suddenly recalled our mangy dog on whom we tried all the non-tinned stuff that we ate. The bastard wouldn't touch meat. The bloody vegetarian. If Kartar's dog too was into organic foods ... but I had no time to work that out. I slipped out and put the dish behind the tent.

I had barely made it back to my bed when Kartar and the dog arrived. I sat up.

'Hullo, Kartar Singh. What an odd time to come visiting.'

'Where's the other fellow?'

'Did you miss him? He went to see you.'

The dog could smell his mistress and whined excitedly.

'Shut up, Moti. I don't like your jokes. Has anyone else been here?'

'Anyone else?' I repeated asininely.

'Answer me.'

'Why don't you choose a better time to come around? I'm going back to sleep. Goodnight.'

Kartar raised the flaps of the tent and went in. Moti was standing guard outside. I brought the soup and placed it near him. 'Here, Moti, drink,' I coaxed. What was that saying about horses and water? We were done for. Kartar's dog sniffed the soup and kept his mouth out of it.

'Unlock the van,' said Kartar.

'Brought a search warrant?'

'Unlock it or I'll set Moti on you,' Kartar threatened.

I unlocked the van. He held the lantern up to the tins of food and scrutinized them closely. Then the darkroom and the drying rolls of film. The rows and rows of photographs caught his eye and he started going through them with compulsive curiosity. How I cursed myself for not thinking of those photographs earlier. I took a bottle of chilli sauce and got out. I poured some into the soup, dipped my finger and mixed it evenly. The dog didn't need any cajoling this time. He lapped up the whole pungent mess.

But the soup was a mistake. Moti was twice as vociferous now about the whereabouts of his mistress. He went into the van, nudged and pushed and whined at Kartar.

'Have you got pictures of me?' Kartar asked after he'd been through the lot.

'No, but if you like I could take some now.'

'Not now, I'm not dressed for photographs. All right, all right, Moti, I'm coming.' Moti pulled Kartar towards the well. That bloody dog. Those pills would have knocked down two elephants by now. But this son of a bitch seemed determined to get to the bottom of the well.

'So this is your famous well.' He leaned over to look into the depths. One kick in his backside, I thought to myself. Suddenly he straightened.

'There's something down there. I saw it move.'

I gave a lunatic laugh and peered down myself, really scared now.

'Something definitely wriggling down there … Moti. Moti.' He kicked the now quiet dog. Moti opened an eye and went back to sleep.

'You just have a dirty mind, Kartar,' I muttered, to give myself courage. Kartar disentangled the end of the rope ladder and was about to throw it down. I undid my pyjamas and started to pee into the well.

'You filthy pig. Have you no shame? Relieving yourself in front of me?' Kartar was infuriated.

'Shame? Why should I feel shame? Are you ashamed of your filthy black deeds? Then why should I be ashamed of peeing before scum like you?' I couldn't stop talking nonsense. Kartar turned around, disgusted. I could see Raghu's feet peeping from under the sheet.

'Moti?' Kartar tried to wake the dog, but Moti was dead to the world.

'Come, I'll take you home,' I said, as I got the bike out. Kartar looked at me gratefully. He heaved the dog on his lap, astride the pillion. Halfway to his house, I stopped the bike. 'Get off,' I said. He looked puzzled, but obeyed. I called out goodnight and left him there.

I switched off the engine and took off my crash-helmet. 'Kushank, Kushank.' I heard heart-rending screams from deep within the well. My heart bled for him. I took my time going there. I peered down. There were two creatures standing like Adam and Eve, but even in the darkness of that vertical tunnel, I could see that they had been turned out of Eden. 'Kushank, can you hear me? What's the matter with you?'

'Hey, why are you still there?' I sounded genuinely surprised. 'It's almost six o'clock and Kanhaiyalal and his people will be here any minute.'

'You bastard, Kushank, you…' He must have been really angry, he was spluttering and the words kept derailing into an inchoate yelp.

'You okay, Raghu?' I was still all concern. 'And the lady with you? Why don't you people put on some clothes, for God's sake?'

'Kushank, you motherfucker, I'll break your balls when I come up, I swear. Are you going to throw down that ladder or not?'

'Hell, why didn't you say so?' I threw down the rope ladder. She climbed up first. Raghu followed with his palm under her buttocks, helping her along. I gave her a hand and she swung over. I put a hand over my nose when Raghu came up.

'Stop covering your bloody sensitive nose, you bastard, it's your pee and it stinks.'

'Next time around I'll pee eau de cologne.'

Next morning at eleven we struck water. As we were breaking the auspicious coconuts, the trucks arrived. With them the shouts of men. Finally Amar, the doctor, the tailor, and the rest of the villagers and Bhishander and Kartar. Moti must still have been asleep. The women hurriedly disappeared from the site.

Kanhaiyalal and his friends stood apart, embarrassed. Amar and the others tied our hands behind our backs. And then the bulldozers and the earth-movers began to fill up the well. It took them an hour and a half to level it.

'Enough, Kushank, enough of this silence now. Talk to me … Look, here's a penny for your thoughts.'

I kept mum.

'Come on, Kushank. Tell me a story. About Christ. Or Atlantis. A brand-new story or a lovely old one. Say something.'

But I didn't.

'I'll leave if you don't talk to me … Don't be so moody today, Kushank. Please. What did we come here for, then? Just because I said something on the phone yesterday, you won't talk to me today?' She was at the end of her tether. 'Angry today because we couldn't meet yesterday. Angry tomorrow because of today's silence and bad temper. Then my turn the day after for having been so sweet and sane these two days. Improving on your performance, naturally. A full seven days' silence just to be one up on you.'

Either alternately, or together, you and I have gone over this so many times before.

But I was adamant.

'I'm off now.' And you left. Knowing what was good for me. I stayed glued to my chair at the Victory Stall. What got into me? Why did some of your schizophrenia suddenly attach itself to me? For weeks you were mean, bitchy, friendly, affectionate, said unforgivable things, made the Mahabharata and the Gita, Tukaram and Dnyandev come alive for me, were nasty and cruel, and through it all I kept my head, refused to be drawn into a fight despite every attempt you made. And then one day, the tables turned and I scooped out my pound of flesh for all those days of quiet and calm.

I knew I would come to my senses when you got as far as the Regal. Then pay the bill and chase you like a madman. And if you had taken a cab? And if you hadn't gone home? And if you didn't let me in? … I ran after you. You were buying two cones of softy ice-cream.

You smiled, not a sour smile. I could have asked the ice-cream man to hold our cones for a moment while I hugged you tight and kissed your lips, your cheeks, your ears, your glasses as they slipped off your nose. I stuffed my mouth with half the cone.

'Tell me a story.'

We returned to the Victory Stall. The young girl at the next table looked like a Maharashtrian. She must have overheard our previous conversation. She and the waiter came wide awake at our second entry and composed themselves for act two. The carefully dressed man she was with, probably from her office, tried to hold her left hand in his right. Her Maharashtrian upbringing brought her flat black handbag smartly down on it.

'But why?' he asked, hurt, trying to flare his nostrils. His whole body seemed to shrink under the weight of that black handbag. My heart went out to him.

'Kushank, will you stop eyeing those two while you are looking at me?' you asked between clenched teeth.

His foot came out of its moccasin and fleetingly touched the foot under her sari. He looked into her face for a reaction. She didn't use her bag again. I almost burped with relief.

'Are you going to be moody again? Or do you want to go and sit with them?'

'No, no, no, no. And I'm sorry, sorry, sorry.'

Your eyes grew large. 'That's enough sorry-ing. You're moody the first three-quarters of the day and sorry the last. And stop laughing. It's a week since you told me a story. Or is there some unwritten law that you can't till I lose my temper or throw a silent tantrum?'

'Tell you a story about a cotton ball, shall I?'

'Very funny.'

'No, really. Shall I?'

You turned away to look at the sea.

'Once upon a time there was a you and a me.'

'And then, Kushank?'

Some stories are for telling, some for keeping to ourselves.

This was my second trip to Banaras.

Sadhan had written, 'Come for a few days, before I go away to the United States. We will have a couple of weeks together and talk.' My four school friends. Rakesh, Raghu, Jitendra and Sadhan. Until a few years ago, Sadhan and I weren't very close.

'Banaras hasn't changed,' I remarked.

He didn't answer. Even after he had been appointed a lecturer, the youngest in his faculty, there was little outward change in him. Dressed in a woollen suit. Receding forehead and aggressive, large, protuberant teeth. He had either stopped expanding or had got himself a new pair of trousers. I remembered his clothes when he was a student at the university. You never knew when the buttons of his fly would pop and hit you in the face.

But I sensed another kind of change. He seemed more relaxed, more at peace with himself. He'd probably still be in the thick of any fracas, but I doubted if he'd strike the first blow.

He had a five-room bungalow on the campus. Only a few minutes away from the hostel where I had stayed with him on the previous occasion. The lovely old red-tiled roofs made me feel at home. There was grass everywhere, like the last time. But it was green and not yet shoulder high. A little playful breeze skimmed over it and touched me lightly as it disappeared. I looked down at my hands. The hair stood up on them. Sadhan remarked, 'Banaras doesn't change, it changes people.'

I didn't understand. For a moment, I thought he was trying to be profound. But I should have known better.

He had wasted an academic year and had failed the entrance exams to the Indian Institute of Technology. So he went to Banaras. Small, slight, vegetarian, south Indian Sadhan. He had spoken little Hindi at the time. Four years in Banaras and he looked and spoke Hindi like a bhaiyya. Thick curved moustache. Body like a steel cable.

'I work like a slave every year to get a first. I've got one now for the past four years. I'll get one when I do my BE next year and also when I do my ME. Then I'll teach for a year. And slave again for a PhD from MIT,' he had said once. And it had all happened. Like clockwork. Now, only the doctorate remained. But there were no doubts about that either. Nothing left to chance.

That first evening, we went for a walk. He stretched himself out on the grass. 'I'm ready,' he said. Then was silent. Ready to take on the world single-handed? I smiled at him. But that wasn't what he meant. Whatever he was ready for had better be ready for him. 'I'm ready for the States. The MIT journal published my latest paper this month.' He drew a cable out of his pocket and passed it to me. 'I can apply for a grant to do research on anything I want. I'll be my own boss and I can ask for all I need. I'm going to take that place by storm, Kushank!' He laughed. Then, turning to me affectionately, he said, 'But you'll always be there, won't you?'

And then the grass grew high and turned yellow. Sadhan was twenty-two again and we leaned over the third-floor balcony of his hostel, exchanging friendly abuse with the boys in the hostel across from us. Sadhan opened the innings. 'Slave of my forefathers, eunuch of the harem, go take a flying fuck at the moon.'

Quick came the retort, 'You bastard. Listen, you, whose cock is like the crescent moon…'

It was a beautiful campus. Vast open spaces, like an open gaol. Very pretty and methodically mad. Sadhan said it was blazing hot in summer and froze the veins in winter. The hostels spread out far and wide. And in those buildings were let loose boys from all over India – from Bombay and Delhi and Calcutta and Madras and Agra. Only one thing was taboo – women. Girls, women, females. And that's all they ever talked about. Twenty-four hours of the day, even as they studied. Studied, swore, and talked about women. Over and over and over. Till the words ran out and tongues fell limp and ears grew numb. Talk, talk, talk, but never a woman in sight.

A third-year friend of Sadhan's accosted me one night and wiped the superiority off my face.

'Yep, that's all we do. Rub our cocks the whole day long. But, superman, all it's going to take to bring you down to earth and make you human is ten days. Tell you what, smart-arse. You get the hell out of here if you know what's good for you.'

The next evening, Sadhan, his roommate Ravindra, some others and I went into town to the movies. A group of girls from the ladies' college came out of the theatre after the matinee. The usually quiet Ravindra turned to me and asked, 'Do you think they talk about us as much as we do about them?'

'I pray to God every day that they…'

The third-year friend, who had confronted me the night before, cut me short. 'Don't worry, Ravi, only another week and the women who cut the grass will be here…'

Sure enough, five days later the women came. I could feel their presence even before I woke up. The air had stopped moving. The atmosphere was electric with the swish of sickles. I laughed and put on my glasses before going out of my room. The boys were out on the balconies. Down below, making you want to throw yourself down in a mindless ecstasy, were dots of shrill yellow, dazzling red, and lime green. The dots moved imperceptibly with the grass and made me dizzy.

My laugh rang hollow. The campus had claimed its latest victim. The women sang softly as they moved forward on their haunches. Occasionally one of them laughed. And the eyes of the watchers on the balcony turned upon her with infinite love. For the next two or three days, the air felt cool and tender, like a shower of rain in the midst of dog days. Faces relaxed and there was much camaraderie. But not for long. Gradually the temper changed. Faces began to show the strain. And God's gift turned sour before our eyes. The women and us. Face to face. All of us so free, yet bound hand and foot. Miles and miles of grass extending to the horizon, and our machismo lying mortgaged with those witches.

We could have touched them if we had leaned over from the road a bit. And then either they or we would have turned to ashes.

Those women must have smelt the acrid smell of our sordid desires. When they couldn't see one another in the tall grass, they made sure they stayed within calling distance. The midday meal was eaten together, giggling, chewing paan, combing each other's hair.

Their simplest gestures and movements turned into screaming sexual signals for us. All day was spent on the veranda, on some pretext or the other. And then the long night, descending like black pepper on an open wound. Restless, agonizing, dismal. Masturbating in the bathrooms to the point of indigestion. But frustrated and dissatisfied more than ever. As their faces became familiar, we picked favourites. Sometimes there were arguments over the same woman. But mostly we dreamed of sweeping down on them on our horses like Genghis Khan and vanishing with one of them into the hills.

The morning found us back on sentry duty. Trying to glimpse a thigh or a breast through the folds of their saris. The topic that caused the most heated debate and gave rise to much anxiety was: don't these women ever pee? And then we went wild with the vision of slit flesh under a thatch of curly hair. But maybe they didn't indulge in that kind of thing. Or they had a couple of extra bladders so they could hold out for ten hours at a stretch.

On Friday evening, as we argued about this for the fifteen hundred and ninety-first time, Murari laughed at us derisively. 'Oh, cut it out. As if you believe the rubbish you talk. I've seen them do it.'

He said it with such confidence, we were struck dumb. What bloody luck! 'Whom did you see? When? Where? How? All of it? Where were you?'

He answered some of the questions, ignored others. We were crazy with envy. And then, a few hours later the doubts began. 'The lying swine. We know him. He and his stories. Who would believe him?' But of course we believed him. He had seen that beautiful landscape denied to us.

The next day we redoubled our efforts. We spied every move with renewed enthusiasm, taking turns. No luck. In the evening Ravindra asked Murari, 'Did you hit the jackpot today too?'

'What if I did?' Murari turned away, whistling.

Everyone of us was listening intently to this exchange. 'Oh, come on, Murari, tell us the truth.' Ravindra's voice had sharpened with frustration and hope.

Murari shrugged and Ravindra was almost at his throat when Sadhan pulled him back and told him to shut up. Murari lost every friend from that moment. Nobody spoke to him, except his roommate. Then one day we plied his roommate with hooch. And he talked.

'That son of a bitch. Calls me his friend. Stares at them for hours through his bloody binoculars, but when it's my turn, pulls them away after a few minutes. Says what the hell do I want to look at them for. The selfish bastard...'

In an instant we had sobered. He too seemed uneasy at how much he had blurted out. But we were smart. We didn't bring up the subject again.

The next day, as we returned from lunch, the sky was rent with blood-curdling cries. They came from the hostel, from our floor. Murari burst out of the room next to Sadhan's, a knife in his hand. There was a crazed look in his eyes. He must have slashed at a mattress. He was surrounded by clouds of cotton wool. The stairs disgorged boys from the other floors.

'You wait here,' said Sadhan, and vanished. For a moment or two, Murari did not realize that Sadhan was standing only a few yards behind him. Then he saw him and raised his hand to strike, his whole body rigid with blind hatred. For a second their eyes were locked, the one unseeing, the other willing him to see. Murari rocked indecisively as his blurred mind slowly brought the world back into focus. He dropped the knife and collapsed on his knees. He was screaming now. Weird, inhuman screams that were more terrifying than his rabid rage of a few moments ago. It took us a while to decipher his cries. 'Who stole my binoculars? I'll kill him. How will I look at them now?'

The next morning Sadhan said half-jokingly, 'Come, let's go to the Ganga. Wash our sins away.'

He'd said it before. 'You've come all the way to Banaras and haven't even been to the Ganga?'

But I had ignored him. I don't know why I agreed today. 'Let's go.'

Sadhan and Ravindra were going on fieldwork to a place a few miles away, near a canal. I took the opportunity to get away from campus.

We left early on our bicycles. The sun was just coming up, like a bump on the forehead. Green and yellow clouds of cut grass lay everywhere. The women hadn't arrived yet. I thanked God, but not quite honestly.

After a while when I looked down, I found that my legs had parted company from my body. Someone had wound a spring and for the next few days they would keep going up and down. Non-stop. Breaking the world record for cycling. A record player played raucous Hindi film songs to stop me from falling asleep. And an audience crowded around me. Through my reddened eyes I saw Sadhan passing a hat round among them. Three coins and a note. Would that buy me a lemonade? Then Sadhan passed me a bottle to pee into. The audience livened up. 'Next time, pass the hat around after I've peed,' I said to Sadhan. 'Let the bastards pay for their curiosity.'

'Hey, you doddering old fool, what are you muttering to yourself?' Sadhan said, stopping by my bike. 'We'll stop if you're dying to have a leak.'

When we got there, my shirt was stained with the butter from the sandwiches. I undressed and jumped into the canal. Then slept a deep sleep under the peepul tree with a book over my face. Sadhan and Ravindra would come up occasionally to see how I was doing. We had brought food enough to feed a small army, but it was all gone by the afternoon. Around eleven, a farmer came by with his cow. 'Jai Ram ji ki.' He stopped to chat.

'Does she give milk?' asked Sadhan.

'She is Kamadhenu herself, God's own gift of a cow,' he said. 'Blessed our family, she has. One drink of her milk will even cure a snakebite! The other day we fed her milk to Yadram's barren wife; the woman will be a mother soon,' he simpered.

We touched her teats reverently.

'What do you call her?'

'Meenakumari,' he said proudly.

'Give us a drink,' said Ravindra.

'Oh no, sahab, her calf hasn't been fed yet. You wouldn't be so cruel, would you now?' He had sized us up all right.

Sadhan gave him a rupee. Meenakumari fed us milk till we burst.

'Now the hash?' I said.

He refused. When we persisted, he promised to bring us some the next day.

Before leaving we had another swim.

A pale moon. Not a cloud in the sky. Then the sun hit the horizon and the sky was bathed in yellow and red. We would ride together for a couple of minutes and then I'd fall behind. Sadhan and Ravindra would wait for me or I would pedal furiously to catch up.

About four miles from the campus we sighted the women. Each with a bale of grass on her head and a sickle at her waist. Long plaits of hair, done up with bright hairpins. Glittering tinsel tikas on their high foreheads. Wiping the sweat with the ends of their saris. No cholis, just the sari hiding the body completely.

I think the three of us saw her at the same instant. She stood alone. The evening seemed to wind itself round my throat and pull it tight. We went mad. The wind stung our faces. We hadn't seen anyone for a few minutes, and then, suddenly, there she was.

She had a large bundle of yellow grass on her head and was tightening her green sari at her waist. As we got closer, her dark face looked extraordinarily beautiful.

Some kind of seismic signal flashed between Sadhan and Ravindra and they shot off like lightning. I was damned if I was going to be left behind.

She stood still, slightly puzzled as they pedalled madly towards her. Then suddenly realizing that they were heading for her, she balanced her heavy load with one hand and ran. Her free arm sliced through the air like an oar, but the distance between them kept on decreasing.

She disappeared into the grass. Sadhan and Ravindra dived in after her. The wind parted the grass and I saw her crouched with her back to us. As Ravindra's bicycle wobbled towards her, she dropped the bundle and thrashed her way deeper into the high stalks. He let go of the handle and threw his arms around her. Her left breast was in his hand, his eyes lit up with the joyous innocence of a child.

Her sickle missed Ravindra's hand and coiled around his neck, half disappearing in it. Sadhan followed close behind. Jets of blood soaked his shirt front. She seemed riveted by the horror in his eyes. She shuddered convulsively and jerked the sickle out.

Sadhan and his bike fell together and Ravindra keeled over with his lolling neck. Red butterflies alighted on the yellow grass.

Sadhan clung fiercely to me as he raised himself. My shirt started to tear. He banged his head again and again on my shoulder, on my chest.

'God, Kushank, and I was going in after him too,' and he fainted to the ground.

She stood there still, the sickle in her hand, her lips apart and disbelief on her face. Her eyes, those large eyes, were terrified and even larger now. Durga's eyes. Her black skin shone like polished ebony. The red stone in her nose ring and the orange sindoor on her forehead. The small, firm breasts still in the folds of her sari.

A drop of blood dripped down the point of the sickle. Golden light filtered from the hostels on the horizon. The grass around Sadhan had been flattened. I crouched and felt for Ravindra's pulse. 'Oh, my God, what have I done?' I heard her say as she turned away.

I gave the cable back to Sadhan and we returned home. The lights had been switched on and the table laid for dinner. I went to my room. My head felt heavy. The bed was made and there was a soft quilt on top. I lay down and must have slept. Till Sadhan called, 'Dinner!'

As I washed my hands and sat at the table, I noticed the woman trying to keep to the shadows.

The red stone had fallen out of the nose ring. And the Durga eyes were gone too. But her incredible beauty still took my breath away.

After dinner Sadhan said, 'Aren't you going to say anything?'

I was silent.

'I'll be away for two or three years.'

She watched us both, motionless.

'Kushank, shall I tell you something? Take Meha with you.'

She didn't blink an eye.

'She's a good woman. She will look after you well.'

However free a man is, he manages to tie himself to something or to someone. Psychology and philosophy may offer a hundred explanations for this tendency, but you can't escape human bondage. Whether you like the bonds or not, whether they're from the past or the present, the point is, you're bound. There are a thousand ways of freeing yourself if you really want to, but you remain tied.

You choose a person to communicate with. In solitude, in a crowd. Whether he can hear you or not. Whether he has forgotten you or you no longer exist for him, you keep talking to him. But rarely can you find two people who talk to each other.

When I first saw you, your eyes seemed extraordinary. Even through your glasses. I had never seen eyes that were so wide, and which hid so much. If I had walked straight through them for a mile or two, I still wouldn't have found you. Yet they were so open, so expressive. When I talked to you, I had the feeling of talking to two people at once.

You had built a wall around yourself, in self-defence against your brilliant and temperamental father. To spite him. It worked. But then you got trapped within the wall.

You couldn't escape from it, you never tried to. It was safe in there. Yet in seeking that safety, you had lost your freedom, your capacity to grow.

I owe a great debt to Fernandes. It was he who gave me courage to leave my secure job, he who introduced you to me, changed the course of my life. I must have spoken to Fernandes for less than an hour, but the meeting proved eventful. Unknowingly, he made me take up my long-dreamt-of hospital project. It frightens me even now to think what small and irrelevant things change the flow of our lives. Do you remember how I met him? They were testing a new drug on a few of us at the hospital. Fernandes sat beside me as we waited for the results. Wrapped in a world of his own. And then he started to talk to me.

'Last night, as I was making an omelette for myself, I remembered something after ten or maybe fifteen years. The nausea I once had for eggs. My father used to cook eggs for my brother and me. He gave us fried eggs and bread and butter in the mornings. And an omelette and bread for lunch. If it wasn't raining too hard, and most of the time it was, he got us puris and boiled potatoes from an Udipi restaurant. Otherwise we had eggs again at night. The choice was limited, since my father could only cook eggs. One way or the other, it was either fried eggs or an omelette.

'My mother was ill and in a hospital at Worli, on the seashore. The dimmest of lights hung from the high ceiling of her room. The hospital was in some old British army barracks. Her room was dark, even during the day. When the tide came in, the surf seemed to crash into the room itself. My mother was very lonely. On the rare occasions that I visited her, she seemed distant. It was the rainy season, and my father often had to walk to the hospital to see my mother and to bring her food twice a day.

'There is nothing in common between a poor man's poverty and the genteel, barely lower-middle-class man's ceaseless efforts to make ends meet. There is nothing to recommend either. The first is a rock-bottom pervasive state. The other too is total, but it corrupts, warps and paralyses through insecurity.

'A genteel, middle-class man may become well-to-do, but he cannot rid himself of insecurity till he dies or kills himself; the second alternative is rarely practised, because genteel environments and insecurity leave you inconclusive and indecisive. And suicide requires decision.

'If I feel threatened again, I'll sell my soul. Or I'll lie down on my belly and open my arse for you to bugger me. I'll only pray that you will have the mercy to bring along a little Vaseline.'

~

I gave up my job and started to interview patients and people at the hospital and to take photographs. My medical friends and the other doctors were lukewarm in their reception of my project. They suspected it involved a criticism of them. When I asked for help from sociologists and others, they knocked me back because I did not have the right qualifications, the right degrees. Your director passed on to you the job of refusing me help. You sifted through the pages of my writing and stopped at Fernandes. I must have been in luck.

'Shall I program this for you?' you asked, unexpectedly. I was slightly bewildered. Only half an hour ago you had told me that you were a punch card operator. But knowing the distaste your institute had for anyone like me, without qualifications and credentials, I accepted your offer. How I foamed at the mouth with amazement at the work you put into my research and the way you transformed it, how I went cold, dumb, speechless – all that is history now.

I asked around about you and discovered that you had done a highly advanced computer programming course a couple of years ago, that you were biding time till your sociology thesis received the final okay. 'But why a punch card operator then?'

I was taken aback by your vehement and angry reaction. 'Because I like it. And it's none of your business.'

Then one day, much later, in a moment of weakness, when you were off guard, you told me, 'When I was in the eighth grade, I didn't come first in my class. My father saw my report and said, "I don't want second-rate children." I turned my back on him and said, "Fuck you." I did the punching course in my last year at university and applied for every available job. And accepted the first one that came along. I go home once in a while, after he has asked me several times. Once at dinner he said, "Why don't you look for a better job?" I looked him in the eye and answered, "I don't mind being a second-rater."'

You are your father's daughter, all right. Other people have brains, you have an acetylene flame instead. But you are so pig-headed about this one thing. Even after you left home, you kept up the battle with your father. He is the pole star in your life and all roads lead to Daddy. When I told you that you reminded me of most of the hippies of this world, you felt I was being unfair. Like you, they too are rooted in the past. Holding their parents responsible for everything they do, for their lack of involvement.

'Fuck the past, and fuck them. Start from now and here,' I said to you. But it didn't have much effect on you.

And the tragedy is that you have such a tremendous capacity for happiness. If only you'd let yourself go. Because when you do, you not only recreate yourself through new experiences, you change everything around you and the world becomes a different place.

'I refuse to get hurt, don't you see? The last one to hurt me was my father. After him I keep everyone at arm's length.'

Yes, yes, I do see. But you are going to be hurt. That's life. Hurting and getting hurt. But it's living and tasting too. I've asked myself, and asked you too, so many times. Why don't you people cut your throats and end it all?

I've never known what the future will bring. Or what fatal message the next moment has in store for me. Which is why I gobble up the present so furiously, squeezing every last drop out of it, stretching my bones, limbs, brains to grab everything I can. But I couldn't argue with you. I lost every time, and in despair became rude.

Then you went away. Travel sets people free in so many ways.

You thrust your hand into your bag, fumbled inside and said, 'Take.' It was six months since you had changed your mind.

'I don't want them,' I said.

You had come back for a month, to see your mother.

You had asked me to meet you at the Sea Lounge because you wanted your letters back. The glass windows cut off the sound of the sea and it seemed as if the red, blue and yellow yachts bobbing up and down on the pregnant waves were beckoning me to go out to them. My constant struggle for self-awareness suddenly sprang a crack and I realized in a calm and inevitable way that I was deceiving myself. However absorbed, however lost you are in a person or a situation, you can never justify your actions by saying that your faculties were paralysed or that you were carried away by the momentum of events.

Not to yourself at least. We did know, didn't we, even after getting engaged and losing ourselves completely in each other, that this wouldn't last?

'You find this whole thing distasteful.' You couldn't resist the remark. And when I didn't answer, you said, 'What shall

I do with this ring?' I almost said 'Put it on the third finger of your right hand and marry me'. We are all Gatsbys. You, Chandani, me and so many others. Looking for our Daisy. Centuries from now, when our love has long been gone, we'll still pick up the strands and start to respin the web, at the faintest of signs. I smiled at my self-delusion. And that irritated you. 'You find me very funny today?'

How can I explain to you that even six months after you said no to me, I am still none the wiser. If you really had been pregnant that time, two years ago, when you missed your period and we were so scared, perhaps I wouldn't have lost you, would I? Suddenly I was disgusted at my self-deception. And surprised. And a little amused.

After taking photographs all day, as I splashed water over my face, you asked, 'Why don't you ever take pictures of me?'

'Because if I did, I'd be left with them and you would go away.'

'Stop making excuses. All those old hags and snotty kids. Why not me for a change?'

'I'm not making excuses.'

'And where would I go? I'll get my degree in two years and come straight back. Or you come with me.' And then you were very quiet. 'I might not even go,' you continued, pouring condensed milk into my tea. And before I could ask why, 'My period is seven days overdue.'

I observed my reactions carefully, closely.

I had always insisted that you go overseas for further study. When the university did not answer your application for two and a half months, I grew impatient with them.

'What difference does it make? Going, not going?' you repeated your favourite catechism.

Then suddenly I asked you to marry me. I wanted you to go, but I wanted you to stay.

But today we didn't refer to it, not till it was time for me to go home. Lying with my head in your lap, listening to Ali Akbar on tape, we barely spoke. Wrapped in our private silences. When the music came to an end and I rose to go, you pulled me back gently.

'Let's get married, Kushank. This month.'

And I sat up and answered. 'You feel so bloody trapped, do you?' For a moment you looked stunned, not understanding. And then you started to shake your head. As if you couldn't believe what I had said. Your forehead creased with dismay.

'How prickly you've become!' you said. You were silent for two minutes. 'No, it's not feeling trapped. I've been thinking about marriage for weeks. That we should live together. I hate you leaving every night. Sundays are too short. And sometimes I don't meet you for four or five days at a time. I want to lie next to you and read as you wait for sleep. Without saying a word. Making a pointed effort to ignore you, lest you get angry. Or suddenly, while talking to you, letting my mouth stray over your body. If I had the guts, I would have moved in with you long ago. But I'm not that strong or fearless.'

You hugged me and traced my mouth with your finger. 'Let's get married. Shall we, Kushank? Before I go to Baroda. Tomorrow!'

You waited for my answer.

'And what about the university? The degree?'

'You can come too.'

'How? Who is going to give me a scholarship?'

'Somebody. Somehow.'

I had to laugh. 'For what?'

'Well, what about your photographs and your research?'

'No degree, though.' I shook my head. 'No, you go and try to find something for me to do.' I walked to the door. 'You go to Baroda for the weekend. I'll ask Rashid, he'll know what to do.'

'You're going to tell him? About us?'

How often you've teased me for trying to hide you, like a secret.

'He will know a good doctor.'

But you didn't return for five days, instead of within two. This has happened a million times before, I told myself. I have read about it in books. At the hospital I had seen women brought in on stretchers, their clothes drenched with blood. But the world's experience has nothing in common with what happens to us, personally. I had tried so hard to come close to you. It had taken so long. In tackling the ghosts from your past, had I now become the latest curse in your life?

There was no point in worrying, so I worried. Why were you so long coming back? Had you already had an abortion? Were you angry? Your letter informing me when you were returning didn't mention the matter at all. I met your train at Bombay Central. And restrained myself till we got to your room. You put your arms around me as we went in and asked, 'Now do you agree that we should marry? Do you?'

'What happened?' I waited.

'About what?' You looked puzzled for a moment. 'Oh, that! You idiot, all is well. No problems.' You grinned.

Seeing the relief on my face, you were contrite and hugged me hard. Without bothering to shut the door. 'Kushank, my dearest. I'm so thoughtless. You were really worried, weren't you? Never mind, let's forget that and find a Brahmin. And an auspicious moment. And we'll get married. This evening. I'll wait for you.'

~

And here you are now. Across from me, on the other side of a cup of Cona coffee. Your favourite kind. To take away the letters you wrote to me. Keeping for yourself the long, rambling letters I wrote to you.

What a long way we have come from each other. The distance is measurable in terms of your first and your last letters to me.

Dear Kushank,

It's midnight and I write to you with Okhon asleep beside me. I was terribly sleepy just a while ago. My legs were numb after sixteen hours on the plane. And then seeing my sister, her husband and little Okhon, after so long. I thought I'd fall asleep at once.

I shut my eyes and feel the presence of another being in the room. He's gone when I open them. If I keep very still he might come back. You're laughing at me, aren't you? But I can feel you here, in this room, near me. Telling me a story, pausing to look for the right word, listening to yourself. I always see you like that when I think of you. And the other picture is of you straight out of the shower – looking so new. Virginal! Even when you wash your face and rub it dry, you look as though you've powdered yourself – you are so pale. Then combing your hair with your fingers, without a mirror. I've never seen your hair stay in place. And when I brush your hair neatly, you look so like an obedient seventeen-year-old that I have to ruffle it again! I can't feel your hand in mine today because you are so thin, isn't that so, Kushank?

There is one last picture of you in front of my eyes. It's four days before my departure and you're writing like a madman to me. It's late at night, but you fill the fourth aerogramme to its bleed before you sleep.

Kushank, thank you, thank you, thank you. The thank you that Madhabi Mukherjee sings in

*Charulata*. I can't imagine a more beautiful way to greet a person in a new country.

I kiss this letter in ten places. Kiss it till it puts you to sleep. Good night and love me as I love you.

P.S. Reading this the next morning embarrasses me!

Like a young girl's first declaration of love!!

But one of us must write love letters. And since your four letters barely mention us, I shall take over the job. Jokes and regression apart, I'll stand by what I wrote last night.

Your Dear John letter was brief and to the point.

Dear Kushank,

You've probably guessed what I am going to say. But I'll say it anyway, I don't want to marry you.

I'd have liked to say sorry, but it seems meaningless.

You hadn't changed. New glasses and your hair more in place. Always a little plump. And the fringe on your forehead. I saw you smooth your grey and navy sari over your rear as you passed a mirror. Then you pirouetted like a mannequin and showed yourself off.

'How do I look?'

'Fantastic.' I smiled.

'Liar. Look at my bottom, it's spreading on all sides.'

'But still fantastic.'

'Me or my bottom?'

You. Truly. You were never beautiful. But being with you made me feel fighting fit. Being with you was like being on a motorbike with the wind whipping my face. A quickening of my blood and a sharpening of my senses.

You stretched my mind, spurred me on to greater heights, impossible depths. You were far more self-willed, stubborn and temperamental than me. There could hardly be a pair more mismatched than us. When I came to my senses, I thought there should be a ban on us, our being together. But who wanted to come to his senses?

I could see through your transparent brown choli that you had finally acquired the black bra you had coveted before you went away.

'My letters?' You put out your hand.

I gave you the bundle I had brought with me.

'And mine?' I asked you. Your face fell. 'The two letters your brother-in-law wrote to me on Okhon's behalf. Do you want those too?' I asked.

'No.'

You removed them from the bundle easily enough, his refined writing was unmistakable.

There's a story about those letters too, isn't there?

When I first met Okhon, she was about three. Like most adults, I've never been able to talk to children. I say hello and smile and relapse into silence or I retreat. At your house in Baroda, as I took off my glasses to rub my eyes, I felt someone staring at me. I put them on again to say hello, but she had disappeared. Later, as I was about to stretch myself out on the bed, she danced into the room again in her red smocked dress, hopping and skipping. 'I can walk, I can talk,' she sang, anticipating applause. I watched her and then stood up to skip and dance with her. That stumped her for a moment, she thought I was teasing her. But soon she couldn't stop laughing. We became firm friends.

Months later, after Okhon had gone abroad, back to her father, I sat playing snakes and ladders with Shatlaj's six-year-old son, Arshad. He was winning, but that didn't seem to make him happy.

'Hey, solemn face, what is the matter?'

'Nothing.'

'Come on, tell me.'

A few more minutes, and he did.

'My birthday is eight months away. How can I wait for so long?' he wailed.

'Now that is tragic.'

'You are laughing at me,' he accused.

'No, I'm thinking about the problem.'

I looked for him after school the next day.

'Two solutions. One, we name every month the same –

June. Then you will have twelve birthdays in a year. The only problem here is, if all months are called June, Aai and Baba and me and all your friends are going to miss out on their birthdays. Now, the second solution – twelve days will make a month. In that case June will come around thirty times a year. And everybody else can have their birthdays too. That's a happy thought, isn't it?'

He chewed over that for a few minutes, his eyes on his shoelaces. Then he looked up with a big grin on his face. 'Kushank, you arc brilliant.'

'Thank you.'

Arshad dreamed of the new calendar arrangements all day.

'And wouldn't it be lovely if it rained Coca-Cola on my birthday? And Gold Spot on Baba's and choco-cone on Aai's and raspberry shake on yours?' he cried ecstatically.

I liked that. When I got home, I wrote to Okhon to inform her of Arshad's and my plans, and of the formation of the new society to spread happiness in the world. Asking her for advice and ideas.

A month later her father answered, in his immaculate writing.

Dear Kushank,

Forgive me for not answering your letter to Okhon earlier. I've been busy with one thing or another.

Okhon is growing up in the Western world, in a society where people have realized the primacy of logic and of rational thought. In the circumstances, it is hardly surprising that Okhon finds your and Arshad's ideas nothing but patent nonsense. She sends her love.

Regards…

That letter really threw me. Aren't we all born fools, anyway? Every now and then you stray for a minute or two and become wise. Then you notice your mistake and lapse into foolishness again. Rarely has a situation made me feel so totally irrelevant.

Without being given even a moment's notice, I was informed that I had become a stranger to the world and its realities. For the first time in my life I felt old. Cast off and even more helpless than when confronted by Prutha.

When almost all our lives are patent nonsense, we can't identify what patent nonsense is. I was reminded of *The Bridge on the River Kwai*. Of the British colonel waving the Geneva convention in the face of the Japanese officer, protesting against the inhuman treatment meted out to his men. Pointing out that the Japanese had gone against the rules! I first saw that film when I was about fourteen, and I couldn't make up my mind whether to laugh or cry. Germans, British, Japanese and Americans, all hell-bent on killing as many million people as they could, and this guy has the temerity to wave a piece of paper and demand justice … Only human beings know the convention of killing their own kind. Raghu once told me of a group of twenty-one adivasis in Bihar who had walked for thirteen days without food to reach a famine relief camp and gorged themselves immediately on arrival, despite advice to the contrary. Only three survived the meal. In Bergman's *Winter Light*, a fisherman wants to opt out of life. He sits in solitude for days and refuses to go to church because he had heard that the Chinese had invented a cobalt bomb capable of killing ten million people at once.

What should one call patent nonsense?

You picked up the letters and said, 'Bye.' I sat where I was. I could see the Gateway of India.

The irony of the situation was so obvious that it turned sour within me.

I begin to disbelieve things when they get exaggeratedly melodramatic. But disbelieving doesn't make them less so.

A sudden shower at the Gateway, swiftly gone. And then the faint sunlight. A light breeze that filled the back of my shirt.

Her brother, she and I. I couldn't look at him.

He had a habitual stoop and walked with his head a few inches in advance of his feet. I felt embarrassed for him.

A little longer and then it would all be over. Half an hour, an hour, maybe a bit more. Then they would leave and I would walk away pretending that I had some place to go.

It wasn't nine yet, and there weren't many people at the Gateway. Just the peanut vendors and the man with the telescope. There used to be only the one then. What could you see through it? At nine or quarter past, we could go to Ali Baba's for a cup of tea. Meanwhile, I tried to make conversation, about films, something equally neutral. It wasn't too difficult. There was no need for it to be.

Some boxing matches last for fifteen or twenty rounds. It's obvious by the fifth or sixth round who is going to win. But the loser still sucks on the slice of lemon, or the bell goes ping just as he is being thrown to the floor. And he picks himself up with his swollen face, on to his toothpaste legs, and staggers blindly to his corner. He ought to be knocked out by the eighth round, but that final blow is not struck, and once again this bruised, blue-green, hulking figure with a mouth and eyes and eyebrows, raises itself painfully on one knee, on an elbow and up again. Once more unto the breach, dear friend. The exhausted winner, hitting out whenever he remembers to, and the loser, exhausted beyond numbness, but always coming back for more. Snuggling up to the winner, like a child to its mother – Come, my pet, come to Mummy. Don't cry. There now. Did the chair hurt you? Shall we kick the chair? Naughty chair, hurting my baby. Pushing a gloved hand into his mouth in retaliation to a stunning blow on the ear. Putting his swollen hands round the winner's waist and pushing his head into his chest. Twelfth round, thirteenth … fifteen … twenty … thirty, forty, fifty … numbers that don't mean anything any more. Just the loser already high with the relentless bashing, getting more and more stoned.

I felt I had been in the boxing ring for the last year and a half. Her father had said, 'She won't believe it, not unless you tell her yourself.' I nodded.

'Will you tell her if I send her to you?'

'Yes,' I agreed.

'Thank you.'

He paid for his dinner and my pineapple juice, and left with his friend.

~

'Are you saying no?'

'Yes.'

'Forever?'

She glanced at her brother. Her father had sent him to guard her. Against me. If he left us alone for a moment I might say something that wasn't in the script. Pretend I hadn't promised. Or she might overwhelm me, make me change my mind. He ignored her look. The wide steps at the Gateway. The raindrops drying fast on the stone. And a hurt Chandani.

I remembered her at the temple of Chatushrungi. In a dark, dark green silk sari. Beautiful Chandani. Incredibly and infinitely. Created for the one blow that would destroy her forever.

It was maybe a year after Aaroti had gone to Delhi. I lived moderately, routinely. A few friends in college, but only one of them close. Rakesh. The English lecture was over. I was making my way to the amphitheatre for the political science class. Someone called out behind me, 'Rakesh Tejani.' I heard the name called out again, and this time I felt someone run up behind me. As I turned around to look I was lifted a clear six inches off the ground by an immense hulk of a man. My book-loaded hand swung against his topmost rib, and I had an aerial view of my books, identity card and glasses flinging themselves helter-skelter to the ground like creatures trying to save their lives in a bomb raid. The man's army moustache kept descending ticklishly on my cheek like buzzing bees. With every inhalation, his pink-lined nostrils seemed to sprout wings and become airborne. Fifteen seconds later, when he exhaled, they softly landed back on his face. His grip had twisted my neck abnormally towards my right shoulder.

'Put me down, please,' I said. My voice sounded like something squeezed out of a tube. But I remained suspended in air. That gave me a chance to inspect his face at a close range. He was a couple of years older than me and a couple of inches shorter. But his Body Beautiful routine had made a pehelwan out of him. Chiselled features, but opaque eyes that might not always register what was happening. Smooth cheeks with a whiff of aftershave lotion. Must tell him later to wipe that bit of soap from his ear.

'Rakesh Tejani,' he snarled. His neck swelled with fury. 'You bastard, chasing my sister. If I see you near Sita again, I'll break your bloody leg, you hear?'

'You'll break my neck right now if you don't let go.' My voice still sounded like a stork's.

'Yes, and every bone in your body too.'

I believed him.

'I'm not Rakesh Tejani, you big moron, haven't you gathered that yet?' The long sentence brought tears to my eyes.

He chewed that over for a moment. Another moment to digest it, then he dropped me. From a few miles off some college boys were looking at us curiously.

I tucked my shirt into my trousers.

'Why didn't you say so before, you twerp?'

I wanted to hit him, but I said meekly, 'Sorry about that.'

'Never mind,' he brushed it away. 'Then who is Rakesh Tejani? Somebody told me you were … You lying to me?' He started belligerently, and I stepped back quickly before he decided to airlift me once again. The principal's son, Madhav, was on the other side of the lawn. I pointed to him.

'How do I know he's Rakesh?' he growled.

I tittered. 'Everybody knows about Rakesh Tejani and

Sita Ranade.' He cuffed me on the ear – 'Watch your tongue' – and started towards Madhav. I watched as he walked up and lit into him.

Madhav's screams brought the sky down. 'Help, help, Baba, Mr Phadnis, help me!' he yelled. And sure enough, came father, the librarian Mr Phadnis, a few other professors, and peons and the gurkha – running to save Madhav.

By evening everyone knew how Sita's brother, Satish, had been beaten up. The gurkha and the principal's other slaves had overdone it, and the principal himself had had to intervene and take Satish to his office.

I got the rest of the details through Rakesh. When the principal discovered that Rakesh was at the bottom of it all, he ordered the peon to find him. The peon traced Rakesh and Sita finishing off dosas and coffee in the canteen.

'Is it okay if I finish eating my dosa?' asked Rakesh.

'Save your wisecracks for your girlfriends, don't try to impress me,' said the peon.

Satish said over and over again, 'A boy in the college pointed him out to me as Rakesh. I wouldn't have touched him if I had known he was your son.' It is difficult to say whether the principal would have asked him to identify the mischief-maker. But I do know that Mr Phadnis had unwittingly let me off the hook when he exclaimed, indignantly, 'And if it hadn't been the principal's son you'd have thrashed him, I suppose? So what gives you the right to beat up any of our boys? And what has Rakesh done, anyway? Spoken to your sister? So have I, this morning. So you want to beat me up?'

There hadn't been much talk of giving Satish over to the police. The principal had hauled up the peons. 'Whatever he has done, we can't take law and order into our hands. Just pray that his parents don't lodge a complaint with the police about the college.'

I was infinitely relieved. And secretly pleased at being one up on Satish Ranade. But I didn't think I'd tell anybody the true story yet, not even Rakesh.

It didn't end there. There was much more to come before Chandani arrived on the scene. Sita didn't come to the university the next four days. On the fifth day, Rakesh dragged me out of the library. He looked like someone whose entire clan had committed mass suicide.

'I have to see Sita,' he said urgently.

'Yes.' I wasn't going to help this dialogue along.

'I think I'll go to her house.'

'Yes.'

'Are you going to say anything else?' he asked irritably. 'You think I'm asking for trouble, don't you?'

'Maybe there's no other way.'

'What else can I do?' he asked. He didn't wait for an answer. 'And I don't want any advice from you.'

'I wasn't going to give you any,' I answered, equally irritable.

'Will you come with me?'

'To chat up her brother?'

His eyes blazed and he walked away. I stood undecided for a while and then went after him.

'Kushank.' He'd been waiting near the steps.

'Bastard.'

'Will you come?'

'Yes.'

That evening his motorbike spluttered outside my room, sounding like an unwilling transplanted heart. He handed me a catapult and a note tied round a pebble. I looked at his worried face and laughed. 'You planning to elope or something?'

'Don't talk like a film star, you ass.' And he showed me the note. 'How are you? Whatever happens, come to my house tomorrow afternoon. Rakesh.'

Rakesh's plan was so crazy that if I had had any sense, I'd have opted out right then. But I know that even if I live to be seventy-two, I'll always be game for anything juvenile and dangerous. I tested the catapult and, fitting a little stone into it, asked Rakesh, 'What shall I hit?'

He pointed to the nearest lamp post, thirty yards away. I smiled and patted my back as I heard the satisfactory *tun-n-n* a few seconds later. And said, 'Let's go.'

It was freezing cold on the back of Rakesh's bike. I made myself as small as possible behind his leather jacket. Rakesh drove down Prabhat Road and turned right towards Law College. Then right again towards Deccan Gymkhana, and we coasted noiselessly down the hill towards Sita's house. Rakesh skid his feet along the street and stopped. There were two lights on in the house, one on the ground floor, probably the living room, and the other one upstairs. He pointed upwards. Two windows and a sixty-watt bulb. One of the window curtains had been drawn. Through the other we could see the pale blue of the curtain on the inside door, moving gently in the breeze.

'Make sure you hit the door curtain,' Rakesh cautioned, 'or we've had it.' I crossed the street to aim from the other pavement. The window had bars on it. I remembered the statistics I had read somewhere – three out of five chances of hitting the bars. At least it wasn't an intricately decorative grille, I consoled myself.

I had just pulled the catapult taut when suddenly a large black elephant of a car pulled out of the lane and came towards us. I thought it would go past, but it stopped next to the bike. Terrified, I shoved that catapult into my pocket and heard the pebble with the note tied round it drop and bounce off the pavement. 'Is this the way to the film institute?' the driver of the car enquired. Rakesh calmly nodded. The driver thanked him, and the car purred a few times before it drove off. I fell to my knees, scrabbling for the note. Rakesh kicked me gently in the arse and held it out.

'Don't let me down,' I prayed as I shot the catapult and hugged Rakesh with a squeal of delight as I heard the pebble hit the curtain and fall to the floor. The next moment we were both caught in the beam of a flashlight. Before I could turn round, I heard a loud bang and my bum felt as though it had been stung by a swarm of bees. It was so sudden and excruciating I couldn't even scream.

'The gutless bastard, can't even shoot straight, probably shit scared of me,' said Rakesh.

'Sure – he's – shit scared – of you,' I mimicked him, writhing in agony.

'What's the matter with you? What are you squirming for?' asked Rakesh as he started the bike and pulled me over the pillion. I'll tell you why. Sita's brother got me instead of you, you swine, I muttered to myself, and then was startled into silence as I felt the sweat break out on my backside.

'I can't sit up, I'm falling off, stop the bike,' I screamed. I don't remember why I was so terrified. Maybe the pain had worsened or maybe it was just the shock of discovering that the sweat was really blood.

But Rakesh drove on.

'Hold on, Kushank. Only a few yards to go. Hang on and count to a hundred and twenty.'

Jane Fonda rose before my eyes, telling Alain Delon, 'Driver, drive slow, we're in a hurry.'

I opened my eyes as we stopped. My body felt as though it had been through the wheels of Rakesh's motorbike. The fog of pain cleared and I saw a sign saying 'Maternity Home' behind Rakesh.

On the operating table I asked Moina, 'What am I doing here?'

'Having a baby.'

I smiled and drifted into pentathol.

Moina removed seven pellets from my left buttock. I couldn't believe it. 'But I only heard one shot.'

'He shot you with a twelve-bore shotgun. Each cartridge has eight or twelve pellets.'

'What happened to the others?'

'I'll ask Sita's brother.'

For the next few days I stayed with Rakesh. In that huge house, the three of us – his mother, slightly deranged since the death of his father, the lovelorn Rakesh and I. And Rakesh's sister, Moina, who came and went. When she was there, I waited for her to go, and when she wasn't, I longed for her.

'Undressing time, Kushank! Get your lungi off and show me how brave you are. Be strong of mind like Hannibal and Attila the Hun. Grit your teeth and don't kick the doctor just because it hurts.' And when I winced with pain, she pulled my hair gently. 'Angry?' She came home three times a day. On her scooter. Twice for meals and once to change my dressing. She was an intern at the maternity hospital and seemed forever rushed.

'Stop hanging on to your buttock. It's not going to run away, you know!'

I shamefacedly pulled my hand away. 'Oh, look, you dropped your Modess!' Horrified, I clamped my hand on my arse. Everything was in place. She smiled mischievously and hummed '*there's a hole in the bucket*...' I slammed the door shut.

One day, she called out to me as she came in through the front door. 'Hey, one-arse, look what I've brought you.' And walked into my room. 'Absolutely new! Complete protection for those difficult days of the month! Untouched by human hands, the ultimate in human technology … Ten times more absorbent because it's got cellulose! Safer … because it has the new blue-as-the-sky plastic shield … Light as a flower. And wonder of wonders … No belt … Self-sticking!'

Her sales talk over, she threw the box at me, turned me over on my stomach, and got down to work.

Walking in the garden that evening, I spied Sita and a friend coming towards the house. I ran to give Rakesh the good news and shut myself up in my room.

I could hear them talking downstairs. Suddenly I felt bored and lonely. I looked out of the window and saw a parakeet take off from the branch of the mango tree and fly into the sun. I missed Moina. But she wouldn't be home for a couple of hours yet.

'Kushank,' Rakesh said as he came into my room, 'come on down.'

'What for?'

'I'll buy you a book if you come down. And Sita wants to say hello.'

He came into my room.

'Don't try to bribe me, I'm not coming down dressed in my lungi. And don't lie about Sita. You obviously want me to do something for you, you selfish oaf.'

'Where have all my friends gone?' he sang. And then, 'Please, Kushank, I beg of you. A matter of life and death. My dearest friend, I need you.'

'Oh, go to hell.'

'Listen, idiot. How can we talk with her friend sitting there? We could go out into the garden if only you would come down and keep her friend company.'

I went downstairs.

'How are you, Kushank?' Sita greeted me.

I wonder if she knows, I thought, and was about to touch my buttock to reassure myself. I stopped though, just in time. 'How do I look?'

'Like the butcher down the street!' she retorted, and introduced me to her friend from Indore.

I leaned forward to hear her better. 'Hello, Sanatani,' I said. Tortured all the time by the thoughts, do they know, does she know too?

They burst out giggling. I quickly ran my hand over my bandage.

But they weren't watching.

'Not Sanatani, you fool – Chandani,' explained Sita. 'Rakesh is waiting for me to go and say hello to his mother,' she went on, 'I'll be back in a minute.' She disappeared.

Chandani was still smiling. I wondered what she thought of me dressed like a bloody butcher. Whatever it was, it could hardly be complimentary. I tried to sit up and look graceful in the unfamiliar garment.

She had a complexion that told you her blood circulation was in great shape. Delicate, incisive nose. Sleeveless choli.

Couldn't read more into her physiognomy since she was seated, but the total effect made me short of breath. Jesus, she was beautiful.

She sat up straight, without resting her back on the couch. Bet she walked just as straight, too. I thought she came across more as an abstraction than anything else. She had come to terms with her astonishing beauty so totally that she was no longer aware of it. So if you had the temerity to speak to her, you were going to be thrown off balance by the sheer and unqualified focus of her attentiveness. No, she hadn't heard of original sin, I decided. I felt self-conscious and vulnerable.

How long would this silence last? I was uneasy. When I couldn't think of anything else to say, I fell back on, 'Would you like to listen to some music?'

'What have you got?'

I brought a stack of records for her to choose from. She wanted to hear the soundtrack from *My Fair Lady*. I put it on and turned around.

Sita's friend was trying desperately not to look at the floor. Every component of Moina's allegedly faultless revolutionary, cellular sanitary towel had declared its independence all over the carpet. The route I had taken on my way to the record player, where precisely I had put my foot down – it was all charted out. By the super-absorbent cellulose, the blue-as-the-sky plastic shield and the transparent paper jacket. Involuntarily I checked to see whether the Velcro at least had remained, and ran.

~

Past the first gate of Fergusson College, past Swarvihar, and still I did not see her. I had lost her and then there she was, just going past Mr Kanade's English, maths, statistics, physics and biology supplementary classes. I had hung around in my room for three days, waiting for her. Then I had stepped out for barely half an hour. She would have to drop in just then.

'Chandani.'

Looking straight ahead as usual. Her face a mask of concentration as she bicycled. Eyes ahead and chin up and back straight. And her feet still on the pedals as she rolled downhill.

I braked as I came up beside her.

'Chandani.'

She woke up and smiled around the eyes.

'Shall we go home?' she asked.

'Yours or mine?'

'Neither. Let's go to Chatushrungi.'

I stuck out my right arm and turned with her. It was dark by the time we got to the agricultural college. Suddenly she vanished from beside me. I looked around for her. She had stopped and got off her bicycle.

Trying to disengage her silk sari from the chain. I tried to help her but wasn't sure what I was doing in the dark, probably making it worse.

Chandani and I on the street. She tied to her bicycle. The headlights of passing cars probed at us.

Then a strong breeze filled up and ballooned her sari over her head and it suddenly came unstuck. Leaving a shred of silk in my hand.

'Oh, hell.'

So green that it was almost dark. Darker than the green of a bottle of Vat 69. Deep and heavy. Only Chandani could wear that colour, like the depths of a forest.

I sat down on the street.

'What's the matter?'

'I wish I hadn't torn it.'

'I'll sew it up again. Darn it so carefully even you won't know it was torn.'

She took a safety pin she had used instead of the last button on her choli and pinned the torn ribbons together.

~

At the foot of the Chatursrungi hill, the municipal council had installed a single yellow lamp, shedding its glow from way up high. We rested our bikes against the lamp post and Chandani said, 'Shall we go right to the top?' And then, seeing me hesitate, 'Never mind, I can go to the temple for darshan another day.' A couple of kids selling flowers followed us up the first few steps.

'Buy flowers for the goddess and she will bless you with a son.'

'When did you come back?' asked Chandani as we climbed.

'On the night of the thirty-first.'

'Then why didn't you come to see me on the first?'

I had one foot in the air as I stopped in surprise. 'Why didn't I come? It was you who promised to come and wish me a happy New Year, that's why I came back from

Bombay. Christ! You really take the cake – and I've been waiting for you to turn up for three days… '

'How seriously you take everything. My grandmother was sick.' Halfway up the hill, we left the steps and sat down to rest. I kept leaning over every two minutes to see if our bikes were safe. She had rested her elbows on her knees and cupped her chin in her right hand.

'Why don't you wait down there with the bikes? Then you can guard them much better.' I thought about it for a moment. She waited just as thoughtfully, then smiled sweetly to drive the point home. 'You could talk to me from down there and I could answer you from up here. Okay?'

The wind had turned colder. It crept softly towards us, then suddenly put on speed and sliced into us, blowing through us, and away. Making goose bumps on arms and legs. Another playful nudge and another swipe.

'Have you ever been to see the goddess at the top?'

'No.'

'The one at Parvati?'

'When I was a child.'

'Did you stop going to the temple when you grew up?'

'We never did have gods in our house.'

Her torn sari fluttered in the wind. I felt a strange curiosity about the goddess. Who had installed her in this place? Chandani was lost in her own thoughts.

'I believe in the goddess.'

I didn't know why she said that. It didn't need an answer, but I said 'okay' anyway. 'What does your goddess look like?'

'Ugly. Ugly enough to startle you, make you stop in your tracks. Want to see her?'

I shook my head.

She laughed. 'You don't have to believe in her to see her.'

'I stay away from gods and goddesses.'

'Why? Because you find them irrational?'

'On the contrary, I think God and superstition are living symbols of man's rationality.'

She looked at me suspiciously. 'You're trying to be funny.'

'No.'

'I've heard a lot of explanations about God and superstition, but this one is new to me. I don't understand.'

'Forget it, it'll only bore you.'

'Don't be so patronizing. I want to know.'

'Come, we'll change the subject. I don't feel like holding forth.'

'Will you stop making excuses?'

It was no use. So I tried to collect my thoughts.

'In the beginning, man had to battle with nature, its superpowers, its unpredictable disasters. They came and went. Nature was always stronger than man, but what worried him most was its uncertainty, its duplicity. The elements that protected him, helped him to survive, would one day suddenly turn round and destroy him. Too much rain caused floods. The sun's heat brought on famine and great fires. Man wanted a neat, regular, tidy world, a world in which cause and effect depended on each other absolutely ... Shall I stop now?'

She didn't understand the question for a moment.

'No, go on. And don't interrupt.'

'But the thing that frightened him most was death. Someone who was alive and talking one moment could be struck dumb forever the next. And nothing man could do brought him back to life – no amount of kicking and thrashing, no long supplications, nothing. Now, if only there was a reason for all this, how marvellous a place the world could be! And then, after ages, man discovered the first cause – God. Omniscient, omnipotent, omnipresent. God took on the responsibility and took the weight off man's shoulders. Yesterday's cyclone – the direct result of God's displeasure. Suresh forgot to go to the temple and was struck by lightning. But I saw him at the temple. Aha, then it's obvious that his heart wasn't in the prayer. That's how desire and covetousness are punished. Slowly, everything was brought under control. God took over responsibility for all major disasters and the minor ones were attributed to superstition. Mustn't look at eclipses, cross a cat's path, and so on.'

'Are you making fun of me again?'

I looked at her and said, 'No, I'm not. This is just one of the perverse contradictions of my mind. I fight superstition because I'm drawn to it despite myself.'

She didn't talk on the way home. I wanted to ask her when I'd see her again. But I had already said too much, too readily.

She'd joined our university soon after we met at Rakesh's house. We studied together for three years, but it was only in the last two that I began to get interested in her. I was attracted to her, but at the same time there was something that made me keep my distance. During those two years, Rashid only met her for three or four minutes. He was quiet for a long time afterwards. Rashid, my loud, boisterous South African friend – the man with a finger in every pie – foreign exchange racketeer, underground political student leader and part time Casanova.

'I don't know how to say this, Shank, it's the kind of thing that has never occurred to me. But I reckon you've got to be clean, really clean, if you're going to touch that girl.'

Two days later, she wrote me a letter.

> Dear Kushank,
>
> I haven't lost faith in my goddess. Will you marry me? I'll come to see you this evening – have your answer ready by then.
>
> Your Chandani
>
> P.S. I may be a romantic, Kushank, but not about the man with whom I want to spend the rest of my life. Don't bother to go into explanations about yourself and I promise we won't get married till we're both earning our living. So think of another excuse.

Left to myself, I couldn't have asked her for another four to five years, no, not in a lifetime. If the distance between your mouth and your belly is uncertain and elastic, your opinion of yourself is likely to fluctuate too. Add to that extreme self-deprecation and innumerable inferiority complexes. And Chandani becomes unattainable.

My experience with life, with the fact of being alive, had one important reference point – what cannot be satisfied is not a need. Whenever I remembered, I let this principle rule my life. But I persisted with my obsession for Chandani.

~

One o'clock in the afternoon. Or maybe two. The sun like a seven-hundred-billion-watt bulb overhead. Sky stretched like a glass disc. Another minute and it would splinter and crash to the earth.

Half an hour ago, Chandani had asked, 'Shall I take you to my favourite place? I haven't been to Vithalwadi for years. Shall we go now?'

And thoughtlessly, I had agreed. Now I was sure that the shattering heat would either puncture our tyres or make Chandani faint any moment. Very little traffic on the way – we turned right at Parvati, and then there was none at all. Some pockets of shade, but even they seared. My nostrils breathed fire by the time we got to Vithalwadi. Chandani's face had turned a bright red.

'Isn't it beautiful? Didn't I tell you? Come, let's cool our feet in the water and then we can go to the temple.'

We left our bikes under the mango tree behind the temple and went to the river bed.

As soon as my feet touched the water, I began to like the place. Small, secluded, a place to worship in privacy. Chandani was quiet as she stood in the water, her sari held up out of the way. I didn't want to break the silence either.

About fifteen yards away, a Brahmin washed his copper lamp and cruet. The copper the same dirty colour as his dhoti.

Chandani said, 'I shall cover myself in copper jewellery when I marry, scrubbed and polished with tamarind. Have you seen the shadows that lurk in copper? Shadows even when it shines and sparkles.'

We dried our feet on the rocks and went to sit under the mango tree. It provided the only shade behind the temple. And all around dry, burnt-yellow grass. Five minutes later, a little boy stepped out of it. Looked uncertainly at me. Paused, and then said, 'He's calling you.'

'What?'

'He said to come,' he repeated, hanging his head.

'Who said?'

'Over there.' He pointed to the temple.

'What for?'

'He said to bring the woman too.'

He led us to the front of the temple. A policeman stood there. He had taken off his sandals and undone his belt. For a moment I thought he had noticed the lapsed registration on my bicycle. But no, I had hired this one, so that must be okay.

'You're coming to the police station,' he said shortly to me. 'You there,' he shouted at the disappearing boy. 'Come here, I need you too.'

'Why should we go to the police station? What for? What are you talking about?'

'I'll tell you what for when we get there. Are you coming?'

'No.'

'Now look, don't get cheeky with me.'

'Cheeky about what? What have we done?'

'Done? Listen to him. Did I do it then? All that kissing and pawing behind the temple? Right next to the gods too. And she isn't even your wife or I'd have let it go. I don't see a mangalsutra round her neck! Showing your thighs in the river – even I had to look away. But that wasn't enough for you, was it? You were about to fuck her, weren't you, when this little boy saw you and called me! And you ask me what for? Come on, you can do all the asking you want at the station...'

'You're lying.'

'I am lying? I, a constable? I'll smash your face in, you bastard. I may be old, but I'm not too old to see what's going on. And that boy, what about him? Does he need glasses too? Or did he dream it? Calling a constable a liar, you just wait till we get to the station. I'll fix you.'

I looked round for the Brahmin. He had vanished in the heat, and instead I saw the ghost of Chandani's yet-to-be-seen father.

When I found out that she had written to her family, I said to Chandani, 'But hadn't we agreed not to tell anyone yet?'

'You're angry with me,' she said anxiously, knowing that she'd broken her word.

'A little. I don't understand the haste. Chandani, all this is so new between us that I want to keep it a secret even from myself. Not just you, I mistrust myself. If we're not careful, not protective, not able to give it a chance to grow, we're going to end up losing whatever it is we've got going for us.'

She took my hand in hers.

'I was so happy when you said yes, I couldn't sleep all night. I wanted everyone to be happy with me. My parents, you, everyone. But it was a mistake, wasn't it?'

I felt annoyed at my peevishness. 'Come, let's forget it. I always exaggerate.'

Five days later, Chandani came to my room late, pale-faced.

Her father had come specially from Indore to see her. To brainwash her. 'Chandani, this is puppy love. You'll soon outgrow it. Then it won't suffice and you'll leave him behind one day.'

Adults have tremendous faith in themselves, even when they lie. Chandani stumbled over the words. 'He didn't stop all day. Over and over he said, of course he didn't want to come between us, but I must not be foolish and impulsive. I told him I wasn't, that we were in no hurry. He laughed and pulled me close to him. "Then you won't see him till after the exams?" He kept on at it. But I didn't agree. Then as he left, he hugged me and said, "Chandani, I wouldn't want anyone to say that you can't face up to the truth. He hasn't told you about his family, has he? I made some enquiries about the Purandares before I came. His family are not respectable. Kushank and his brother aren't his father's children. And Kushank's aunt is a prostitute in Bombay…"'

I looked at Chandani and found her searching me.

'It's not true, is it, Kushank?'

The corner of Hindu Colony, where we lived, nine o'clock at night. Mavshi walked the street, her face smeared with lipstick and rouge. Suddenly Baba twisted her hand behind her back and kicked her. 'Hand over the money, slut,' he snarled. But I was too young to understand the implications of the scene at the time. Then one day, there I was myself, the stricken hero, spurned by his beloved, making his ravaged way to the whorehouse, to seek solace in the arms of lust. But like the man in the fable, my search turned into the discovery of a diamond in the dung heap.

'Kushank.' My aunt looked into my face in the dark. 'Oh my God, how did this happen?' She held me to her breast and cried, 'Don't worry, I'm not the only one in this street. Come, I'll take you to Sona.'

I said to Chandani, 'Maybe,' and went out of the room.

~

I looked at the constable. He was older than my father. He stroked his short beard as he talked. The gesture must have comforted him. His mouth suddenly slit open and he spat a long snake of betel juice at my feet.

His calves were tightly bound in puttees. And above them a knot of varicose veins. My eyes refused to leave his face. He continued to talk. The tobacco had yellowed his moustache. My gaze turned opaque as I stared at it.

'Come on, hurry up, I haven't all day to waste on you lot. I have a million things to do … Are you coming?' And he twisted his moustache. No doubt he had children. Maybe three sons and two daughters. He must have been a grandfather for at least seven years. I felt sick in the stomach, as if I had swallowed the yellow-brown tobacco. But I couldn't throw up. There was nothing to throw up, nothing in my stomach, my mouth or my head. I reached for my wallet – three rupees and thirty-five paise. I put them on his palm. 'I won't let you off so easily the next time,' he growled as he walked away.

The memory of Vithalwadi has never left me. There are only one or two things that can shape the pattern of your life once you have grown up. Vithalwadi is one. I remember every detail of what happened at Vithalwadi vividly, but I have never been able to explain it.

Much later, one day, you and I returned to your room late at night. You shut the door and sat on the bed. And with your head in your hands, you started to cry, silently, without taking off your glasses. The only time I've seen you cry. After a couple of minutes, I couldn't stand it any longer. I thought if I took your glasses off, I'd know why you were crying, and I forced them off. I'm not sure yet if a woman's tears make a man feel helpless or more manly. But I felt as though I had failed to protect you when you had been in my care.

'What's the matter? Tell me, what is it?' I asked you.

You shook your head wearily and shut the bathroom door behind yourself. What's the matter? What a futile question. If you had said then Vithalwadi is the matter, would I have understood? All of us live in our particular contexts. Whether they are chocolates or a dark garage. Each of us has this space – it makes a circle of three hundred and sixty degrees. We can describe it, but there is no way to penetrate it.

After the exams, Chandani went home to Indore and I to Bombay. One morning there was a letter for me, in an unfamiliar handwriting. On Chandani's father's letterhead. It was brief.

> Shri Kushank,
>
> My daughter does not wish to marry you. Even if she did, she would be helpless against my opposition. I'd advise you not to try and see her. Have the intelligence and wisdom to realize what is good for you.

Chandani could write to me, but there was no way I could send her a letter. So I started my visits to Indore.

As I slept in the upper berth of the third-class compartment, someone stole my glasses. They had cost sixteen rupees and I had had them for six years. Their resale value was almost nil. Their loss made my trip to Indore hopelessly indistinct.

The incident was symbolic. Everything I did in Indore had a feeling of fumbling in the dark. My world shrank, my sensations shrivelled. I felt suffocated. I couldn't wait to get out of Indore and return to Bombay.

I didn't know this town and had no idea where to start looking for a cheap place to stay, or where to meet Chandani. I booked into a scruffy hotel, had a shower and went in search of the psychology department at the university. It was eleven o'clock when I got there and I discovered that her first lecture wasn't till two-thirty. I waited. Tried to decipher the words in my book, but without my specs my eyes hurt and I gave up.

Chandani arrived in a red and blue Irkali sari. A slight tremor passed through her when she saw me. For a quarter of an hour I tried to get her to talk. But without success. So I dragged her into a cab, took her to the hotel. The manager and his friend looked at us knowingly as we went up the stairs. The walls of the five-by-eight room were made of thin plywood. They stopped four feet short of the ceiling. I latched the door and made Chandani sit on the stale sheets. The tears ran down her cheeks and I felt helpless. I didn't know why she cried, but I wanted to take her away – out of that filthy room and the unfriendly town – to my father's house.

'Chandani, why did you ask me to come?' I asked again irritably.

'Don't be angry. I felt I couldn't go on. I wanted to see you.'

'Do your parents treat you badly?'

She laughed so strangely, I wanted to bang her head, my head, our heads against the wall and end it all.

'Why don't you answer me?'

'What will you do if I tell you?'

'Take you away.'

She pulled me to her and kissed me. 'You're such a romantic fool, Kushank. If we live together now, without jobs, without money, we would lose each other in no time. Don't you know there's no love on an empty stomach?'

I had the feeling of being spied on. I turned round and saw the hole in the wall. I stuck my biro through it. A yelp on the other side confirmed my suspicions and I quickly went into the next room. The manager stood there, rubbing his eye.

I slammed my knee into his stomach and banged his head on the wall till Chandani and an employee of the hotel separated us.

I put down some money on his desk on the first floor, picked up my case and we left.

The film had already started, but there was another couple going in with us. The usher's torch vanished somewhere in the darkness.

Vague, cotton-woolly outlines of Dilip Kumar and Vyjayanthimala appeared on the screen, in front of an indistinct Taj Mahal, crooning their love. Suddenly she floated away from him and danced by herself. Memories of the acute embarrassment I'd felt as a child when I was caught dancing alone made me squirm.

The couples on either side of us were in various stages of amorous sport. I didn't fancy the idea of the dark theatre as a bedroom much. As I narrowed my eyes to hear Dilip Kumar's voice better, I felt Chandani start to laugh beside me. Nobody could stop her now, she would laugh for at least the next forty-five minutes. 'What's the matter?' I asked for the thousandth time. And she answered, between fits of mirth. 'You look so comic concentrating on the film without your glasses!' And I forgot all my reservations, shame, embarrassment, and drew her to me.

Who needed whom to lean on, at that moment, I wondered.

We'd started to argue about what to do, where to go, as soon as we'd left the hotel. So many roads closed for fear of being seen. Finally, we had decided to eat and then go to the film.

Over the meal, Chandani cold-bloodedly described the scenes at home. I didn't want to believe her, but she kept talking. When she spoke of something especially bizarre, I remembered the things her father had said about my family. I didn't want to hurt myself any more, so I only half listened.

For days no one spoke to her. When they did, they called her a slut, whore, bitch. If she was near enough, they would grab her by the hair and beat her black and blue. Every few days, her mother staged a fit and her father reminded her of his diabetes and impending heart attacks. All due to Chandani, of course.

As Dilip Kumar sang, with great rectitude, '*Mujhe duniya*

*waalon sharaabi na samjho/Main peeta nahin hoon, pilaayi gayi hai...*' we left the theatre before the film was over. Chandani to return home, and I to Bombay.

I soon learnt to live like a rat in a gutter. Sticking my head out of the hole, a quick, furtive look around, a little frightened scampering, and back into the dark again. I even looked sneaky. Among Chandani's father's various gifts to me, self-hatred and self-disgust were the most noteworthy.

There were two more trips to Indore in store for me. The second time I met Chandani at about ten in the morning. She seemed surprised to see me.

'Father made me write to you – that I wouldn't marry you. For a week, all day and part of the night, they told me such awful things about you and your family that finally I broke down and agreed to write the letter. But I changed my mind the next day and wrote another, to cancel the first one. You must have left before it got there.'

Once again games of hide-and-seek. Another scruffy hotel and another film show.

For ten months I had been looking for a job. Answering advertisements, dropping into friends' offices to see if there was anything going. Then I stopped looking and decided to finish my degree. I went to Indore to tell Chandani, but I couldn't see her for three days. I camped at the university all day, but she didn't come. Then putting aside fifteen rupees for my return ticket, I spent the third night on a bench at the railway station.

When I finally saw Chandani on the fourth morning, she was listless, dull-eyed. 'If I hadn't seen you today I was planning to come to your house,' I said.

She shook her head slowly. 'They'd have humiliated you terribly.'

'I'd come prepared for that, so I wouldn't have minded.'

'But I would have.'

I looked into her face and was suddenly very tired. Chandani said, 'Let's walk, someone might see us and tell my father.'

I didn't move.

A large black Dodge stopped and the driver stepped out carrying a bag of grain. A shower of yellow wheat in the sun and hundreds of pigeons rose and wheeled and scrambled for the food. Fluttering like balloons tied to the rear wheel of a bicycle. Within a couple of minutes, not one seed remained on the ground and the pigeons had disappeared.

Chandani was still struggling to get through to me. I looked at the sea. The sun was getting warmer.

'I'm going to get some cigarettes,' her brother mumbled, and walked off.

And still there was nothing to say. As if overwhelmed by the mass of the Gateway in whose shade we stood, Chandani's voice flickered into a whisper every now and then. The sea continued to wash the stone steps every few seconds.

'Remember we agreed that if one of us wanted to break it off, we'd see each other first to make sure that's what we wanted?'

I looked at her and nodded. She found it difficult to talk and there was no time to choose the right words. 'I wrote to you once refusing to marry you, and you came to Indore at once to see me, to make sure.'

She took a deep breath and smiled helplessly.

'It's my turn now – I came because of your letter. But I don't know how to make you change your mind, Kushank.'

Then her voice slipped and she crashed down. Still standing. Without whimpering or sobbing. With her head bent. Just trembling. And every few moments, a new thought or grief would gather her up in a seven- or eight-storeyed wave that smashed her down and left her utterly broken.

Then she stopped.

'Why not, Kushank? Why? What happened to us?' she cried, as if her insides were being wrung out.

Her father said, 'If you want to marry her, you must do it right away.'

His friend smiled at me encouragingly.

I said no.

'No? What do you mean?'

'Don't want to marry.'

'Now or ever?'

He stared at me from behind his glasses. But turned his gaze away when I looked back at him. His face wasn't fat or flabby, but it looked as if it slid down weightily. A thin and delicate mouth. Flowing in the direction of the rest of his face. With streaks of betel juice pointing the way. When he spoke, you felt he was walking through filth. But he was not concerned about picking his way carefully, on his toes, without getting his heels dirty. He spoke slowly, but the words threw up muck every which way.

I looked at him and felt spent. This was the first time we had met. But we had played cat and mouse for a long time. For the last two years, Chandani had pleaded with him, 'But how can you abuse him when you haven't met him?'

'I won't ask you again,' he warned me.

At twenty, twenty-two, you are still innocent. In years and in experience. But it doesn't last long. A few more years and we all become common or uncommon swine, bastards, motherfuckers. If they get you before you grow up, you are simple, innocent and stupid. When they are about to squeeze your balls, you are dumb enough to feel disgusted, and you squirm with distaste instead of kicking them or bashing their heads in with stones and running away. But it can't go on for two whole years, you think, people can't keep it up, you think. And you still cherish foolish hopes of changing them, making them understand. But once you lose your balls, you have lost them forever. You can't find them, not in your head, not in the sky above.

'Look, you're making this decision, I'm not making you do it.'

'No.'

His mouth fell open. I explained. 'No, you are not forcing me into making a decision.'

'But are you ready to say that?'

'I just did.'

'Will you write it down for me?'

On stamped paper? Witnessed by the head clerk of the Supreme Court?

'Or Chandani won't believe it.'

I wanted to pat him on the back and tell him, 'Relax, the game is over.' I agreed to write it down for him.

'He has your letter in the safe.' She tried to make me smile.

'But I'd addressed it to you.' And before she could answer, 'Okay, I know, don't say anything.'

'You haven't changed, even after two years.' And then, softly, almost as if she didn't want me to hear. 'Don't change about me either, Kushank.'

A ship blew its siren at the Alexandra Docks and then appeared round the corner. Puffing and blowing. In front of the little island across from the Gateway. Still bellowing painfully.

'Do you want to see her through the telescope?'

She said yes tonelessly. She steadied the dirty brass barrel, closed her left eye and peered through the telescope. 'There's no ship.'

'That's not possible, memsahab. Close your left eye properly and look again.'

She tried again according to his instructions.

'It's dark, that's all.'

'How can it be dark so early in the morning? Let me look,' and he bent to look through it. Straightening up with embarrassment, he added, 'Sorry, very sorry, I forgot to take off the lens cap. Now look.' He adjusted the focus. 'First-class view. Everything – the sea, the ship, the little boats…'

The ship steamed away into the sea.

Chandani had walked away, saying, 'Never mind.'

'Don't do this to me, memsahab, you are my first customer. Here, take five minutes. I won't charge you extra.'

She smiled.

He was upset now. 'Look, you can see it for free. I made a mistake, but I said sorry. The sea is so beautiful in the morning. And the telescope shows you what the eye cannot see. Please…'

I paid him.

I wanted to sit down, but the steps were still wet. I found the least damp spot and said, 'Let's sit.'

Chandani was impatient. Her brother would be back any moment and she hadn't said all she wanted to. A couple of times her lips moved with a half-formed thought or sentence. But the silence persisted. And beside her I was cold and unresponsive. Reflecting on her plight.

Suddenly she brightened. 'I'll wait for you. Wouldn't it be terrible if you change your mind and I wasn't there!'

I continued to stare at the sea. But the clanging bell of the fire engine kept coming closer and closer. And the red warning light shone unflickering in the middle of my forehead. I kept shaking my head.

'Why not? How does it bother you? I'll wait. I'll get a job after the exams and live away from my parents.'

'It's no use.'

'Why not? I won't force myself on you. If you decide to come back, I'll be there. If not, well, that's that.'

She stopped suddenly, looking incredulous as she was struck by some new thought. There was no telling how she would stab me in the back with a brand-new, totally unselfish idea. But I needn't have worried.

'Is there someone else?'

'No.'

She came back with renewed enthusiasm. 'Then there's no problem. You don't have to decide anything right now. Don't even think about me or marriage or anything. I won't either. We'll just wait and see.'

When I still didn't answer, she laughed brokenly. 'Look, no strings. If you meet someone else, you don't have to worry about me.' And then, 'Is that okay?'

Chandani's brother must smoke a rare brand of cigarettes. I was grateful to him. But I wanted him to come back now. We still had to go through the charade of that promised cup of tea.

'Kushank,' her voice woke me up. She seemed lost in her thoughts too. 'Why don't I understand? It's all over, isn't it?'

The wind was cold, so she covered her head with her sari and turned my face towards her.

'I don't want to live any more.'

I don't know if I had expected that. But even if I had, she had caught me unawares. She said it simply, without guile, and suddenly we were in enemy camps.

She had brought out her last weapon. And that too not as a threat.

No holds barred, I said to myself. My mouth tasted bitter.

She could do what she liked. I had said no, she was only putting into effect the consequences of that decision. Maybe it was her last-ditch effort to make me change my mind. Be that as it may, whatever the reasons, they were hers. I was going to fight her now, with whatever came to my hands, truth, lies, anything…

'Couldn't you have thought of anything else to threaten me with? Why didn't you tell your parents that a year ago? It might have helped then. But we're all so shrewd, like little kids. We know who to touch with our tears, who will console us with chocolates and who will ignore us.' And then I laughed horribly. 'But of course you couldn't say that to your family, could you? They were always one up on you. Fits, heart attacks, hypertension, they knew the whole repertoire backwards. I remember you telling me that your grandmother always used the word suicide in English because it sounded more solemn, more effective.'

And as I spoke, her whole body shrank. Her hurt eyes and her helpless hands. She reached for my hand.

'Oh God, Kushank, how they have hurt you. You don't believe what you're saying, do you?'

I had been trying to shame her, but she'd stripped me clean with one stroke. I saw my face fall.

The telescope man was staring at us. I stared back at him. What do you do with Chandani? This Chandani who loved Le Douanier Rousseau and Hieronymus Bosch and then doodled silicone-busted women and ball-less men. And unexpectedly went to the heart of the matter. Out of the blue she would say something so deep that if you had a mind to it, you could be wiser by a good six months in an instant. She must have had her share of intelligence. Nothing extraordinary though. She worked all hours in short spurts and managed to maintain her grades. She rejoiced in soppy music, second-rate historical romances and mythological plays. Pleased with herself, she blended perfectly with the emasculated society around her. And yet without really being aware of it, she would draw away unobtrusively from it all, fathom something profound and terribly precious, only to disappear once again into the mainstream.

'Don't change the subject.' I had to get this over with before her brother returned. And I turned venomously upon her. 'Have you nothing to live for but me?'

She found my question unnecessary. 'No, nothing.'

I hated her then. I found her revolting. Die then, I wanted to say, Go on, die, die, die, die.

'You'd have installed me in a shrine, made me the centre of your life, suffocated me. And marrying you I'd have fallen every half minute. And neither of us could have borne that for long.'

'But, Kushank, I want to die because you won't marry me.'

That shook me and brought me to my senses. For two years this woman had loved me. Without doubts or reservations. Constantly. Then I had admitted defeat. But she hadn't. And I was using her as an excuse for my anger with myself.

Her brother had been hesitating by the arch of the Gateway for five minutes.

'Kushank, please.'

She was free. I had no right over her now. But I went on shaking my head.

Her brother had started to walk towards us.

'You made your decision,' she said. 'Now don't interfere with mine.'

Nobody has the right to live another's life, least of all me. How many years had I believed that, yet I went on shaking my head even after her brother had reached us.

She wrote to me, several times. But I didn't open her letters. After four months, she gave up on me.

Whatever you do, the first time is the only innocent time. You can say this is my first ninth love affair and it can bring you applause in a second-rate comedy, but it's not the kind of line that helps you to reconcile with yourself. My father had said, 'It's not enough to be good once. You've got to be good all the time.'

Whatever prompted me to say no to Chandani, and however relevant or true my reasons were, I lost whatever good there was in me. Not altogether. But a little. Once you turn your back on something, the next time becomes easier. And once goodness has gone, you become dehumanized and there's nothing left to salvage.

Isn't this my hindsight talking? Sometimes when I find that I'm beginning to look a bit too much like myself for comfort, I pull out a platitude and hang on to it for dear life as if it were an emergency chain on a train. For example, you're always wiser after the event. Or some such.

I came to see you on a Friday instead of the usual Monday. You were about to go out with your deep-voiced friend with the thick glasses. So I left the tapes on the table and turned to go.

'What is it?'

'The songs from *West Side Story*.'

You had mentioned, in the only reference to your private life, that you have never been able to get the Leonard Bernstein soundtrack. 'Really?' Your face lit up. 'But the record lasts only forty minutes. What's on the rest of the tape?'

'I filled it up.' And I left.

A week later, I stopped my trips to the hospital. I'd take a couple of months of hard slog to finish the project. But I wanted, I needed, a break. I was tired, tired of working sixteen or seventeen hours a day. Ten long months of proximity to a hospital and its inmates had infected me with its abysmal despair. Abuses, faith – real or blind – hocus-pocus, bootlegging, ignorance, bribery, corruption, dirt, total resignation, death – Indians rarely have an overdose of these. Neither did I. My father too had raised Ankush and me on the same diet of perverse obstinacy, love and insecurity. But I, the flesh and blood symbol of the younger generation's aspirations, kept looking for a silver lining, for the legendary Maharashtrian ray of hope in the pervasive futility of that hospital. There is only one kind of poverty in India. Black. Without the faintest taint of grey.

I decided to go to Banaras. Twenty-four books, one for each day. I'd be lucky if I read even one. A pair of everything, starting with underpants – one to wear, one to wash. Glasses. Six enormous handkerchiefs, large enough to be used as towels, borrowed from my father. A very limited amount of money in my pocket. I should have hitchhiked as usual. But I was mentally bushed and I could see before me a long stretch of being kicked from pillar to post in search of work when I came back.

I came to see you three days before I left. As I entered, you said, 'I loved the tape. Tomorrow, Saturday, will you come to lunch?' You seldom joked or wasted words. Our meetings had been strictly for work. Bitten by some wayward and impulsive bug, I had left my job. But the first flush of enthusiasm, the devil-may-care defiance had almost been wiped out when you came to my help. I was grateful to you and unsure of myself. Distance had always been basic to our relationship. And now an invitation to lunch? I was startled. I heard what you said, but I didn't believe it. For a full fifty seconds I didn't react. And the moment passed. When I had collected myself to say yes, you said, 'Forget it.' I thought you were having me on, but I was wrong. Dead wrong. 'What happened?' I asked.

'Nothing,' you answered.

I asked again, and again, but the answer did not change. I was furious with you. And with myself. I left. It was going to be a long time before I learnt to accept your withdrawals with any degree of composure.

One night in Banaras, when Sadhan's woman brought me a cup of Bournvita, I asked for an inland letter form. And wrote to you – such minute writing that you'd have to hold it under a microscope to decipher it. Filled it up with happenings at the hospital, experiences, arguments, anecdotes. Not a word about our last meeting.

Back in Bombay, I wondered uneasily if you would speak to me.

You smiled and the gods showered me with blessings. 'Come back in a couple of hours. Then we'll go to my place.'

It started to rain on the way to your room. It was the first time I'd walked along Marine Drive in the monsoon. I didn't understand why you smiled as I tried to shelter myself under my umbrella. Then the wind turned it inside out and I understood. You were revelling in the downpour.

'Come on.' You crossed the road to stand at the sea wall. I stopped beside a tall building for protection. As if the pandemonium of the wind and rain were not enough, the waves had gone berserk, flaring like white peacocks on heat. I was afraid you'd lose your balance and fall in. But you were in your element and lost to the world. When you came to and turned around, you saw that I hadn't moved.

'Why did you stay back there?'

My teeth chattered.

'Are you okay?'

I shook my head.

'Does that mean yes or no?'

'Why do women's shirts have buttons on the left?' I asked, buttoning the dry shirt you gave me.

'Because parrots are green,' you answered.

~

The sea is yours, just as much as the sun, moon, frogs, snails, revenue stamps, Gold Spot, cupboards, cats, Rock Hudson, marigolds, raincoats are not yours. But the sea, yes. He is your responsibility. Are you keeping an eye on him?

Monsoon, but no rain. The sun dead. Flying charred-paper clouds. The sky behind. The colour of spit after brushing your teeth with black Monkey Brand tooth powder. The sea down below. Tightly packed. Like an army posed for D-Day. Crouching stealthily, waiting for your signal. Seven, six, five, four, three, two, one, go!

You beside the sea. Like a demagogue. The water eager to catch every word you utter. You against the parapet, your eyes roving far and wide, your body expectant, and then the long, long loping waves, surging towards you, showering you with thousands of white bouquets. The wildly flaying arms of your mob. Impatient to reach out and touch the feet, the hair, the eyes of their superstar, their second saviour, their Saibaba.

The dimples in your cheeks slipped into your eyes. Utterly drenched, you strained your ears to catch the sound of the next behemoth wave. And then, the crash of brass cymbals. And the sea about to engulf you.

The reclamation project is devouring whole hunks of the sea. At the Gateway, across from the Victory Stall, at Cuffe Parade, at Nariman Point. When will you be incensed enough to unleash the fury of your seas over Bombay?

'I won't open the door,' you said.

'I'm coming.'

'Don't be foolish. I'm a paying guest here. And you know there is only one front door. I'm not going to open it.'

You were not one to change your mind.

'I'm coming,' I repeated, and rang off.

As I took my first step, I felt as though I were swimming.

With every footstep in that sticky, tarry darkness, the night's rags seemed to attach themselves to my body. The first night of the blackout.

Since I was a child I have always frozen at sudden, blinding darkness. When I enter a dark theatre, my first instinct is to hold on to the usher's hand. I started to walk faster. The air was freer at Marine Drive. This was the second time I was coming to your room. It was an hour since I had phoned. I thought the gurkha would stop me. But he was busy gossiping with his pals. Coming up in the lift, I felt foolish.

It was half past ten. You'd mentioned that your childless landlady and landlord were terribly orthodox. There was still time to retreat. I fumbled for the bell.

The door was slightly ajar. The bolt had been deliberately moved forward.

You were waiting. Your reading lamp brushed against the floor and shed a small circle of light.

You held my hand and led me to your room. Smiled and said, 'Didn't I tell you not to come?'

Later, much later, at the Lodhi Gardens in Delhi, in the fogged twilight, you asked me, 'What difference does it make?' What made me feel so hopeless was that you meant it. There is no falsity in you, no theatricality.

What can I say to you? Push your glasses up to the bridge of your nose once again and say to me, Didn't I tell you not to come? That's it. Just hearing that makes a difference. A whole lot of difference.

Then I left. After being with you for a minute and a half.

'When do you go to Delhi to show your hospital manuscript and the photographs to that foreign publisher?'

'Next week.'

'How long will you be with him?'

'All my life.'

'Stop being funny.'

'Two days.'

'Then come and meet my train on the third.'

I looked at her intently. 'Very funny.'

'Don't you ever believe anything I say?

'Okay, the trip's cancelled.'

'Are you really coming?'

'I was. I'm not, now.'

'Your slave begs forgiveness.'

'Not enough. Rub your nose in the dirt.'

'Really?'

'Yes, with a friend.' My face fell just a little.

'She has some business in Delhi, you won't even see her. You listening to me?'

'Yes, yes, yes. With my ears and mouth open. Can't you see me floating five feet in air?'

I met you seven hours after my train had left. It was five minutes to five, so you asked me to wait. Then, 'What on earth?' You frowned.

I tried to tell you the whole drama in a few words. Rashid and I at the railway station. We had plenty of time, so we bought some cutlets and stood eating them. Five minutes before the train left, my body began to swell and my throat to contract. Rashid pushed me on to a bench before I became unconscious and ran to find a doctor. Afterwards he said, 'That bastard of a station master refused to call a doctor. I told him that if we didn't get help immediately, it'd be too late. Don't exaggerate, he said, we'll do all we can. I jumped into a cab and knocked on the door of four neighbourhood doctors. But they wouldn't come either – afraid it would turn out to be a police case, not wanting to get involved. Finally, one guy agreed to come. He shot five injections into you. By now the station master had produced four more doctors from the railway hospital. And would you believe it, Shank, the fourth actually gave you a B-complex shot!'

Rashid wanted me to go into a hospital and postpone the trip to next week. But I didn't agree. I argued and bullied the station master into giving me a ticket on the night train.

'But why? So we wouldn't have gone. What difference does it make?'

You were shocked by my rapacious desire to live every moment of my life. I felt you found it nauseating. How I loathe myself for this gluttony and uncertainty. But this is all I have. One life. One you.

I grabbed your hands and shook you, crazily. 'It does, it does, it does. It makes a lot of difference.'

When I met your train in Delhi, you were a long time emerging from the carriage. I thought you had changed your mind. Then you appeared, holding a case. 'Hullo, Bones,' you said and moved on.

Your friend behind you. Her case looked heavy, so I picked it up. She thanked me, but gave me a strange look.

'How was the trip?' I asked politely.

'Mind your own business. The cheek! Trying to act fresh with a girl!'

You were helpless with laughter. The woman was as flummoxed as I. Finally you said, 'My friend didn't come.'

At the open-air theatre in Delhi, you broke the slab of chocolate into two and passed me half. As your fingers touched mine, you said, 'You're frozen.' Then you rubbed my hand between yours. 'Warmer?' you asked.

~

As the sun set in the Lodhi Gardens, your mood changed too. A cotton wool mist floated among the trees. It was cold.

I loved the gardens, the space, the trees, the ruins. But not now. It was too quiet, too isolated.

'Let's go,' I said.

'I want to see the night fall.'

'It's not safe here at this time.'

'You go then, I'm not afraid of the dark.'

A few quiet minutes and then you began to talk. 'One cold winter night at eight o'clock, my father told me to walk round our house in Baroda because I was afraid of the dark. Even now, our house is secluded, far from the main road.

Every year the gardener used to kill a snake or two in the garden. I went out and hid myself behind a pillar and hung on to it. I knew my mother would be trembling with fear too. She was not permitted to cry, but I could hear a faint sobbing. My father came out to check on me and called my name. When I didn't answer, he caught me in the light of his torch. "You big, hulking ten-year-old coward, I'll get rid of your fear once and for all." He locked me inside the empty garage. I must have cried for about three hours. Then I shut up. I stopped crying after that. I resolved that I'd never let myself feel anything – joy, sorrow, fear, weakness. I would let no one come close to me. Not even my mother. Her helplessness and softness had done nothing but provoke my father. At five-thirty in the morning, my father unlocked the doors. "Well, lost your fear now?" I looked at him and said, "What difference does it make?"'

~

'Bones, teach me to ride a motorbike.'

'But I don't know how to.'

'Then learn, so you can teach me.'

I looked at you.

Your hands gripping the handles. There was a vrroom in my head as your right wrist moved to accelerate. The bike sped like a comet. Your hair flying parallel to the road. Your eyes freaking out on speed.

'When do you want to learn?'

'A week from today!'

I had driven a motorcycle only once before. At school, when I was thirteen, there was a man who used to rent motorcycles to people with licences. When Raghu pestered him long enough, he would let him have one for half an hour. One day I sat in the front and Raghu behind me. 'Brake,' he yelled. But the crowd of kids ahead confused me and I accelerated instead. The crowd scattered and soon we were on the deserted Vadala road. Flying on it. On the way back, we ran into my aunt who had come to school to pay her son's fees. When I got home, my father said, 'Don't ever do that again.'

I overrode every reservation and objection that Rashid could muster and made him teach me. Every day, three hours, for six days.

On the seventh day, I came to your room. You were ready in your jeans, a scarf round your hair. From Victoria Gardens to Malabar Hill to Kemp's Corner to your institute via Queen's road.

'How soon will you learn?'

'How many days did you take?'

'Six.'

'Me too.'

Every evening from eight to ten, I taught you. Either from Cuffe Parade to the R.C. Church or from Khar to Santa Cruz.

'Where to?' I asked you on the seventh day.

'To Poona.' You laughed.

A woman riding a motorcycle. Without a licence, too. I must have been mad. I made you wear a leather jacket and hid your hair in my beret. Poona was a hundred and twenty miles and several hair-raising hairpin bends away. It wouldn't have occurred to you to choose an easier place to go to.

I filled up the tank and drove as far as Khandala. The wind cut through me and I was terrified. The lights of Khopoli blazed in the valley, but I didn't dare admire the view. Without reducing speed, I threw some coins at the shrine in the Ghats and prayed to the god within to save us. I cheered up after two cups of hot tea at Lonavla. You were feverish with excitement. I touched your elbow to ask, 'Are you okay?'

'Yes, fine. Don't worry.'

You kicked the bike to start it and it was transformed into a whirlwind. I was filled with a strange peace. When I drove the bike, I was very conscious of it. But you had become one with it. Riding it, you were oblivious to everything else. By the time we got to the Valvan Dam, you had started to accelerate.

I hugged you tight round the waist and leaned forward to shout into your ear, 'I don't want to die.'

You shouted back, 'Can't hear you.'

I yelled from the deep end of my belly button, 'I don't want to die.'

'Not even with your arms round me?'

'No.'

'Oh, I love you, Kushank, I love you.' The wind threw your words back at me. I thought you hadn't heard me.

'Not even with my arms round you.'

'I know, I know. That's why I love you!'

The next time we met, the scene had changed.

As soon as I came in, you said, 'I think you ought to stop seeing me.'

'Anything else?'

'Can't you understand? I don't want to see you.'

'That's your affair.' I laughed. 'But I shall continue to see you.'

'It's no good. It's already gone too far. It'll be easier if you leave now.'

'Easier for whom?'

'For both of us.'

'I'm not going.'

'Oh, yes – you are.'

'Not unless you throw me out.'

'Don't underestimate me.'

'I never do.'

'Please, Kushank.'

'Sorry, but I'm not leaving.'

'Don't be stupid. Look, I'll say something I'll regret and hurt you.'

'You've trained me well to cope with that.'

'Now you're trying to get back at me.'

'No, I'm not.'

'Will you leave if I tell you why?'

'No.'

'You fool. Don't you understand? I don't want you to get any closer to me. Every time I see you, I forget my years of resolutions. I forget not to let myself feel anything and get involved with you. And then one day this will be over too and leave me hollow and naked.'

'I'm not going.'

'Don't you have any self-respect? God, you are shameless.'

'You're damned right.'

~

Honour and self-respect, birds of a feather. God knows what truth is in them. We've known each other for years. We've invented a thousand ways to stunt and cripple ourselves. Yet perhaps the most effective and prestigious among them is this bogey of self-respect. We've burnt our innards and wasted our lives in its name, discovered something called revenge, argued, fought wars and world wars, all for the sake of honour. And I, the son of my forefathers, I too have often been trapped by it.

After my mother died, I started eating out. My father gave me money every month and let me fend for myself. If I asked for more, he gave me more. But I didn't like to ask too often. Then I had to go hungry. I had got used to two-day fasts. But sometimes, my head and stomach would play havoc. There's a point up to which hunger is unbearable. Cross it and then it's easy. But when I'd missed three or four meals, I felt a string wind itself round me and start to tighten. The world swam before my eyes and there was a numb humming in my brain. Slowly it grew into a tight vice around my head and I turned into an irritable, snapping dog. I stuffed my ears with cotton wool, but the humming grew worse, and finally I dropped in on my friends, Prachinti or Jitendra. It was my third meal in four days at Jitendra's.

It was almost midnight, but I knew they ate late and anyway, however late it got, I was sure of getting a meal there. As I reached for my second hot chapatti, Jitendra's mother said something angrily, in Sindhi. There was a sudden silence at the table. Jitendra's little brother and sister stared at their plates. I had never learnt Sindhi, but

I did know enough to interpret what she had said. 'Hasn't he a home to go to? Here, every day … Is this a home or a restaurant?' Only Jitendra continued to eat calmly. I thought of pretending that I hadn't understood. But my face had paled.

'Ignore her, Kushank,' said Jitendra. 'Mother says whatever comes into her head.'

The only difference is that she says it, while all of you only think it. But I had never enjoyed the game of sharpening words to cut people down.

I finished my dinner. Not hurriedly. No. When you are grown up, it becomes a matter of honour to retreat with grace. Like the hotel manager in Gulmarg, I told myself, 'It's all right, it's all right.'

Later, driving me home, Jitendra said, 'Don't let her worry you. After all, I'm the breadwinner in the family, aren't I?'

At least my stomach was half-full that night. Gradually I stopped going to his house. If I was ravenous and if Prachinti wasn't at home, or if her family were on a starvation diet, I thought yearningly of the meals at Jitendra's. When I could bear it no longer, I gave in and went to his place. But just once or twice. And those meals left a bitter taste in my mouth before I'd even eaten them.

With you, I have never let my self-respect intrude. I had worked it out. The meaning you brought to my life lost its colour when you were no longer there. As long as you were with me, I wasn't going to let go of you.

~

You didn't speak again that day. I lay and read Anouilh's *Poor Bitos* for a few hours and left.

The next morning, very early, walking past your amazed landlady, I knocked at your door.

'You?' But it was a month and a half before you gave in.

'Want to get married?'

'Whom to?' you asked.

'Me, of course,' I answered, as I lolled on the bed and stretched my legs towards the ceiling. 'Just us, you to me, and me to you. Without letting anyone know.'

'Really?'

I shut up. Wasn't it an unwritten rule between us never to talk of marriage?

My clock stopped ticking with the thought that we could have gone through our lives without my asking you the one question that mattered. I felt numb. Not at the thought of your saying yes, but at how stupid I must have been not to have realized till now how much I loved you.

It had seemed a perfectly natural question to ask, yet I was beginning to feel unsure.

'I wasn't joking.'

'I know.'

'Will you marry me?'

You were quiet, for almost an hour.

'When do you want an answer?' you asked.

Just as I was about to say something, you added, 'And don't say right now.'

'Then when?'

'Kushank, how did we get here all of a sudden?'

'Will you?'

'Have you really thought about it?' And then, as if that sounded utterly irrelevant. 'When I return from Baroda. On Monday.'

'Tell me, tell me, tell me,' I said, as soon as we got home.

'You're mad.'

'Yes, mad. About you.'

'Don't be theatrical.'

'I'm not. Honestly.'

'Want to get married?'

'Yes, yes, yes!'

'I'm staying the night.'

You gently placed the stylus on the edge of the Faiyaz Khan record. Then looked up. Now what had I gone and said? But I looked back defiantly. You said, 'You will have to use one of my saris as a lungi.' And then, 'If my landlady finds out, I'll have to look for another place.'

You closed the door.

You had a shower after me and drew the curtains.

'You want the light on?'

I shrugged.

You left the reading lamp on and came to lie beside me on the bed.

'Shall I undress myself or will you do it?' you asked.

'I will.'

'Do you remember the first time you held and kissed me? You'd come back exhausted and lay with your head in my lap. Suddenly you pulled my head down. The next day at the institute, I felt dizzy every time I thought of it.'

I kept mum.

'You're laughing at me.'

'Why do you always smell so good?'

'It's the soap.'

The answer was so like you that I burst out laughing.

'Nobody says that to me when I use the same soap.'

'You idiot.' And you hugged me.

Your body felt cool. I thought it was because you had just stepped out of the shower. Your embrace was always so cool and soothing. Whenever I was exhausted after a long, hard day's work, the memory of your body against mine gave me strangely pleasant gooseflesh. I always had a shower as soon as I came to your room and then interrupted whatever you were doing to push my head between your breasts and sleep. When I woke, the first thing I saw were your pink nipples.

'How often are you going to make love?' you used to ask.

'Till you can't stand me.'

'There's no chance for you, then. I'll never tire of you.'

You were weird. It never occurred to you to go through the paces of coyness and stylized resistance demanded by Indian tradition. There never was any false modesty about you. You were utterly unselfconscious in your lovemaking. All your dos and don'ts and taboos fell away. Arguing and fighting with each other as we did, we never resorted to lovemaking to resolve our differences of opinion. You taught me to make love without haggling over it. You gave happiness so generously, your mind and body had accepted making love so easily and unreservedly that there was no you, no me, no intellectualizing, no preconceptions.

I was a deep sea diver with a flaming torch in my hand. It was a fantastic light, lighting you from a great distance, burning me up at the same time. The tide came in with every breath I took and we were picked up by a wave. The sky so wide. I was a bird flying very high, very far. My wings stilled. Then I folded them and the earth rose to meet me as I sped towards it. As we lightly touched, you retreated. I was going to have to fly higher. I wheeled and soared again and suddenly you were with me. The universe within our embrace with Parvati's clasp round Shiva. How simply all bonds fell away and were transmuted into pure rhythm. It spread from us, in ever widening circles, to touch the centre of the universe. Free, free, free. The sky was freed too, and, with the sea, was absorbed within us.

She wouldn't live long now. Only a day or two. Then an end to her darkness. Forever.

I'll find a note under my door. To inform me that she's passed away.

It would have been more seemly if I had waited till she died and then decided matters either way. But I'm not going to the funeral. She knows it. As I was leaving this evening, she asked, 'Will you be back?'

I didn't think fast enough. I was about to stutter, 'I beg your pardon?' when the daughter from Cochin arrived and entered the room without knocking. 'How are you, Mummy?' she asked, embracing her as she lay on the bed.

'How do I look?'

'Ill, very ill,' she blurted and then, collecting herself, 'but you're going to get better now. I'm sure of it.'

She smiled. 'That's sweet of you, dear. But Kushank is more honest.'

The daughter from Cochin looked at me resentfully. She said, watching me closely, 'Why? What did he say to you?'

'Nothing. He didn't say a word.'

Even when a person is dying you can never tell how long he'll take to die. In fact, you can't be sure he won't change his mind at the last moment. But Kaku was going to die. Even if there weren't enough medical reasons. It was merely a matter of time. Since it wasn't a very bad attack, the two daughters who lived in Bombay were in a fix. I'd have liked to sympathize with them, but you can't tell with people. If I said, for instance, that the dying should have more consideration for the living and do away with the element of uncertainty, one of the daughters would probably have rolled up her eyes and passed out. This despite the fact that they had taken her to the free municipal hospital on the last two occasions. Worse still, since symbolic gestures like fainting go over my head, one of them might have lectured me feelingly on my heartlessness, or their filial love, or their sense of duty. No. I wasn't going to risk it.

This time, taking courage into their hands and hoping for the best, they had brought her to a private hospital. When I caught one of the daughters off guard, I could see the lines of worry on her face. Worry about the unnecessary expense. Their mother was dying. At home or at the municipal hospital or at a private one. Somewhere. What difference did it make? They must have talked about sharing the expenses on the way back from the airport with the daughter who had just arrived.

Her mother's words had stung the daughter from Cochin. Kaku was never going to change. Certainly not now, on the threshold of death. She mumbled savagely to herself, 'If I were honest, I wouldn't have left Cochin.'

The past disappointments, quarrels, jealousies, every emotion that had been mulled over for years, but not given speech, suddenly rushed to the surface. Within a few minutes of all of us coming together again. And Kaku, Kaku, who had been blind the last six years, watched it all. For a long moment, the silence stretched and swelled in the room.

'No. That's not true.' Her voice was stricken as she wrenched her hand out of Kaku's. 'I came to see you live, not die.'

If Kaku had decided to live, things would have really become complicated. But, for the moment at least, the girl really meant what she said. To ask for anything more was to expect far too much. All our lives we wander around carrying this heart of ours with us, even survive thanks to it. And then, one day, someone wants to take a close look at it. And we discover that we're not sure we like what we see. We can expect what we like from ourselves. But to judge others is a luxury we certainly can't afford.

After that, the two didn't say much to each other. Later, she went out with her sisters, saying she'd be back to spend the night with her mother.

We were left together again. With one difference. Fifteen years ago, Kaku could see the dark. Now she didn't have to close her eyes to do so. I could stare at her. Her eyes were wide open. The muddy eyeballs moving restlessly, testifying to their blindness. I tried to shut out her eyes by closing my own tight. But her eyes were everywhere. Behind my eyelids. Locking me inside a cataract. I wanted to stick my tongue out at her. But I remembered the last time I had done that.

'Sticking your tongue out at me, eh? You cheeky little runt, have you no respect for your elders? You thought I couldn't see you in the dark, eh? I've seen a lot like you. I have three daughters, each worse than the next. And I've straightened them all out. Shameless brat, aren't you, even after such a thrashing. But I'm not tired yet, I'll give you some more.' She wasn't in the habit of lying.

If I'd got up to switch on the light, she'd have fired a battery of questions. 'Who is that? Kushank? What is it? Do you want to go home? Are you bored? Of course you are. You feel tied down, don't you?' And once she started, she'd remember her daughters, and then God help me. How those girls hated her. No, it was even stronger than that. They found her revolting. They had tolerated her while they were young. They teach you that much at school. They were at university, or looking for jobs, when their father died. They thought that they'd have to be nice to her until they were on their own and free. But it didn't work out quite that way. Their mother refused to cut the cords even after they had married and left home. She had discovered a new fad – illness. Every few months. Drawn out. Useless. Like a curse. A fad only the rich could afford.

Royelle, Sabatienne, Chezyl. But the mother insisted on using their Marathi names – Urmila, Sanjayi, Premangi. And not just at home. In public too. On purpose. How ugly she had become. But what was unforgivable was that Mummy had married Papa.

I didn't have the courage to switch on the light. I hadn't even seen her for months because I couldn't cope with her harangues. I was going to sit quietly in my chair as if I were strapped into a straitjacket. Quietly. Without moving. Till her daughter returned. Silence. My right foot went to sleep, the leg felt like one with elephantiasis. I rested both feet on the floor and wriggled my toes. Kaku seemed lost in her inner world. She wouldn't worry me any more tonight.

'I didn't expect you to come. I thought about you a lot. But that was no reason why you should come.' Was she unaware that Sanjayi had gone out of the room? She spoke slowly, but clearly. Would she understand if I explained to her?

'Is it windy outside? If I walked out on the balcony, a breath of wind might touch me too, mightn't it?' she pushed back the quilt and half sat up. The effort tired her, silenced her for a while.

I got up to draw back the curtains at the window and asked for a bit of breeze. The curtains were motionless.

'Will you switch on the light? I want to hear the click of the switch.' She closed her eyes and listened. 'Once again, please.' Her eyes were open now. 'Do you know, I sometimes feel that it's my eyes that come between me and the light … Will you pluck out my eyes? Gouge them out with your fingers? How often I've wondered whether you'd come or not. Now you've come, but what's the point? I want light and that's not possible. And without light, there's no forgiveness. Do you think the distance between us is a little less now? I know I can't fool myself … But tell me anyway.'

And I said, 'Yes, it's all right between us. It's always been. For the past fifteen years.'

She smiled to herself. 'The forgiveness is in me. Not in your words.'

I returned to my chair. Even if I had to spend the next four years with Kaku, in the same room, I wouldn't have minded it now. We could have talked now, unendingly. There was nothing left to say. I rested my head on the back of the chair and had a catnap, but woke up when I heard Sanjayi's heels tapping down the corridor.

I could hear her talking to the nurse outside.

'What do you know?' asked Kaku.

'Nothing.'

'Did you ever tell anyone?'

'No.'

I said goodnight to Kaku and Sanjayi and left. Chocolates are for keeping quiet.

~

After that day, I went home late every night. And left very early in the morning to avoid the messenger who would bring me news of Kaku's death. And despite all these precautions, what if she decided to die between midnight and six o'clock in the morning?

On the third night, I stepped on a piece of paper in the dark. At the front door. Goodbye, Kaku – I said as I switched on the light and read the note. Sanjayi's bold writing showed through the imprint of my shoe. 'Dear Kushank, Will you come over to the hospital? Mum wants to speak to you. Sabatienne.'

Talk to me? What about? Didn't we talk the other day? A final talk? If you want to change your mind about your departure, do so. But don't involve me in it. Owing to unforeseen circumstances the death of Mrs Reghla, alias Kaku, has been postponed. The stars were not quite right. I switched off the light and vanished in Kaku's darkness. Purandare, you have no sense of death. Maybe not. Or maybe too much. I wasted a couple of hours in idle nonsense, talking to myself.

What does she want? My answers haven't changed, even if her questions have. And if she didn't have any questions to ask? I was losing faith in my own prescience. If she died before I saw her, I could never live it down. I locked up my room and left. I'd better hurry if I wanted to catch her.

It was a quarter to one in the morning, but the train was crowded. With night shift workers? Maybe. There is never a reason for crowds on the suburban trains in Bombay. If four million and sixty-seven thousand cobalt bombs were dropped on the earth, and if they killed off all of humanity, the local trains of Bombay would still have people hanging on to people hanging out of doors and windows. More people got on at Mahim. I was scared now. Terrified that these people wouldn't let me get off the train. They'd block all the doors and I'd throw myself at them again and again, over and over, trying to get out. Till Virar, the last station. The train stopped at Khar and I was the only one on the platform, the others had vanished in the night.

No cabs outside the station. I started to walk, hoping to pick one up on Ghodbunder Road. My head down. Not looking left or right. Counting my paces. That's supposed to shorten the distance.

Ghodbunder Road. Nice clean road. Want to lick it? Four cars. Not one of them in the desired yellow and black livery. My chappals in my hand. Walking barefoot. Faster, almost running now. And if a dog took a bite out of my calf? Slow and steady does the tortoise walk. And if Kaku dies before I get there? That's her problem. I don't think of the fourteen shots in the stomach. Run. From far away, I saw that there was no light in Kaku's room. I don't believe in symbolism. But in the documentary, the kerosene flame killed Tilak. The flame died and he died. What are you going to do, Kaku?

'There's a switch on your right.'

I stood panting at the door, my tongue licking my dry lips.

'Aren't you going to turn on the light?'

What difference will it make? I switched it on. She lay looking at the ceiling. Her legs pulled up to her stomach under the sheet.

'Won't you say something?'

'Yes.' Horrible. My left eye too will go off at a tangent. All it needs is time. What's the hurry anyway? We're all in the process of becoming caricatures of ourselves. And you're in the vanguard, Kushank.

'Can't work out what the old woman wants now, eh?' She smiled sourly. 'Do you know, I feel so well. You should have heard my daughters' silence! … What are you thinking of now? That old Kaku's mind is wandering again? I wish I had the key to starting conversations with you. But you've always been the same. You and your silences. At Bangalore too. I thought then that you were just cussed and rude, so I ignored you. All right, I thrashed you. And now? I can't hit you any more, right? But I've become wiser with age. Your silences weren't as simple as that. Relax. I won't ask you any questions. I'll talk. You're used to that. To listening.'

I switched off the light. Bitterness was contorting her face in strange ways. 'No. Not a word out of you. Always a monologue. Between us. But then, again, that's not entirely true either.'

I couldn't work out what she was getting at.

'It wasn't like this in the beginning. I had three daughters. But they weren't enough. You were my favourite. And not just because I didn't have a son of my own. So many of my husband's friends had sons. And in your own family, there was Ankush. But you? Everything you did was so spontaneous and blunt. Anger, joy, love. Everything a little exaggerated, a little greedy. I remember a letter you wrote to your father once.

'Dear Baba, There is an influenza epidemic here. Sanjayi had a temperature of a hundred degrees, I only had one degree.' She suddenly stopped short. 'Kushank? Kushank?'

'I'm still here, Kaku.'

'Fed up? I've waited for you all day. Fourteen hours. I wasn't sure if you'd come. I tried not to think about it. That made it easier to wait. The hospital clock kept track of the time. But it would have struck even if I'd been deaf. What did you do with your mother's ashes?'

'Threw them to the wind, from the hills in Khandala.'

Balancing myself in the rocking train. Trying to find a spot where I could be alone. Putting on an indifferent face, leaning out of the carriage as we emerged from a tunnel, looking down at the valley of Khopoli. I loosened my fingers and the packet flew away. It clung to the carriage behind mine, then came adrift, opened up and the ashes scattered away.

'I won't take too long now.'

Her feet slid down the mattress. I had never known her to be so still.

'Will you throw mine into the sea?'

I thought of the receptionist downstairs. She had dozed off, resting her head on her folded arms. Waking with a start when she heard me coming in.

'Who do you want?'

'Mrs Reghla, on the second floor.'

'Is this any time to come visiting? Come in the morning.'

Sanjayi came down the stairs. Her eyes darker than the darkness round her.

'You win,' she hissed bitterly.

Still the same language. I could see myself as a child, tugging at my father's sleeve at the movies, or at a play, every few minutes. Comedy, tragedy, farce, bullfights, it didn't make any difference. The only question I always asked was, 'Who's winning?'

My father's exasperated voice when we got home. His hand on my shoulder. 'You ask me once more and I'll never take you out again. Do you understand?'

The next time around, while my father was totally engrossed in the film, despite all my self-restraint, I would spring the question, 'Who's winning?'

But I'm not playing any more. I don't even know what the game is. I don't want to know. Then I can't win, can I, Sanjayi?

'I don't want to wait any longer.'

Kaku's toes peeped out from under the sheet. How short she was. And ugly. Baba said she was very beautiful once. Maybe. You have to take people on trust some time or the other.

'I got tired of waiting for you. What if you hadn't come after all the rows with these people?'

Her paralysed face twisted with pain. 'First my daughters, and then the padre. They didn't believe me when I said I don't want to be buried. Sanjayi, Premangi, they think I'm reverting to Hinduism just to spite them. The padre has different arguments, says there is no such tradition. You can't give up the religion you embraced when you were married, he says. I'm sorry, and shakes his head. Cremation is out of the question. Think. Think coolly. And straight after that he says, I'm in no condition to make decisions anyway. Says, I won't let you do anything against your own interests. You'll only set a terrible precedent for people of the next generation. Once again religion and God. Fools … them and I. What do you think? Do you really think I'm being drawn back into the fold of my original faith? No, I promised I wouldn't question you … Maybe I am going back. But I'm not abandoning any religion. And what will God say? I don't know. He'll have to make up his own mind. I can't hear him yet. When I persisted, the padre suggested to the girls that they should get me certified as being unsound of mind. Pay someone to do it. I'll pay for it if you can't, he says. God will bless me for my good deed. And all this in my room where I could hear them. When Premangi refused, I'll excommunicate you all, he threatened. But Sanjayi stood up to him and said they wouldn't be coerced into anything.'

She was quiet for a while. Then her voice seemed to come from a long way off.

'There's nothing left now, is there? No way to reach them. Only malice in their hearts. Not a very pleasant legacy. No, not a very pleasant memory to take with me either. And along with me, they hate you too. Because I asked for you. You still haven't answered me. Even though I've spoken so much. It takes more than blindness to find your way in the dark.'

'It's free,' he said. He wore khaki shorts and a navy blue shirt. I looked blank, so he explained, 'For the staff.'

'Yes.' There didn't seem much to say.

'Not bad, is it? Perks for the staff?' He raised a brow in question.

Must you talk? Get stuffed, you and your sociability.

'Perks for the family too?'

I realized my mistake too late. He had taken me seriously.

It hadn't occurred to him before. He scratched his beard for an answer. Then came to sit beside me.

'Don't know.' He shook his head. 'Don't know about that.' And then, 'I must check that out. I haven't quite made up my mind about myself yet. This electric cremation bit, I mean. I don't like the rush. You hurry all your life and then hurry again, while leaving. Now if your hand or arm were cut off that would be a different story, wouldn't it? Well, that's an idea. You know I'm just full of them. Got a trick up my sleeve for every occasion. Just imagine, that way I'd preside over my own last rites. See that observation hole? I'd be watching myself from there. Carry my ashes to the Ganga too. Come, you really ought to take a look inside. Won't get to see such an inferno in your life. Here now, gone the next.'

'No, I think I'll stay here.'

I could hear a fountain through the trellis behind me. This would be a good place to sleep. When you were tired. Like now. Alone, or with a woman. Because there's a fountain nearby.

'Why?'

'Because I feel like it.'

'Your mother?'

'No.' Yours, you bastard.

'Relative?'

'No.'

'Someone else.' He nodded to himself understandingly. 'Her today, you tomorrow. At least you'll know what's in store for you. Stumped you, eh?'

Yes. You have. I have no answer to that. In the centre, the fountain. A fourteen-day-old moon up above. Far away, the sounds of a Ganapati procession. Crowds. So many obstacles on the way here. This road closed. That one open only to small vehicles. An auspicious day you chose, Kaku. A couple of wreaths. How many of us in all? Seven, including Kaku. A few tears. It was getting late. They all had to get back. Bye, Kushank.

Him and me. The rails that had taken Kaku's body into the furnace. The red conflagration behind the thick metal doors, seen through the mica peephole. Hot air around us. Drops of water from the fountain on our backs. Bye, Kaku. My mother used to say that in Indian films a man was never really dead unless his body was shown burning on the funeral pyre. But you've changed it all, Kaku. From the age of the handcart to the age of electricity.

'Did you bring an urn?'

I didn't answer.

'Or at least a box of some sort?' he queried me again.

'No.'

'No? What will you take her in, then?'

'Don't know.' Please, Kaku. Can't we stop now? I'll take you away tomorrow morning.

He looked at me contemptuously. 'Sit down and wait then ... Came with three women and didn't even think of bringing an old tin,' he muttered to himself.

Four women. Kaku.

Towel? Not on the hook. I sat looking at the boat in the bathtub. An inadvertent splash had put out the flame. The oily smoke had turned the boat into a black smudge. Where was my towel? I sifted through the damp clothes on the floor once again. Kaku's towel wasn't there, either. And it would be no good calling out to her, she wasn't at home.

'Come on, hurry up. I told Mrs Swaminathan we'd be there by eleven.'

'I'm not coming.'

'Now what? You said at breakfast that you would.'

'No, I want to stay at home.'

I thought she was going to lose her temper. But she only sighed. Then smiled and pulled me to her.

'I know. You want to play with your new boat, right?' My eyes were fixed on the floor.

'Say yes, or I won't light the wick for you.'

'Yes.'

'And promise me you won't touch the matches?'

'Promise.'

'Even if the flame goes out?'

'Yes.'

'And don't go out in the sun. I'll be back by one. If you're hungry, eat some grapes. Look at me, Kushank, not at the boat. Did you hear what I said?' And then, 'I'm off. I guess you're going to have that boat on your mind all day today.'

Towel? Dripping wet, I shot towards my room in search of a towel. If I don't look around, no one can see me naked. On the left of the house, an open field with a fence. On the right, at a distance, the Srinivases' bungalow. Nothing else around. Blinkers on my eyes as I run. Taking a long jump into my room, I froze mid-air. My eyes dropped and slid into my stomach. Devouring everything. Greedily. My every pore examining, absorbing. Our neighbour, Aminara, from the Rustoms' house, which Kaku had forbidden me to go to. She wasn't wearing a choli or a bra like Kaku did. Flint sparks pulsating in my head. Two purple grapes, their ends winding up to erect points under Kaka's repetitive fingers. The next moment his long slim body descended on her. He seemed to have got stuck. The cleft between his white buttocks rose in a line with my nose and crashed down. Foreshortening to a sharp pinnacle to plunge deep once again. Her tight body unravelling with his. Breathlessly sucking him down, ejecting him, up and down and up again. My taut body echoing her yearning, abandoned moans with sharp spasms. Her eyes opened in a toxic haze. Pomegranates burst in the sky. Red seeds exploding inside me. It went on agonizingly and I couldn't have enough of it. Her eyes focused on me. I kept tearing out of myself, my pole-vaulting penis arching to a fine breaking point.

'Look, look,' she cried, the disbelief in her voice as breathless as me. 'Look how it's risen. The littlest darling I've ever seen. I could lose it in the palm of my hand.'

Kaka had become conscious of me. Tall Kaka. Fair and pink-skinned Kaka. White soft hair falling over his brow. He was God. Indra, or Vishnu. Sometimes both. His hand had stopped moving. Midway. His red eyes welling up with anger.

'What are you doing here?' he didn't raise his voice.

'Having a shower.'

'Obviously,' he said drily. 'Why didn't you go with Kaku?'

'Kaku?' Who was Kaku? 'Because ... because of the boat.'

'How long are you planning to stand there?'

Aminara was watching me. I tried to cover myself with my hands.

As she bubbled over with laughter, Kaka's gold chain slid over her left breast and glittered in my eyes.

'Are you going to answer me?'

I ran.

My body had dried. But I was still in the bathroom. Naked. My legs hurt from having stood there for so long. The clock struck half past twelve and the bathroom door opened.

'Come out. Aren't you getting dressed today?'

Kaka's deep voice reverberating in the mountains.

'Here,' he made me put my hand out. A ten-inch-tall chocolate Father Christmas, wrapped in cellophane. Tied with a red ribbon. 'Eat it before it melts.'

He raised my chin gently with his right hand. Then a flashing, staggering, powerful slap across my face. Stunning me. My ear began to swell. 'Eat it. Chocolates are for keeping quiet.'

I had started to vomit violently by the time Kaku came home. Clutching the remains of Father Christmas's sticky snowboots. Rolling in the chocolate mess. Pulling at the roots of my stomach. For hours I lay palely dead. Then with a demonic force, I rummaged through my viscera. It was three days before I could purge myself of the fever.

'Goddammit,' Kaku fumed, as she wiped my face with a wet cloth. 'Why didn't you stop him from eating the whole bloody chocolate?' They glared at each other. I had the feeling she'd have liked to throw up all over him. And that wouldn't have satisfied her either.

'I thought he liked chocolates,' he mumbled.

Suddenly, she pulled me up by my hair. For a second

she imagined I was Kaka. I screamed and she let go. 'O you fool, you clown.'

The next day, as the doctor packed his bag, I heard him say, 'You'd better send for his father. He's going to die.'

Kaku sat at the head of my bed. Like someone with lockjaw. 'Let him try, just let him try.' And the jaws shut again.

When I got out of bed seven days later, Kaka was laid on slabs of ice. My father had come. Kaku was still sitting. Beside Kaka this time. Cables, trunk calls, coffin, wreaths – everything was arranged. Only the three girls had yet to arrive. Kaku didn't speak. Not even when her daughters came. She called me to her once at night. As she waited for her daughters. In the light of the candles.

'It's midnight. Happy birthday, Kushank. These candles are not for you. But next year you'll have candles. Twelve. Learn to breathe deeply. You'll have to blow them all out with one breath ... Go to your father now.'

She came in the afternoon. Her misty eyes like a georgette scarf. There was nobody with Kaka, except Kaku, whose chin was sunk into her chest. She lit the candle she had brought with her, placed it on the wooden plank at the foot of the coffin, went round Kaka once and stood again at his feet. She looked at Kaku. I wanted to make Kaku vanish. But without looking at me, Aminara had rooted me to my place. She stood without expression. Motionless. Till Kaku raised her head to look at her.

The living room in Kaku's house was huge. It seemed bigger the day they took the coffin away. In fact, Kaka had never left that room. He was still there. But since he had decided to remain invisible, he had to stand behind me. Even now, so late at night. I lay with my head in my father's lap, half asleep, so he stood behind my father.

How long were those people going to sit here in silence? When Baba asked Kaku to come into the room, it was about a quarter to twelve. Soon the clock would strike half past and Kaka would open the bathroom door. But still they sat. And we were catching a train home early tomorrow morning. My mother should have been here. She made everyone go to bed early the night before a journey.

Kaku, at least, had some excuse. But what was the matter with those three? Since their father's death, they had begun to treat me as if I didn't exist. How they had spoilt me once. Kushank, have a chocolate. Kushank, a book for you. Let's go to the movies, Kushank. Kushank this and Kushank that. And now, if I wanted to be with them, they looked at me suspiciously. 'Did Mummy send you?'

Like a fool I asked, 'Where?'

'What do you mean, where, you idiot? Here, to us.'

Despite their insults, I persisted. 'What for?'

'Shut up and go away. You won't understand these things,' Sanjayi said with utter disdain, her chin in the air. And they started to whisper together. I ran away and from a safe distance yelled at them, 'I'll tell Kaku on you. I'll tell Kaku everything!'

'There, didn't I tell you?' Premangi muttered in English. 'That little rascal is a spy.'

I would have to ask Baba what the last word meant. But I yelled back, all the same. 'Yes, yes, I'm a pie.'

I was almost asleep, it was so quiet. Baba cleared his throat, but his voice was hoarse.

'This is going to be difficult. You'll have to help me.'

I opened my eyes when nobody answered him. Premangi and Urmila sat on the red carpet and Sanjayi behind them, on a chair. In the opposite corner, Kaku sat alone. She had removed her glasses and dug two fingers into her eyes. Since Kaka's death she had been digging her eyes out. As if to reach deep inside them.

'One of you will have to stay here.'

Sanjayi glared at Baba. 'What for?'

Baba said angrily, 'Do I have to plead with you to stay with your own mother?'

'You'd be wasting your time,' answered Premangi, barely concealing the contempt in her voice.

'Stop being theatrical,' Baba said, controlling his temper. 'I wish your papa was here to straighten you girls out.'

'He isn't. And you can hardly blame us for that, can you?' Sanjayi said.

Baba looked at her. 'You're the youngest. You'll stay, won't you?'

'Me? Give up my studies? No, I can't do that.'

He looked at Urmila's cold, set face and gave up.

'Right then. Kushank will stay here.'

'No! No!' I jumped up to hug him. 'I want to come home with you.'

My hands hugged his feet, but he ignored me. And without looking at Kaku, I knew I had cracked the blank emptiness on her face.

When I woke up in the mornings, I could see the rooms. Kaku, rooms. Baba back in Bombay, rooms, me, rooms. I crossed myriad thresholds, but there were always more rooms. As soon as I stepped out of bed, I was smothered by rooms. At night, going to sleep, I slipped out of the rooms. When I woke up, they were back. Chains and chains of rooms. To the left, to the right. In all the eight directions we had learnt at school. Even when I referred to them in

English. At the end, a room, in the middle, a room, ahead of me, a room, Sanjayi's, Premangi's, Urmila's. Kaka's and Kaku's room. The guest room, the kitchen, the balcony, the terrace. Had they always existed? Even before Kaka died? Right at the beginning? When I came here on holidays? I roamed from room to room, calling each one by its name. Counting them. But as soon as I closed my eyes, they escaped, slipping away like wet cakes of soap, multiplying themselves, inside my head. Back to back. One-walled rooms. Crouching behind doors. If I touched them, they would retreat like snails in the wind. Like gas balloons, free, floating in space. Oh God, I forgot to count the dining room. All over again, from one besotted room to the next. Till I came to the kitchen. Waiting for Muthamma to notice me.

'You going to stand there all your life?' And after some time, 'Lost your tongue?'

'Muthamma...' I stopped.

'Hurry up and say what you have to. I haven't got all day to waste. Now, you going to talk?' she threatened.

The dam within me burst. 'Muthamma, can you count?'

'Count? Count what?'

I pleaded with her in agony, 'Rooms.'

'Oh Rama. Oh Lord above, I swear to you by the God Venkateshwara and the Lord reclining on the serpent, I'll call your aunt and tell her all. How you plague me. Just because fate has kept me illiterate. Just you wait. I'll call her. Now.'

'Tell Kaku?' I was terrified. 'No, no. Muthamma, I'll touch your feet, but please don't tell Kaku, say you won't?'

Even as I pleaded with her, my voice took on a demented edge. Rooms. One-dimensional, monochrome, antiseptic, hygienic white, albino white, bitches, swine, gaseous, drifting.

And Kaku in black. In a sari or a dress. Even her choli was black. Hardly ever saying a word, embedded in the sofa. Getting up for meals. That's all. Her monolithic silence absorbed everything around her.

At first, people used to come to visit. Kaku's strange silence diverted them from her to me. To ask questions, to shower me with affection. They expected me to cooperate and answer their trifling queries with such compulsive enthusiasm that I felt that Kaku was unfairly passing the buck to me. She sat with her head down. Then suddenly her eyes would surface. For an instant. If their eyes met, the visitors would invariably become restless and be in a tearing hurry to leave. I never understood the momentary distrust that passed across her face, but it got under my skin. There was something symptomatic about my helpless journeyings through these rooms. At the bottom of them, there was Kaku's doubting uncertainty. The visitors stood up and left. To forget and never return. But they never understood that when Kaku looked at them, what she saw was not them at all, but her own disbelief and doubt. A suspicion which was pervasive, degenerate and self-destructive.

To pass the time, I sometimes loitered in Srinivas's huge radio workshop on the ground floor. I got to know some of the mechanics so the security man didn't drive me out. They gave me blackened radio valves and used-up bulbs to play with. From there I went to the tobacconist's. His pipes had never moved out of their glass case. The owner greeted me. 'How are you, son?' he would ask, and go back to his dark brown, expensive pipes. The eighty-foot-wide street outside and the still, quiet afternoon without any traffic. And lunch at whatever hour I wanted it.

Evenings came late, very late in the afternoons. And then the children came back from school – Sambodh and Sushiksha Srinivas, and the Rustoms' son, Jamshed. It takes four to make an evening, or a Sunday. Sundays were one long evening. They started in the morning. The rest of the week I wandered lonely, sometimes swallowing my tears till my throat hurt, but mostly dry eyed. Bored. In the archway between the Rustoms' and Kaku's houses.

Then in the afternoons Sanjayi appeared. Sometimes Kaka too. My mouth gaped and memories of past holidays crowded into my mind.

She had climbed on the bed and draped herself against a bedpost. Her arms raised, her armpits revealed, she let her head loll to one side and said, 'I'm Jesus, Kushank. And you're the Romans. And the Jews. Now, quick, while I've got these nails in my hands and feet.'

Disengaging her left hand, she pointed to the basket on the floor.

'You must put my crown of thorns on my head. To kill me.'

'No, no, you're not Jesus or anything. Get down.'

'Kushank – no, Romans, how dare you? You must kill me now.'

She stamped her foot with rage.

And started to moan. In sharp pain. Her hands and legs ran with blood, as in the holy pictures.

'No!' I started to scream. 'I won't let you die, Sanjayi. Promise you'll come down?'

'I'll die now and my Mother Mary will cry over me. Hurry up, Kushank, and hand me my crown.'

'No, I won't.' I banged my head on the wall, in hysterics now. 'I won't let you die, I won't.'

Kaka grabbed me and scolded Sanjayi. 'Get down at once. You and that sadistic convent school of yours. And stop crying, Kushank. Crying like a girl. Forget Christ. Come, I'll tell you the story of Ulysses and his gang.'

~

A cool wind, and rain. I had undone all the buttons of my shirt, as instructed by Sanjayi. She came in, walking with tiny steps. Water, mud, the queen's feet. I swept off my shirt and threw it on the ground with a flourish. Sanjayi gave me a smile of sweet condescension. 'Thank you, my lord Raleigh.' My eyes were fixed on her. I was overwhelmed by her beauty. My newly visible bobbing Adam's apple had frozen midway.

'Kneel, stupid, I'm going to make you a knight.'

On my knees. Only in my shorts. Ready to chop off my head for the queen. Her ruler touched my left shoulder, my head, my right shoulder. 'I, Elizabeth, Queen of Britain and all her domains, dub thee knight. Arise, Sir Walter Raleigh.'

The problem was Kaka. We never could decide in which pantheon to place him. The Rani of Jhansi, the Pope, Thor, Padmini, Christ, Arjun, Scarlett O'Hara, Achilles – we could be all these. I liked being the god Dattatreya best, because of his dogs. But he always looked like such a sissy in all the coloured posters that I kept my preference to myself.

Although the games depended on our moods, I felt sometimes that I was being discriminated against. The girls could be Helen or Juno or St Francis or Akbar. But when I wanted to be Joan of Arc, Sanjayi laughed at me and said, 'Oh, don't be silly, you can't be a girl!'

'You're not to look me straight in the face, Kushank.'

'Why not?'

'Because you might put the evil eye on my beauty. I'm Padmini. I told you not to look, you fool. You may, however,' she said as if she was doing me a great favour, 'look at me through a mirror.'

But, Papa? Sanjayi pronounced the world's most beautiful 'pa'. Breathlessly. Softly. Like blossoming petals.

'Pa-pa,' she said. She let it float like a feather on a faint breeze. While saying Papa, an ecstatically happy Sanjayi would spread out her arms and let go of herself from the twentieth storey of a building to fall into the arms of her beloved father. Papa, who read a hundred and ten pages an hour. Who had been everywhere, done everything. Rode horses bareback. Papa of the puff as you blew slow motion bubbles in the air. Our hero, Papa.

That's why we couldn't ever decide who he was. Sanjayi often said that he must be Christ. But though Papa was a Catholic, he admired Krishna more than Jesus. He could recite the Gita backwards, forwards, horizontal, vertical, transversal and while fast asleep. Spouting passages from it at every opportunity, like a ticket inspector in mufti producing his badge of identification. Krishna was beautiful, but Sanjayi said, 'He's not a patch on Papa.' Krishna was blue. Kaka was fair and tall, with a wide forehead and thick, dense hair.

'Hey, don't you want your lunch today?' shouted Muthamma, breaking into my reverie and dragging me up the stairs. 'You know very well that your aunt won't eat till you come up, but that doesn't bother you, does it?'

There she sat, unwieldy and immovable. It was because of her that Sanjayi had left me and vanished. Like a buffalo, up to her neck in black muck. I wanted to hit her, kick her, dance on her head.

'Why do you wear that horrible black? When are you going to stop this nonsense?' Oh my God, what made me say that? They were almost the words of my impatient, no-nonsense mother, and like her, I too regretted instantly.

I thought she was going to box my ears. We ate in silence. The silence of an incipient earthquake. I had asked for it and I was going to cop it. I'd get flattened today.

'Finished? Get dressed then. We're going to the movies.'

In a pale blue blouse and a white textured sari. After that, Kaku went to the movies two or three times a week, with one of her friends.

But I never went to the movies with her again. She didn't ask me either. That first time I was so bored with the Hindi film, I made her come out of the theatre with me nine times to go to the toilet. The tenth time, she got a cab and brought me home.

When she went to a matinee, she came home by about half past six. I locked the door at four o'clock, hung the key round my neck, and went down to wait for the other children to come home from school. But then came summer, and she started going to the evening shows.

I was only halfway through my dinner when the front doorbell rang. When Kaku went to the movies in the evening, the food was invariably cold. 'Eat at half past seven, you understand? Don't wait for me.' I took hours over my solitary meal. Kaku always had my favourite dishes cooked on the days she was going out. But without her, every mouthful lingered and turned to sawdust in my mouth. I chewed, but could not swallow. Sushiksha and Sambodh had to go home at seven to do their homework. A little later, Jamshed left. Then there was just me. Climbing the twenty-four steps, unlocking the door, quickly shutting it behind me. Nobody could come in. Except Kaku, who had her own key. So who could this be? I could see the lights at the Srinivases' house. The bell didn't stop. Drilling into my ears. What if he pounced on me? Through Premangi's room and into the balcony. What if he climbed in from there? Kaku's room, Urmila's. Shall I shout for help? And if no one hears me? Worse still, he'll know that I'm at home.

Pulling the lavatory chain. Waves of water churning around in the bowl. Foaming, fanning, spewing. Drowning out the jangle of the blasted bell. How I love the sound of water. But I can still hear it ringing. Pull the chain again. But the cistern hasn't refilled yet. Leaving the lavatory door open, I ran to the bathroom. Turned on all the taps there. Then the one in the kitchen. Run, run. He's behind you. To the loo in Kaka's room at the other end of the house. Pull the lever of the flush there. Like a dam bursting its walls. All the chaos in the universe within the vortex of the whirlpool in the bowl. Gone underground in a trice. And before the bell could stab me again, running back to the first lavatory. Again and again.

Pull, pull. Where are you? Kaku? Aai? Baba? Won't you stop that bell? Ankush, please, please?

He came the next day. One foot in plaster, leaning on a walking stick.

'I rang for half an hour. Then I left. Heard the chains being pulled and water running in the bathroom. So I was worried and leaned on the bell for five minutes.'

'Kushank, come here a minute.' I didn't want to see him. But Kaku called again.

He was tall, Kaka's age. Searching my face, waiting for an answer.

'I don't know, I wasn't there.'

He laughed. 'Don't lie, boy. All the lights were on.'

'Where were you?' Kaku's tone was unexpectedly sharp.

'I tell you he was at home. Must have had his friends in here.'

'Did you go out after dinner, Kushank? To the Srinivases'?' Sharper now.

'No.'

Then pointedly, 'To anybody else's house?'

'No.'

'All right. Go to your room.'

Sushiksha came shouting and dancing, to get his brother. 'Hurry, Sambodh. We're going to the movies. Daddy's got the Murphy radio agency. He's taking us out to celebrate.'

Sambodh swung his cricket bat round his head. 'Yippee! Now we're going to be rich. And I'll have a bicycle!'

'We're going to see *Captain Horatio Hornblower*. Tarararan-tara.'

He began to mime scenes from the trailer. 'See Hornblower on the high seas. Tarararan-tara. See him secure his lady love from the slave king. Bang, bang, bang.'

I saw the sea and the ship. Tarararan-tara. The wind blowing the ship on to great rocks. Waves crashing against the ship. Shipwrecked. And in the centre of the storm, cool and steady – Hornblower. He looked like Kaka.

'Sambodh, will your father take me too?' I asked, before I could stop myself.

'I'll go and ask.' He ran away and returned immediately.

'Yes, yes, everybody can come. Jamshed too.'

I burst into the living room. The Swaminathans were there, talking to Kaku. But my eyes only saw Hornblower and the storm.

'Mr Srinivas is taking us to the movies!' I yippeed like Sambodh. 'He's going to be very rich and buy Sambodh a bicycle. He's got the Murphy agency.' I chattered on like a parrot. 'See Hornblower fight the sea,' as I slashed with my sword, left and right. 'Can I go?'

'But Mr Swaminathan was going to take you for a drive in his new car,' protested Kaku.

I was crestfallen.

Mr Swaminathan picked me up and laughed, 'Tarararantara. I can take him another day. Let him go with his friends. I wish I could go too!'

Kaku made me get into my best clothes. I could hear guffaws from the living room, where Mr Swaminathan imitated me. Kaku tightened the belt round my shorts and zipped my jacket.

'Kushank, you didn't ask them to take you, did you?'

In my excitement I said yes.

She held my face in her hands. 'You won't ask people to take you out again, will you?'

'No, never.'

'Go now, and tell me the story tonight.'

'You're not going,' growled Jamshed. He hadn't changed his clothes.

'Why not?'

'Because my mother says I can't go. And if I can't go, you can't either.'

'Oh go away. Kaku said it was okay. See, she let me wear my jacket. Of course I'm going.'

I turned away, but he twisted my arm behind me.

'Don't you dare. You take one step and I'll tell Kaku.'

'Tell her what?' But the wind had already gone out of my sails.

'Don't you remember? Last Tuesday? Don't you?'

I was sunk. 'No, don't. Please, I won't go to the movies. But promise you won't tell?'

'I'll tell if I want to. I'm the boss around here, right? And you'll do what I say.'

'Boss? Balls. You're only a tattletale. Come on, fight me if you have the guts.'

He twisted my arm until I cried out.

'Tattletale, eh? Repeat that and see if I don't tell your Kaku!'

I went upstairs after the Swaminathans had left. Jamshed came along.

'You didn't go?' Kaku asked with disbelief. 'What happened?' I didn't answer.

'Then where were you all this time?'

I still didn't speak. 'But why didn't you go? It must be at least an hour since the show started.'

'I didn't feel like it.'

'Liar!' Kaku was angry. She kept looking at Jamshed, preening himself.

'How could he go when I ordered him not to?'

'Is that why you didn't go? Because he told you not to?' Kaku shook with anger.

'Isn't that right, Kushank?' Jamshed stuck his thumbs nonchalantly into his belt. 'You didn't go because I told you not to, isn't that the truth? When I said that I'd tell you everything, he stopped arguing. True, Kushank?'

I looked at him. I was past despair.

'Tell me what?' Kaku went rabid.

'He came to our house on Tuesday night. The coward. And he kissed Pervez on the lips. In front of everybody.'

'Go home now,' Kaku told him quietly, without opening her mouth. He was frightened and began to run. 'Ask him if you don't believe me,' he shouted before he disappeared. 'Ask him.'

~

Kaku and I. In the living room. She couldn't make up her mind what to do with me. And I wasn't going to look at her to find out. The minutes passed, my eyes fixed on the floor, hers willing me to look up. Then she got down to work. We turned the house upside down. Kaku's blows landed accurately. Slaps, kicks, chappals. I started to run. Then I stood still. Sat. Rolled round on the red carpet. She was never going to stop. She didn't. My leather belt in her hand.

'Why did you go? Didn't I tell you not to go? And hadn't you promised me? Speak, you lying rascal. Why don't you answer me? And what did they tell you?'

They have an awful house, Kaku. Dirty. Not clean and white like ours. Huge beds and wardrobes that reach the ceiling. Yellow lights and yellow walls. I love you, Kaku. I didn't want to go. The chain in the lavatory broke. The Srinivases' house is so far off and the bell which went on for miles and miles. And behind it the man. Jamshed's people laughed. 'Don't be embarrassed,' they said. But I didn't speak. Not at all. They called Jamshed's little cousin. Pervez. In a green organdie flowered dress. She's six. Very shy. 'Look, here is a new friend for you,' they said and pushed her towards me. 'She is a doll. Aren't you a doll, Pervez? Kiss your new friend. Tell him you like him. Go on, kiss him, Pervez, kiss him,' they hissed. And their house is airless. Thick curtains on the windows. Dark lampshades on every lamp. Our house is much brighter. We have large windows. Air. Balconies. Floods of light. Jamshed's father uses a piece of string to hold his trousers up, instead of a belt. His vest is stained with food. And Aminara saying, 'Kiss him, kiss him on the lips.' Pervez hugged me, frightened. I put my arms round her and kissed her lightly on the lips. Chocolates are for keeping quiet.

'Why don't you cry?' Kaku's belt and mouth working. 'What did they tell you? Cry, go on, cry. What did they say? Tell me what you know.' She was suddenly on her knees beside me. Shaking my shoulders. Sobbing. 'Tell me, Kushank. Tell me what they said. Did they talk about Kaka? Did they tell you lies about him? Him and Aminara? Did they? You could tell me if you cried. Cry, Kushank, please. Listen to me, won't you?'

Kaku in a paper packet, and me. On Marine Drive. My legs trembled and my stomach heaved. I had never walked along the flyover before. I had ridden over it in a cab or in a bus. There are no cars here today. People who walk here for exercise are missing tonight. Holding Kaku in my hand, on the brink of Bombay. Pausing to rub my eyes into wakefulness.

I know this place. This isn't a part of the flyover, but the parapet below it. I can't see the cockroaches, but I know they are there. They live in the cracks between the stones and tickle your feet with their whiskers. And further down, there are rocks and crabs and the tetrapods. Those tetrapods that saw me drown. Exam time in Poona. Past midnight, when I switched off the light and went to bed. Into the sticky green sea of words and sentences from the book on politics I had been reading. So sticky and thick that no waves moved over it. And I, up to my neck in it. Not far from the shore, but far enough for my feet to be off the ground. Struggling desperately to escape the glutinous green that stretched as far as the horizon. The sea would neither swallow me nor let me breathe. And the leviathan tetrapods watched. Primeval, terrifying, forever plumbing the depths of my consciousness. Like fat, swollen, indolent four-headed penises. Discarded, useless. Dragging me deeper and deeper. I loathed them, but I could not kick them away.

The place where you're born – the town, the village – means a thousand things to you. Every spot, every corner holds a memory. Here you stamped your feet, banged your head and cried, there you threw stones to bring down the mangoes. You played doctor behind the schoolhouse, sat for your school-leaving exams a few yards away. Learnt to swim in the Mahatma Gandhi pool, got married at the Town Hall. Every event, every memory is a dialogue between you and the place where you have lived. And although your city, town, or village may never play a leading, or even a secondary part in your life, the fact that it is always present makes it the fourth dimension of your consciousness. My memory holds a lot of Bombays. But the Bombay of the tetrapods is not one of them. That Bombay exists separately, and has an independent life. It is physically there. You can go and see it, touch it to make sure it's real. But that's all. That's the extent of your control over the Bombay of the tetrapods. From there the action passes into its hands. It is subterranean, symbolic and archetypal. And therefore responsible for whatever you are.

After years and years in Bombay, you stop seeing it. It's like someone with a permanently open mouth, you never know when it's swallowed you. If anyone asks you what Bombay is like, you don't recall those millions of other

Bombays from your memory, and even if you did, they wouldn't be the real Bombay. You could spend a lifetime without knowing the Bombay of the tetrapods. But it is a part of what you do, what you are, what you feel. It is thanks to the tetrapods that I can walk along Marine Drive, read the newspaper in peace at home. Without them the sea would have bitten off large mouthfuls of Bombay every few minutes. But there is a price to be paid for holding that shore, and every person in Bombay pays it. Knowingly or not. By carrying the tetrapods in your body, in your mind, all through your life.

There is one other way of keeping your self-awareness alive in Bombay. Through those red and green lights. Screaming at every crossing. Your eyes forever glued to them, as if your life depended on them. And when the green light comes on, whether you want to go in that direction or not, whether you want to cross the street or not, whether your father pops it or not, whether you want to go to the toilet, whether the war in Vietnam ends, lepers take over the city, lotuses bloom out of vaginas, rhinos vanish into ping-pong balls, what does it matter what's on the other side of the street – get out of my way, you motherfucker, you son of a bitch, out of my way, can't you see any moment now the light will turn red and we will all get left behind on this side of the street…

And after half past nine, no red and greens. Just one eye to all of Bombay. Orange. Blip, blip. Like the tick of a sad, neurotic wreck. Maybe you see it, maybe you don't. Maybe you exist and maybe you don't, no matter. Just that hiccupping light, and its regular, everlasting orange jerks fill the night.

Come on, Kaku, let's go. To Chowpatty beach. Your last trip. The P.J. Gymkhana on the right and then the Taraporevala Aquarium. No more fish and chips for you, Kaku. The Government Ladies' Hostel. Long balconies hung with festoons of girls. Their heads turned towards the crowd and the noise. My head feels like a large cipher. Hollow. I'm tired, Kaku. Not hungry any more. Just numb and stupid. I want to sleep. Here. Shall I sit down? The big clock says it's twenty to twelve. Here's Charni Road Station. Shall I catch a train and go home? Speak to me, Kaku, or I'll go to sleep. On the street, forgetting everything. Postpone your work till tomorrow. How much longer do I have to walk? I won't move on if you don't talk to me. I'll become permanently horizontal. And tell those people to stop that racket. To be quiet. Absolutely. Or I'll hit them across their faces. Let me sleep. Just this once. I won't ask again.

Bastards, won't even let a hungry man sleep. Drums and bells. To add to the noise. Public weddings. That's what we need. Of all the boys and girls in Bombay. Ages ten to twenty-five. All at once. Compulsory. And then no more weddings for the next ten years. No shouting, no celebrating. But not today. We'll get you all married tomorrow. Go back to your homes today. I have to see Kaku home.

Am I getting closer to the crowds or are they growing? A hoarding on the Charni Road Bridge – Asha Parekh announcing, 'I use Lux to keep my skin soft and lovely'. I do too. But it doesn't help. Hasn't yet. The bhelpuriwalas and the kulfis look blue in the neon light. Shall I have a kulfi, Kaku? Sweating, jammed crowds.

I walk into the sand. Ahead of me, the rhythmic chants of thousands of people. A sharp elbow digs into my side. A tremendous human wave comes pouring down the Opera House Bridge. Screams of people being trampled upon. Then a short respite and all of Bombay gets shoved fifteen feet towards Chowpatty. And I suddenly decipher the chanting ahead of me. It's the Ganpati immersion day. Ganpati! What a day you chose, Kaku.

Straining to breathe, raising my face to the sky. My neck will stiffen forever. And holding Kaku aloft, in my left fist, above this heaving multitude.

I can't hear a thing now. A fast-moving circle of people hand in hand. Slowly the drums, the cymbals, the whistles, the lejhim, the pakhawaj – I'm playing them all. Every note rises from within me. That's why it is so still and quiet out here. These ecstatic dancers, some with their trousers tucked up, some with dhotis wound tight, shirts sticking to their backs, dancing and swaying with their elephant-headed god – all plugged into me.

Round and round in circles. I'm caught up in the maze of whirling bodies. Being sucked in. I dance because I have no alternative. Like the rest of them. God doesn't just stand and watch when you are caught up in the delirium. He puts his hand into yours. Swaying, bending, twisting, weaving complicated patterns. Compulsively and of your own joyous will, he makes you dance. Switches roles. Possesses you and makes you lose yourself in his godhood.

I feel the beat rising in me like a deadly poison. But it's a stranger intoxication. Dazzling, delirious, preternatural. As you get high on it, you feel you've finally discovered the mysterious connection between life and its meaning. As I floated away into a trance, I had a vague notion that I was no longer in danger of losing my personality. I had long since become a medium. I had short-circuited time and space and entered the land of my primal ancestors. I was face to face with archetypal forces that make myths more meaningful, inevitable, and more powerful than both reality and rationality.

I had never danced before. But now the rhythms of all the primitive dances in the world came to life through me. Look, Kaku, I can dance. Without anybody teaching me.

Shadowy, steaming, hypnotized faces in the eerie neon light, the quickening concentric tempo, whirling sky above, the sea, Chowpatty, a drum in my ear, clouds of pink gulal flung everywhere, the paper packet snatched from my fingers. No, you can't have that, that's my Kaku. Kaku scattered in the wind over bodies, over me.

Uproar, chaos. Wails and shouts. 'Ashes, ashes, black magic, witchcraft…' Looks like a south Indian. Long live Shiv Sena. The first blow knocked out three of my teeth. Don't talk shit. The bastard's a Muslim. Look at his eyes. Throttling me. Check his penis to make sure. Don't allow the motherfucker to desecrate Lord Ganesh. Jai Bhavani! Long live Shivaji! Sirens, police. What evil spell has the son of a bitch been casting? Blows, sticks, arriving at the police station with a torn lip, bloodied, black and blue.

There is just one new thing in the world. Pain. We have suffered it since the first man appeared on earth. Millions of times from the beginning of time and yet we never tire of it. All of us motherfuckers, we never got used to it, never got so godawful pissed off with it that we pushed it over the precipice, stabbed, strangled, killed and murdered it.

If you asked me what is the freshest thing in the world, I'd say pain and suffering. Are they the same? Which came first? I don't know. But there is nothing more urgent, more intimate, more inescapable. Brand-new, fresh, crisp and totally in command. It may be just two minutes since you were driven by a shattering, screaming, shouting burst of pain. But that doesn't make you any wiser to the one that's following on its heel. If the same spasm repeats itself ten times over, it's just as new as the first one. Because pain and suffering have no memory. You may have seen and experienced everything, but for pain and suffering, there is only the first time – act one, scene one.

This is my second trip to a police station. They all look the same. The colours of the uniforms change. A picture of a smiling toothless Gandhi on the wall, and the current president. It was Radhakrishnan in Banaras, here it is Giri.

Then they beat me. How these people beat you. At Chowpatty and here at the station. Beat you, beat you, beat you, beat you, beat you. Kicks, iron rods, rats down your legs, sticks, boots … I don't remember any more. Singly and collectively, they keep beating. Putting their boots into my kidneys, shoving lighted cigarettes up my nose, poking my swollen testicles with the butt end of a pencil, breaking the bridge of my nose, blue, black, green, purple, they beat you, beat you, beat you … they never stop.

Name?

Address?

What party do you belong to? Religion?

Muslim?

Hindu?

Name?

Address?

The same questions again. The same forms to be filled.

'Move. Get out of the way.'

I couldn't figure out their ranks, but his voice must belong to someone above an inspector at least. All the others, in their khakis and navies, came to attention.

'Will you take the responsibility if this man dies, Nene?' he spoke, with hardly a glance at the others.

'He's not going to die, sir. I've dealt with the likes of him for years.'

'Are you getting anything out of him by beating him to death?'

'Not a squeak out of him yet, the bastard. Not even his name.'

'Did you check if he has a tongue?'

He's laughing at me, Nene thought.

'Did you?' he repeated calmly.

Nene peered into my face.

'Open your mouth. Open it, I say.' Forcibly opening my jaws – 'Yes, he does' – greatly relieved. 'Don't be fooled by him, sir, I know these people.'

'Constable, pick him up. Gently.'

'And the forms?'

'You've had long practice, you can fill them easily.' Then, shouting, 'Gently, I said. Help them, Nene. I want the prisoner's back at least two feet off the ground. If he whimpers once, someone will suffer for it.'

'Won't let me sleep, the bastards. Devils, not humans. All of them,' the man in the cell complained loudly.

They put me down. 'Does it hurt much?' the officer asked. And then, 'Constable, water.' The officer opened my swollen lips gently and pushed in a Novalgin tablet and then some water.

'Couldn't you have found another cell? Why mine? Why the crowding in here?' my cellmate was still ranting.

'Try to sleep now. You'll feel better in the morning.' He thought for a while and made me swallow another tablet.

'Is he a political prisoner at least? I want to see the superintendent immediately,' my cellmate had to shout since he wanted the superintendent, wherever he was, to hear him. The men who had brought me were leaving. Locking the cell door. And then the door in the corridor. I was to get used to that routine, those sounds. Ear-splitting sounds of metal on metal. From every floor, every wing, every cell. An inhuman sound. Vastly separated from the world.

'Constable, I'm not going to spend the night with this man in my cell. That naked light keeps me awake all night, and now this man's horrible face. Did you hear me, inspector? I'll scream all night, keep you awake too. Complain to the court. Is anybody listening?'

He had climbed up the metal bars of the door. Hanging from there for a minute or two, like a monkey.

'Shit, they wouldn't care if you murdered me. They'd be relieved. But you don't need to make the effort. Just looking at you is enough to turn a man into a ghost. They've wanted to get rid of me for a long time, anyway. What's your name? Damn it, haven't you a name? Son of a bitch, not a word out of him.'

Then screaming into my ear, 'Can you hear me? You are understanding English? Yes? Not Marathi? I am introduce. My name Phanse. Phanse like the jackfruit. You understand? Ha, ha. Answer me.' Then back to Marathi. 'Are you dumb or deaf, or both? Why don't you speak? Who do you think you are? You're no better than me. Maybe your father is a big shot, but that's no reason to be uppity. I'm a leader. Of all the bank unions. And I'll be the leader of the dock workers' union too, in February. If you are so important, what are you doing here? I bet you're a thief! Stealing from the poor. I can see it. Look at your trousers. You can't fool me. I know they're polyester. How much did they cost? Sixty? Eighty? Answer me, you swine. That's the way to fix you moneyed lot. They didn't beat you enough. You should be starved. And whipped. Twenty-three lashes an hour. Without letting you die. Shameless, you are. Swallowing all abuse, all insults, and still no word out of you. Struck dumb, are you? I'll wager there's not a word out of you when you're robbing the poor too. Not like me – the honest don't have to keep their mouths shut. Who sent you? Tell me, scum. Don't think I'm a simpleton. I might look it, but I'm not. Did Mr Contractor send you? Speak, you bastard. I'll silence that contractor forever when I get out of here. Or did Soares send you? He's a right traitor, that one. Talk sweet and stick a knife into your back any day. I know them all. He's scared that I'll take over the dock workers' union next year. Of course I will. Not even his father can stop me. Did he send you? Open your mouth or I'll bust your face.'

His face fell for a moment. For years he had been defeated by the obtuseness of words, and the defeat still rankled. For everything that had gone wrong in his life, for everything unpleasant that had happened, he knew who was to blame. The world. And part of his quarrel with the world was that language didn't fathom his precise meaning, that words didn't say what he wanted them to. In desperation he said, 'What I want to say is open your mouth so you'll be able to speak. Answer me or I'll tear your tongue out.'

He stood up and came towards me where I sat slumped against the wall, and brought his right foot down on my left hand, balancing himself on one foot. Then he fell over and smiled an embarrassed smile. He took my left hand in his and started to sob, breathing snot noisily. 'Did I hurt you? Does it hurt?' As he looked, he saw my hand swell before his eyes. Terrified, he let go of it. Then he broke down and began to bang his head on the bars of the cell. 'Aai, what have I done now? God, save him.'

I shut my eyes. He was shaking me. 'Will you forgive me? I swear I'll never do it again. You have forgiven me, haven't you?' And anger filled his eyes again. 'How many times do I have to ask you the same things? Why do you pretend to be asleep? Do you think I don't know?'

It took me a long time to surface after he had kicked me in the back. Then I was out of the water and had hit the air. I could breathe but couldn't force the air down my throat. My eyes bulged and my ribcage came apart at the seams. Then I lost control over my body and the breath flowed in.

I moved my leg and found that I had wet myself. 'Oh, God,' I whispered. 'This can't be happening, can't be.' And as I shook my head, I thought of you. We were at Berry's and you had asked, 'What difference does it make.'

It was not a question. Only the certainty of a full stop. Then blackness and no more pain. Was it hours or days of unconsciousness? All I know is that it was a time without pain, without myself.

Patent Nonsense: Three Auto-Biographies

Praise for *Seven Sixes Are Forty-Three*

The Great Deceiver Is One's Own Mind
RITU MENON

*Seven Sixes Are Forty-Three*, forty-three years later KIRAN NAGARKAR

P.S.

Insights, Interviews & More ...

# Patent Nonsense: Three Auto-Biographies*

## #1

Early in his career, Kiran Nagarkar was sacked from his post as lecturer in English because he failed to pass every student. Sacking has, indeed, been a way of life with him. On the rare occasions when he has escaped this fate, the companies he worked for have gone bust and folded up.

As a bilingual author, Nagarkar works in Marathi and English. He writes novels, plays and screenplays; film, theatre, social and literary criticism. All of them very occasionally. He has yet to win the Booker, the Whitbread, the Pulitzer, the Nobel and India's highest honour, the Bharat Ratna (not that he has won any of the lowlier awards either).

Nagarkar is in the Guinness Book of World Records as the author of a novel that is considered a milestone and a classic in Indian literature and which took just twenty-seven years to sell one thousand copies. Can Dan Brown ever

---

* *What difference does it make?*

match those incredible figures? Incidentally, the rumour is that Nagarkar was the sole buyer of all the thousand copies.

Oh, one last thing. He is close to six feet tall, wears ankle-length clingy crepe silk harem pants and has great legs.

#2

Born in 1497, Kiran Nagarkar lives on a private island off the coast of Bombay a.k.a. Mumbai with his fifth wife, seventy-one children, fourteen cats, twenty-one dogs and five platypuses. In his spare time, he breeds crocodiles and Komodo dragons.

A technological wizard, he is credited with the invention of the re-usable condom, the hexagonal wheel and a supersonic aircraft that travels below the surface of the earth. One of India's leading entrepreneurs, he has recently started the world's first fool-proof and fail-safe 'Disappearance Service' whereby you can have anybody bumped off anywhere in the world entirely by accident. Needless to say, for a price. (For further details contact www.happyaccidents.com)

As a pastime Nagarkar writes children's books, metaphysical tomes like *The Spiritual Dimensions of Knitting with Seven Needles*, hard-core pornography and books on how to manufacture WMDs in your backyard or better still, in your kitchen.

#3

Kiran Nagarkar is perhaps the most prolific author the world has seen. No other author has written under as many pseudonyms as he has. Amongst his various pen names are William Shakespeare, Kalidas, Jane Austen, Gabriel García Márquez, Barbara Cartland, Jackie and Joan Collins, Salman Rushdie, Saramago, M.M. Kaye, Tukaram, Louis-Ferdinand Céline, Don DeLillo, Goethe and Shobhaa Dé, to name only a few.

Amongst his most well-read books are the Bible, the Gita, the Torah, and *Chicken Soup for the Mentally Unchallenged.*

*Stolen from the unofficial Kiran Nagarkar website*

[*Seven Sixes Are Forty-Three* is memorable for its] irreverent and incisive style … its alternating moods of comedy and despair, its bawdiness and violence, its rejection of all pretension and solemnity.

… Rendered hilariously in this impeccable and racy translation – the comic episodes give the novel an extra dimension, steering it away from bleakness and solipsism.

– Meenakshi Mukherjee, *The Book Review*

Nagarkar has a very tight, economical style [in *Seven Sixes Are Forty-Three*]. He also has an uncanny skill in combining the bizarre with the mundane, the tragic with the ridiculous, so that you cannot help chuckling one moment and are chilled to the bone the next. … The truth is not always as simple as seven sixes making up forty-two. Often it amounts to forty-three. … *Seven Sixes* is a book that shocks you, makes you laugh, sets you wondering and thinking. It is a book that provides sheer reading enjoyment.

– Jai Nimbkar, *Indian Review of Books*

This book is going to be a literary landmark. It breaks a good deal of new ground in form, subject matter, as well as language. The words [Nagarkar] chooses, the sentences he constructs are so delightfully right for his purpose, that one cannot imagine the narrative being told in any other way. He has no qualms about showing two irreverent fingers to hallowed rules of grammar and syntax. He strides straight into a roomful of words, picks and chooses the ones he wants and strings them together in the strangest juxtaposition so that one gasps at the result, but understands the import immediately. So total is his use of language that one cannot possibly pick a phrase here, or a sentence there by way of illustration. All one can do is to liberate oneself from orthodox notions of language and allow the author to carry us on the crest of his ebullient, verbal waves. … Nagarkar's protagonist is young, vital, mature, and filled with the sap of life. … Kushank lives gluttonously. The avidity of his taking exactly balances the generosity of his giving. He recognizes pure goodness as a tremendous force that can be put to total flight by a single denial. Pain has its place in the general scheme of things, and it must be kept in place. The Kushank attitude is thus a totally positive attitude. There is no flabby self-pity here. Pity destroys life, and Kushank wants to live it. Nor is there the smallest element of sentimentality. Only a strong, forthright compassion.

The slimness of the book is therefore deceptive. It is slim not because there is less material there, but because the immense amount of variety of material is so tightly packed. In fact, if one has to pick a quarrel with the author at all, it will be on this point. Did he have to say so much in the span of a single novel?

– Shanta Gokhale, *Free Press Journal*

Kushank is as ambiguously real as the Prince of Denmark. … No aesthetic theory can explain Nagarkar's novel. And yet, the spark of creative fire illumines every crevice of this tangled mass of monologue, and Kushank looms as close to us as Hamlet, and finally becomes ourselves.

– Prema Nandakumar, *The Book Review*

Written in the first person, *Seven Sixes* is a novel about an urban, middle-class, educated, partly-westernised Indian named Kushank, a young man who, having seen poverty, illness, suffering and death, must come to terms with himself and his environment. How easy then, to identify with such a familiar character.

– Minakshi Raja, *Financial Express*

*Seven Sixes* still emerges as an eminently absorbing, unselfconsciously written book. … Whether his protagonist relives the shattering experience of a loved one's death or whether he has bawdy memories of the sexually starved boys' hostel existence, humour is never too far away.

– Gouri Salvi, *The Pioneer*

Kiran Nagarkar's *Seven Sixes Are Forty-Three* does not represent any style, system or genre. Or, for that matter, anything that can be generalized. It is the ticking of a very original mind, recorded and played back. It is the private view of Kushank looking at himself and at the world. In the telling of his story, Kiran Nagarkar has broken all the accepted rules in the book, to advantage.

– Sai Paranjpye, *The Times of India*

... a stroke of genius ... a vast colourful, brutal, depressing yet comical portrait of a disintegrating Indian society ... Downright revolutionary when it was first published in 1974, no one in India had dared to write before in such an avant-gardistic, drastic and impetuous manner.

– Alex Rühle, *Süddeutsche Zeitung*

... a raging, but witty reckoning with poverty and love doomed to founder ... Sensitivity and humour, a protean imagination and a literary voice, both varied and flexible, characterize this work.

– Angela Schader, *Neue Zürcher Zeitung*

An altogether different kind of novel. Neither does it have a plot-line, nor is it the story of one person's life. Its central principle is a particular point of view – since it is the inescapable fate of mankind to belong to the animal species, it is only through the experiences of sex, physical suffering, and pain that one comes to realize this condition acutely. We have no option but to endure it. In the end all that human beings can do is to live every moment with the utmost integrity: the 'integrity' to keep the entire gamut of one's experiences at the very core of one's being. The language of this novel is inseparable from living life in this fashion. It is precise and naked; it does not try to hide or embellish anything.

– M.P. Rege

This story of Kushank, told through flashbacks, jump cuts, and a variety of other techniques, leaves your head spinning. It is a crazy piece of work. Hats off to Kiran!

– Bhau Padhye

The pedigree of the humour in *Saat Sakkam* is different. It is born of the fragmented incoherence of life and the shadow of death. It hints at compassion and the tragic, and yet it eschews all sentimentality. What this novel suggests is that perhaps the true leitmotif of life lies in an absurd combination of something terrible and simultaneously humorous.

– R.B. Patankar

# The Great Deceiver Is One's Own Mind

Ritu Menon

In 1967, at the age of twenty-five, Kiran Nagarkar wrote the first three chapters of what would later become his trailblazing novel, *Saat Sakkam Trechalis*. The three chapters were published in a Marathi literary magazine, *Abhiruchi*, edited by Dilip Chitre, after which nothing more was heard of them till Mauj Prakashan, a major Marathi publisher, published them as a 'book' in 1974. A little aside here about an incident which was responsible for the long gap before *Saat Sakkam* was published and would have fitted in perfectly with the tone and spirit of the novel itself. Soon after the first seventy pages were published in *Abhiruchi*, a publisher in Pune printed them in book-form and was hell-bent on publishing it. It must be noted here that in those days – very often today also – the concept of a written contract was alien to the Marathi publishing world.

It took seven long years for Nagarkar to return to the book. When he finished it and sent it to Mauj, they were happy to publish it but couldn't, because of a paper famine in Maharashtra at the time! It was sheer luck that Nagarkar's boss at his place of work was able to access the paper required by the printer.

*Saat Sakkam Trechalis* erupted on the literary scene and took the Marathi literary world by storm. It challenged literary conventions, language, subject matter and decorum, and made no concessions to accepted narrative form. It defied – or rather, bypassed – the unities of time and place. It had no beginning, middle or end. It didn't even have a story, really speaking. What it had was daring. It had energy and a passionate intelligence, and an abhorrence of hypocrisy of all kinds. It had a way with words, with deft characterization. It cut through to the bone and laid bare its protagonist's predicaments – real and imagined, emotional and intellectual. It exposed life's underbelly. It caught you by the throat and wouldn't let go.

Most Marathi critics panned it, a few others thought it broke new ground and took the Marathi novel into unchartered territory. It is one of Marathi literature's most remarkable and enduring novels, and the only one Nagarkar wrote in Marathi apart from his extremely controversial play *Bedtime Story*. It took twenty-seven years for the first edition of a thousand copies of *Saat Sakkam* to be sold; and though it won the Hari Narayan Apte Award for a first novel and is today considered a landmark, it never set a trend. Understandably Mauj refused to bring out a second edition. After an inexplicable (he calls it criminal) gap of fourteen years, Nagarkar wrote other novels and plays, but he wrote them all in English. Yet he is part of that small group of writers in the country – Qurratulain Hyder,

Kamala Das, O.V. Vijayan, Girish Karnad, Arun Kolatkar, Dilip Chitre, Nabaneeta Dev Sen, K. Satchidanandan are among those who come to mind – who are truly bilingual, creative and skilled in two languages.

Just one day before Nagarkar made his foray into *Saat Sakkam*, he wrote his very first short story in Marathi titled 'Toh', but to this day he wonders why he did that, after all it was English which had been his sole medium of communication for a decade and a half. Nevertheless, he did, and before he knew it he was writing *Saat Sakkam*. At the time, many writers he knew were going back in search of their 'roots', it was something in the air. But he took a decision then that he has never deviated from: he would chart his own course. 'I am half-baked,' he says, 'I am neither this nor that. Or to put it differently, I am this, and I am that.' And although he may not have been looking for roots, the 'knowledge that a language can just throw you' was exhilarating. He had no normal acquaintance with Marathi, but it proved to be a turning point in his understanding of the all-encompassing significance of a language, any language. 'I had not inherited any of the Marathi traditions, I just had to find my own way. I was extremely lucky.' But this freedom from tradition, this nonconformity, cost him his place in the Marathi literary environment.

In 1980, *Saat Sakkam Trechalis* appeared in English as *Seven Sixes Are Forty-Three,* in a clever and accomplished translation by Shubha Slee. It was published by the University of Queensland Press in Australia, and by Vikas Publishing House in India, this time to critical acclaim. As an experimental novel *Seven Sixes* had no real precedent, even in English – it was edgy, innovative, unpredictable. One of its main characters is absent, she never appears in the book except as an anonymous 'you'; and Kushank, its protagonist, could well be one of Indian fiction's first anti-heroes. The novel itself had the freewheeling on-the-road sensibility of the Beat poets, but with an undertow of despair and anger. Nagarkar says that at the time of writing he had hardly any exposure to cinema, yet the technique he uses is cinematic.

The discontinuous, episodic, narrative style of *Seven Sixes* was not something he consciously sought, but he knew 'somewhere at the back of my mind' that one, he had a very distinct, very definite way of looking at the world and two, that the character who is never present in the novel, is the link. 'These two things were my thread – my take on life, and the fact that Kushank is always talking to this other person who isn't there.' This idiosyncrasy is captured in the title, a line picked up from Nagarkar's novel by Dilip Chitre when he published the first few chapters in *Abhiruchi*. Nagarkar thought it was perfect, because of course, 7x6s doesn't add up. But does it ever add up? he asks. Does life always make sense? 'Whatever happens around you, often doesn't add up.'

So is the novel autobiographical? Is Kushank, who has just graduated, searching for meaning, wandering, seemingly aimlessly, through life, also the young Kiran, desperately looking for work, hired as a tutor in a college at Rs 350 per month, knocking at the doors of thirteen or fourteen ad agencies in search of a job? 'No question,' says Kiran, 'the book is only half fiction. A teacher had actually said to me: "What nonsense is this, 7x6s are 43!" He was most abusive.' The hospital scenes in the novel are based on his own experience, but the Banaras bit is complete fiction. What he managed to distil, however, was the outsider angst of a young Indian, urban, middle-class male at odds with himself and with his world, so that the fractured, disconnected rhythm of the novel is the only credible, believable narration possible. As Nagarkar says, can anyone claim that his life is completely coherent?

Two years after *Saat Sakkam*, Nagarkar wrote a play called *Bedtime Story* between 1975 and 1977. Conceived even before the declaration of the Emergency of 1975–77, it was the result of what he calls 'the rather belated but traumatic loss of my naiveté, of waking up to my own callousness towards the terrible injustices perpetrated around me'. The reality of poverty, of greed and inhumanity, even as he says, of righteous rage that subsides almost as easily as it rises. Nagarkar believes that whatever happens anywhere in the world, we are all responsible. This personal notion of responsibility and accountability became, over the years, 'one of my basic tenets for practising that business called life'. What he fought against, resisted with every fibre of his being, was 'the malaise from which most of us suffer: apathy ... If we don't take a stand and make our voices heard against the violation of human rights, brutality, prejudices, hatred and persecution of the powerless,' he says, 'we are squarely responsible for the consequences of our inaction'.

Nagarkar's *Bedtime Story*, like many others, takes its cue from the Mahabharata, from four oft-repeated, often-told stories: Karna, Ekalavya, Arjun and Draupadi. It is interleaved with a contemporary tale, its characters named after those in the epic – Arjun and Ekalavya, with Ekalavya as the Dalit trying to escape his station in life. The central trope in *Bedtime Story* is that of betrayal and violence, a violence that is as shocking and egregious, as abhorrent as Dronacharya's demand that Ekalavya cut off his thumb and present it to him as gurudakshina. But Nagarkar's play goes further – in the end, there is real and physical violence, on and off stage, and it engulfs the audience: we are all participants, the playwright says, and all violence is war by another name.

It was not allowed to be performed, first by a legal censorship ban and then by the far more pervasive extra-legal one. The State Censor Board in Maharashtra demanded seventy-four cuts in the script; fundamentalist Hindu outfits threatened producers, directors, actors and Nagarkar, too, if they dared to stage it. Street censorship prevailed, and for seventeen years *Bedtime Story* lay in cold storage. It was staged finally by a small band of intrepid players called Abhivyakti in 1995 – but in the meantime, between 1977 and 1995 (when his next novel, *Ravan & Eddie* was published) Nagarkar didn't write another story, play or novel.

Nagarkar puts down the eighteen-year hiatus in his writing to his incredible workload as a creative director at MCM. It was a young agency, elbowing its way into the fiercely competitive world of marketing and advertising, and the pressure to outperform was intense. But could he also have been discouraged by the reaction to both *Saat Sakkam* and *Bedtime Story*, felt a little demoralised? Quite possibly.

At MCM, Nagarkar had the great good fortune to work with fellow writer and poet, Arun Kolatkar, as iconoclastic as himself, brilliant and versatile. Working with Arun was inspiring, even though Nagarkar says he never 'taught me a damn thing overtly. But did I really believe that he never taught me anything? I mean, I was in the company of one of the finest poets, we were together for at least ten or twelve hours every day, how could I not have learnt some really worthwhile things?' Besides, writing advertising copy had its own discipline: 'You have to be compact, at the same time you have to give the full story in as concise a manner as possible. This mattered to me.'

No one reading the sprawling, rambunctious, exuberant *Ravan & Eddie* and its sequel, *The Extras,* or that great river of a novel, *Cuckold,* would apply the adjectives 'compact' or 'concise' to them. But for sheer virtuosity of language and a delight in stretching his imagination as far it will go, Nagarkar's later novels are a departure from both *Seven Sixes* and *Bedtime Story*. He had found himself as a storyteller and forged an idiom that suited his idiosyncratic, yet clear-eyed perspective on life. The form his novels took reflected this.

*Ravan & Eddie,* published almost twenty years after *Saat Sakkam*, was originally a screenplay in English. And an incomplete Marathi novel with at least a manuscript of seventy pages. It was abandoned and picked up again many years later to be completed as a novel in English. Chawl novels seem to be par for the course these days, but in the mid-1990s, Nagarkar's gritty, unsentimental, yet utterly hilarious romp through Chawl No. 17 in Mazagaon was probably first to celebrate Bombay as 'not a one or five-ringed circus, but a circus with twenty, thirty or maybe fifty rings. Chaos is its element and it thrives on it. I wanted to get the essence of that mad, adrenaline-filled city's DNA into my story.' It's unlikely that any other city could have accommodated that equally unlikely pair, Ravan and Eddie – can one even begin to imagine them in Delhi or Calcutta? Of course not. Because Bombay is where you can hope to make it, even if all the odds are stacked against you, if you're as poor as a church mouse, with even poorer prospects. And Bombay is where the two friends end up as extras – in Bollywood, naturally, for hadn't Ravan pawned his mother's gold earrings to see *Dil Deke Dekho* seventeen times, and wasn't Nagarkar himself an ambivalent fan of Hindi cinema, and especially of Shammi Kapoor?

But *Ravan & Eddie*, written after the destruction of the Babri Masjid in 1992, sounds the alarm regarding the steady advance of the forces of Hindutva. Through a clever transposition and a wicked appreciation of the ironical, Nagarkar ensures that it is Eddie who becomes a child member of the Mai Boli Sabha and develops into an accomplished pehelwan, and that Ravan embraces Western cultural mores. All this, together with the sundry alarums and excursions of the duo in preparation for their interim careers – Ravan, the xylophone player in the New India Brass Band, and Eddie, leader of the Bandra Bombshells. Their Big Break would come later.

Once he resumed writing, Nagarkar wrote with little interruption, and *Cuckold*, published a mere two years after *Ravan & Eddie*, dealt with another of Nagarkar's preoccupations – the hiatuses in history, and in memory. The erasures. The protagonist of *Cuckold* asks: 'Do you really think one can wipe out people and events that easily?'

Writing being an act of retrieval, how important are these gaps in history for him as a writer? Terribly central, he believes. 'There are so many small things seeded within you, and you don't even know about them. The Ekalavya story comes to us as the iconic relationship between a guru and his student. It took me a long time to understand that if there is a self-made man, it is Ekalavya. He teaches himself. And in my interpretation of the Eklavya episode in *Bedtime Story*, you know what happens – *jaisa guru, vaisi gurudakshina*.

'Take Arjun – we talk about the Gita all over the world but here's Arjun saying, I will not fight this war; I will not spill the blood of my cousins. We don't want to admit that maybe Arjun had a better grasp of things than Krishna, because Krishna is justifying war at any cost. For me these are the incredibly complex and revealing moments.'

So, retrieving, but also recasting. And sometimes recreating. *Cuckold* excavates history to recover the heir apparent whose misfortune it was to be married to the saint-princess, Meera. Misfortune, because while there is not a corner of India that doesn't rejoice in Meera's bhajans, or a film that doesn't feature a song about her love for Shri Krishna, not a singer who doesn't sing her – no one knows her husband, Maharaj Kumar Bhojraj of Chittor, cuckolded by the Blue God, Krishna.

The idea itself is startling. Why would one want to bring to life a shadowy figure, and then pit him against a god he has no chance of besting? Nagarkar might well respond by saying, why not? And as one immerses oneself in the story, it becomes very clear that this is no simple restoring of a disappeared royal to history. The novel's scope is ambitious, its scale grand, its execution brilliant. The American novelist, Gore Vidal, called Cuckold, 'a sort of fantastic marriage between the Thomas Mann of *Royal Highness* and the Lady Murasaki', and our own Khushwant Singh believed it was 'the best by an Indian'. I cannot think of anything similar having been written in any language (unless it's Qurratulain Hyder's *River of Fire*) that is as breath-taking in imagination, and as supple and mellifluous in its telling. Apart from the riveting historical tale Nagarkar tells, there is the sheer pleasure of his language, and the complexity of the conundrum that lies at the heart of the story: who is cuckolding whom?

Unlike *Seven Sixes* (and even *Ravan & Eddie*), *Cuckold* is simultaneously linear and circular–linear because it progresses in time, following Maharaj Kumar's life from childhood to adult to householder and warrior, preserving historical chronology; circular because through the princess (Meera) it transcends time, circling back again and again to an eternal riddle: how is one to relate to god if one is a person of faith, but not blind faith? How is Maharaj Kumar, a Rajput prince whose creed is war, to square with his pacifist inclinations? Nay, convictions. How is he to deal with his wife's inexplicable but undeniable, passionate love for Krishna? All the mundane realities – battles, alliances, betrayals, intrigues, victories – are given full play, but beneath them lie the irreconcilables of emotion versus reason, mortal love and the love that has no human object, that feeds on itself; and the ultimate futility of placing one's trust in any human relationship. Meera got it right, Nagarkar seems to be saying – till you get to the end, and then the twist in the tale hits you between the eyes.

'An author is not always aware of the implications of everything he writes,' says Kiran, 'some things I'm deeply aware of, but others...' The re-imagining of Kabir is central to *God's Little Soldier*, since it provides a total counterpoint to everything Zia is or does. Fifteen months after *God's Little Soldier* was published, Nagarkar found himself writing one extra chapter. It was a crucial insertion towards the end of the book because Zia's assistant, Yunus, understood, intuitively, that Zia desperately needed to be betrayed.

Two other strands, light and dark (or should one say, dark and darker?) are woven into Nagarkar's novels: a kind of ferocious despair at the state of the world – he enumerates the reasons in the introduction to *Bedtime Story*, published finally in 2015 after thirty-eight years in limbo – and our general tolerance, or denial, of it, the kind of response which to him, is 'patent nonsense'; together with a kind of fatalism, expressed again and again by his characters in the phrase, 'What difference does it make?' The protagonist denies this sentiment emphatically except at the very end of the book when he ambiguously recalls the question. The first proceeds from Nagarkar's belief that each of us is responsible for whatever happens anywhere in the world, that we cannot claim detachment. The second is best captured by an insight that Ravan arrives at in *The Extras*: 'At some point in his film career, he grasped that the metaphor of broken geometry applied as much to life as to cinema. Reality was nothing but what your perceptions made of it … He had learnt that the great deceiver was not the screen but one's own mind.'

Does Nagarkar think that he has been able to reconcile these two, either in his life or in his writing?

No, no, he says, we never do.

*New Delhi, 2016*

# Seven Sixes Are Forty-Three, forty-three years later

Kiran Nagarkar

If I had thought like a sensible person for two minutes, that's right, just two minutes, *Saat Sakkam Trechalis* would never have been written. Whatever happened was because of an absence of thought. To write a novel, and that too in Marathi … surely I would have realized that this was completely beyond my ability. And *Saat Sakkam* would have been dead before it was born.

I studied in a Marathi-medium school till the fourth grade … after which my entire education was in English. I'm not sure of how people think about this today, but in those days, once you joined an English school, studying Marathi and Hindi were akin to paying for all the sins you had committed in the last nine hundred and ninety-nine lives. I was in Mumbai's Xavier's College for the first year, but after that my parents sent me to Fergusson College in Pune for the rest of my undergraduate education. The friends I made there were all English-speaking ones.

I met Dilip Chitre in the year 1966 when I was studying for my master's in Bombay University. He had translated my short story

'The Moon Had to Be Mended' into Marathi which was then published by his father in his magazine *Abhiruchi*. Some time later, Dilip told me that Chitre Senior had asked him to edit the next issue of the magazine. I got back home and wrote my first and last short story in Marathi called 'Toh' ('That Man'). The next day I started *Saat Sakkam* with the first line, 'He had once again come home drunk…' I was not sure how long the novel would turn out to be, but Dilip published the first eighty-one pages of it in the following issue of *Abhiruchi*. The title came from a line he had picked up from the novel.

By the time I had surmounted the proverbial seventeen hundred obstacles, seven years had gone missing. Finally it was published in December 1974 by Mauj Prakashan. Prof S.P. Bhagwat, the head of Mauj, was my publisher and editor. He had a keen eye, and was just the right person to teach me the art and science of editing. It was he who showed me what a world of difference changing the placement of a single word or sentence could make to the text and context. I was worried that he would not approve of my uninhibited depiction of sexual matters but I discovered that these fears were completely unfounded.

If after publication, *Saat Sakkam* got unstinting support and was able to create its own identity in the Marathi pantheon, it was because of the committed backing of the two people who I have always thought of as my gurus. I called both of them 'sir' as we Indians tend to call our teachers though only one of them, Prof R.B. Patankar, taught me for two years when I was doing my master's while the other, Prof M.P. Rege, never did.

I recall Coleridge saying that one would have to be a stone not be influenced. The question is how does one quantify or begin to understand the precise ways in which Dr Patankar or Prof Rege influenced me. It's no different with the authors who I think of as my lodestones. My own writing is so different from theirs and yet I have no doubt in my mind that I would have been a very different person and writer without them.

I rarely mustered enough courage to talk to Professor Rege. One would be hard put to find a more sophisticated thinker, one so devoid of arrogance or self-importance, or as much at ease with both Western and Indian philosophy. He had a delightful and utterly disarming sense of humour. I cannot forget two of his off-the-cuff remarks: 'Arre, Kiran, you must understand that students learn despite their teachers' and 'Only those people who don't know their own subject, tend to use highly convoluted and opaque language.'

Have you tried peeping into Dr Patankar's mind? Like the Champs-Élysées in Paris, all the avenues in his head were so straight and wide, they reached right up to the horizon. Each of the intersections was at perfect right angles. Everything was clearly articulated and in its place. There was no confusion or chaos. On a clear day, you could indeed see forever. Not just that, the heavens in his head were never clouded. While I was doing my master's, I recall him telling me, 'Any language is as powerful and rich as you make it.' When I look back at *Saat Sakkam* and look at the favourable reviews – talk about the partiality on the part of the author – I realize that the critics seem to think that I followed Dr Patankar's line of thought literally. While I did this quite unconsciously, Sir's teachings have surely shaped my opinions and knowledge of literature and language in innumerable ways.

Compared to my limited acquaintance with my mother tongue, my ignorance of the vast treasure-trove of Marathi was and is truly staggering and yet the planets in the zodiac were more than generous to me in the matter of my vernacular work. There was enough vocabulary in that mine called the brain to write one novel and two plays. The wonderful thing is that the more you tap into the deep bowels of the mind, the more gold you discover. But I also have to confess that if I didn't find a word when I knocked on my head for help, I instantly ran to Veerkar's English–Marathi dictionary. The fact is I race with as much alacrity to the English dictionary and thesaurus.

~

I've already mentioned at the start of this introduction that I started writing *Seven Sixes Are Forty-Three* only because I didn't think things through. Now I am about to contradict myself. Every writer perforce seeks his own path and each one has his own internalized set of rules. I don't know about tomorrow, but to this day, as far as my writing's concerned, I haven't been able to divorce myself from acute self-consciousness. Philosophy, sociology, research or painting are not my chosen fields. My genetic coding is that of a storyteller. I like to think that a storyteller is but an extremely sensitive medium. Egotism or self-absorption and storytelling are deadly enemies.

The sole focus in the novel the writer is working on has to be on the characters in it, the ups and downs in their lives, the intricate intermingling of their relationships, and where they reach by the end of their story. Obviously the choice of words, style, tone, humour are very much part of the endeavour. Anything and everything beyond the framework of the novel is extraneous and a distraction. Only when an author is able to create characters who are antithetical to his temperament with as much fidelity and sensitivity as those who figure in his comfort zone and with whom his sympathies lie, will they come alive.

Needless to say, in my imagined world, content dictates form, style and pitch. The choice of language as also the internal dynamics depend on the characters, the context and the situations they find themselves in. In the laws of writing which I had framed for myself very early on, there is no room to show off how talented I am, my flair for fancy language or my capacity for wordplay; or to shove in all my research because I want to impress the reader.

Here is the eternal paradox of art. The painter, sculptor, writer, in short, the artist is considered the creator. But if you don't let your characters breathe or allow them to lead their own lives while you assume the role of the overall controlling intelligence that infuses the work, what you will get are not living, flesh-and-blood characters but puppets.

When talking of *Seven Sixes* there's at least one point that is incontrovertible. The telling of the story, the technique and the language are totally cinematic. In my family, we didn't watch too many movies. What I saw were primarily the imports from Hollywood but almost no Hindi movies. During the 1950s and '60s, even Hollywood films used jump-cuts and flashbacks sparingly. The French New Wave directors of the 1960s, Jean-Luc Godard (*Breathless*), François Truffaut (*The 400 Blows*), and others, broke the mould of linear narrative with jump-cuts, freeze frames and other avant-garde techniques. Mexican director Alejandro González Iñárritu took it to a new level with his film *Amores Perros* by interweaving three parallel stories with rapid switches from one to the other and lightning jump-cuts. All three plots raced at breakneck speeds. They criss-crossed each other, moving from one track to the next, in what appeared to be an utterly chaotic and delirious fashion till they reached the finish line.

What became clear in retrospect was that the script-writer, the director and editor were in total control and masterminding every move. The whole film had been elaborately choreographed and it was only when the action zoomed towards the end that you got the whole picture and everything fell in place. And you had a different kind of film experience.

I wrote *Saat Sakkam* between the period 1967 and '74. It was written thirty years before *Amores Perros* was released. Unlike the three tracks in the movie, *Seven Sixes* had at least ten or eleven parallel tracks. I could then understand why many readers at the time would have found the going tough after reading the first few chapters. Isn't it curious that when reading a mystery where the author goes to great lengths to deliberately plant misleading and false clues, readers are more than happy to hang in there till they discover who the murderer is on the last page? I can only hope that the current generation, brought up on a diet of the Bourne series and other breathlessly intercut action-films, will take *Seven Sixes* in their stride and enjoy the fragmented ride with its mercurial changes of mood and ups and downs.

There were endless discussions and debates amongst critics whether *Saat Sakkam Trechalis* could be called a novel at all. Their main grouse was that the shifts and switches left one confused. 'Why can't Nagarkar write a simple, linear story?' was the question they asked again and again. The second debate was whether the main language could be called Marathi at all. (In this context, Jayant Dalvi wrote in his monthly column 'Thun Thun Pal' for *Lalit* magazine: 'We hear Kiran Nagarkar's *Saat Sakkam* is being translated into English. But should it not be translated into Marathi first?') Other critics thought that the language of *Saat Sakkam* was quite unique and different from standard Marathi and some wondered why I didn't use this splintered and flexible language, style and technique in my later novels. My answer has been that I don't wish to repeat something simply because it has been successful. Each novel demands its own style and treatment.

I have no desire or itch to experiment for the sake of experimenting and novelty. But I do believe that experiments which lead to discovering something new must be tried in all fields. It was thanks to Virginia Woolf's *To the Lighthouse* and *Mrs Dalloway* that we came to understand how the most unconnected or incoherent things get linked up in the most natural fashion and become what was called the stream of consciousness. Mumbai is not a one or even a five-ring circus. It is a circus which has twenty, thirty or more likely fifty rings. Chaos is its element and it thrives on it. It was my endeavour to capture the spirit of this mad city which survives 24/7 on adrenaline. And that was the reason I felt the need to evolve an altogether new technique and treatment. We realize much later in the novel that right from page one, the narrator Kushank is talking to a character called 'you'. The irony is that 'you' has vanished from his life a long while back. Does one ever stop talking to someone just because he or she has disappeared from one's life?

It is the bounden duty of a critic after studying a work of art closely to declare whether it's trashy, demanding, best left unread, haunting or just plain knock-out good and a 'must-read'. It's only on the strength of a careful reading of a novel, for instance, that he can say what the book is about, its central theme, point of view and its ethical axis. He must be able to substantiate the why and wherefore of these conclusions and back them up with proof from the text itself. While doing an extensive and in-depth critique of the work, he must cite the principles of aesthetics that he's applying. For me, one of the most important aspects of analysing a work rests on the primacy and fidelity to the text itself. Deconstruction and other schools may differ radically at times on this point to the extent that the decoding may be done without reference to the written word. In my book of norms, the reader–critic has to base what he has to say on the evidence within the work itself as the touchstone of any work of art and not on the prejudices and predilections of the reader. Surely you too have asked the question every once in a while whether the book reviewed by the critic is different from the one written by the author. There is, however, a wrinkle that cannot be ignored. If the novel is recondite or dense, it is more than understandable if different critics may not only see the work differently but reach irreconcilable conclusions. What happens fairly often though is that the critic has not paid attention and done a cursory reading and has a skewed perception of the novel.

Let me take an example from *Saat Sakkam* itself. 'What difference does it make?' is a sentence that crops up time and again in the novel. The character who is referred to as 'you' in the book poses it repeatedly. Kushank's answer is emphatically the same every time. 'It does, it does, it does; it makes a huge difference'. It's only at the very end when Kushank is in the throes of agony after having been bludgeoned, beaten and tortured that he recalls the question that 'you' had asked so many times: 'What difference does it make'. 'It was not a question. Only the certainty of a full stop. Then blackness and no more pain. Was it hours or days of unconsciousness? All I know is that it was a time without pain, without myself.'

If at the very end of that episode Kushank had not felt a sense of utter despair, the whole novel would have been proven to be false. *Seven Sixes* has many devastating, tragic and helpless incidents and situations and several Marathi and English critics at the time claimed that *Seven Sixes* was a novel about alienation, extreme pessimism and without light. They didn't just stop there, they said the protagonist Kushank was a cold fish, indifferent to whatever happened around him. Whether *Saat Sakkam* is a single track-and-themed work or is it that the critics had single-track minds can only be decided by the reader. But how does one explain the deliberate and selective ignoring of entire chunks of the novel? How come the ebullient spirit, the mad humour, the energy and vibrancy, the intensity and velocity of the narrative which were highlighted by other critics were completely missed or denied by these readers? Aren't the words, the treatment, the ambience and the events, the interrelationships, the tone and tenor, the most important factors when judging a work of literature? Even when the situations are at times ghastly, doesn't the outrageous black humour make it well-nigh impossible to keep a straight face? One would be singularly opaque and dull not to notice that Kushank is an extraordinarily greedy man. Since his desire to live every moment is so insatiable, there's no telling how Kushank will react to any situation. When you talk of the human animal, is it remotely possible not to be confronted by internal and eternal contradictions?

Many critics pilloried me for the three quotations [by M.P. Rege, Bhau Padhye and R.B. Patankar] on the front and back covers of the novel. They accused me of shamelessly promoting myself and self-aggrandizement. One of the critics knocked me down by saying that while my name stood for a ray of light, I was busy pretending I was the sun itself. It might be worthwhile asking whether this was just a pithy comment or was there a bit of envy in it? Oddly enough, when the same critics buy books by foreign authors and read them, they have no problem seeing four or five pages of quotes and blurbs. Marathi critics must definitely prefer double standards, one for foreign writers and another for local ones.

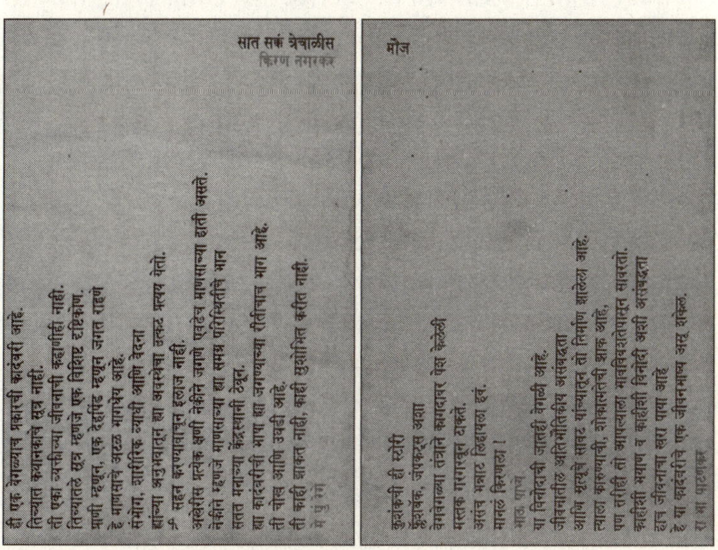


Arun Kolatkar designed the cover of *Saat Sakkam Trechalis* for Mauj Prakashan

The curious thing is that when my publisher, S.P. Bhagwat, decided to publish the book, he said he was game for a cover in colour. I immediately gave the good news to Arun Kolatkar, who was my friend and working partner at the advertising company where the two of us worked as a creative team, and requested him to visualize and design it. Unfortunately, after the job was finished, S.P., or Shri or Pu as he was known, said there was no money for the cover in colour. That's why it was decided to do a typographical cover and I had to run to Dr Patankar, Prof Rege and the controversial Marathi author Bhau Padhye.

Apart from the kind of hypocrisy that comes naturally to so many of us, the critics kept arguing and debating about what kind of creature *Saat Sakkam* was. There was no storyline in it. Was it a novel, a collection of short stories, or was it a mongrel of some sort? Everything else like – what is this creature trying to tell us, why is the author using such unusual language and form, what is the nature of the humour in it and why is it so different – all these question were secondary or, worse, irrelevant as far as the critics were concerned. The most important thing for them was the label. Unless they were able to stick it to the text they were reading, it was impossible for them to proceed. You might ask the question whether the task of criticism is to explore and come to grips with the meaning, content and the whole texture of the work of art or to find a label? Whether the critique of a work should concern itself with the quotes and blurbs on the cover or with the work itself? Needless to say there was no getting away from the fact that their obsession with secondary and banal matters foxed me and I even began to wonder whether I had completely misunderstood the function and purpose of the act of literary creation and criticism. What is marvellous though is that Arun's cover is still as fresh and powerful as it was then.

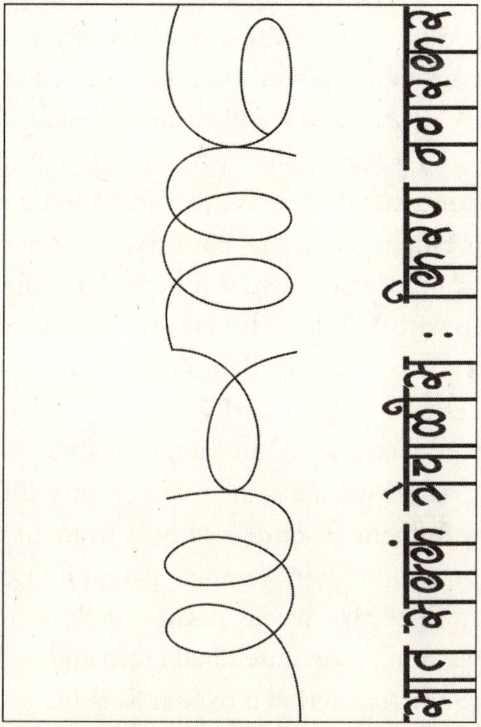

Prabhakar Kolte designed the cover for the book's fortieth edition

Now I am about to make a rather odd observation. I'll never be able to repay the debt I owe to *Saat Sakkam*. My first reason is that it drew me back to Marathi. Truth to tell, it taught me that every language is priceless. My new-found love for Marathi did not reduce my crush on English by an iota. But one thing became crystal clear. Just because you are married to one language doesn't mean you have to divorce it when you take up with another language. Not just one, you can carry on torrid affairs in public with as many others tongues as you want. Do you remember that song from *Mughal-e-Azam* which Anarkali sang: '*Pyar kiya to darna kya?*' (What's to fear when you fall in love?)? It's my misfortune that despite the fact that there are twenty-four major languages in our country, I know only two. If I had had any sense I would have had a really intimate relationship with Hindi. Why Hindi alone, I would have made sizzling love to Tamil, Bengali, Malayalam, Kashmiri, French, German, Italian and several other languages – indeed I would have put Don Juan to shame.

Looking back from a distance of over forty-three years I realize how influential some leitmotifs from *Saat Sakkam* have been in my life. For example, 'patent nonsense'. The reason why these two words occupy such an important corner of my mind is because I had taken an incident from my own life and transferred it to *Saat Sakkam*. It was about a little girl called Okhon from abroad whom I had met at my neighbour's and had befriended.

This is how that episode reads in the novel.

*Months later, after Okhon had gone abroad, back to her father, I sat playing snakes and ladders with Shatlaj's six-year-old son, Arshad. He was winning, but that didn't seem to make him happy.*

*'Hey, solemn face, what is the matter?'*

*'Nothing.'*

*'Come on, tell me.'*

*A few more minutes, and he did.*

*'My birthday is eight months away. How can I wait for so long?' he wailed.*

*'Now that is tragic.'*

*'You are laughing at me,' he accused.*

*'No, I'm thinking about the problem.'*

*I looked for him after school the next day.*

*'Two solutions. One, we name every month the same – June. Then you will have twelve birthdays in a year. The only problem here is, if all months are called June, Aai and Baba and me and all your friends are going to miss out on their birthdays. Now, the second solution – twelve days will make a month. In that case June will come around thirty times a year. And everybody else can have their birthdays too. That's a happy thought, isn't it?'*

*He chewed over that for a few minutes, his eyes on his shoelaces. Then he looked up with a big grin on his face. 'Kushank, you are brilliant.'*

*'Thank you.'*

*Arshad dreamed of the new calendar arrangements all day.*

*'And wouldn't it be lovely if it rained Coca-Cola on my birthday? And Gold Spot on Baba's and choco-cone on Aai's and raspberry shake on yours?' he cried ecstatically.*

*I liked that. When I got home, I wrote to Okhon to inform her of Arshad's and my plans, and of the formation of the new society to spread happiness in the world. Asking her for advice and ideas.*

*A month later her father answered, in his immaculate writing.*

> *Dear Kushank,*
>
> *Forgive me for not answering your letter to Okhon earlier. I've been busy with one thing or another.*
>
> *Okhon is growing up in the Western world, in a society where people have realized the primacy of logic and of rational thought. In the circumstances, it is hardly surprising that Okhon finds your and Arshad's ideas nothing but patent nonsense. She sends her love.*
>
> *Regards...*

That letter threw me. It's not new to me to behave like a fool. For a minute or two we lose our way and become sensible and wise. And then soon afterwards we find our way back, and revert to being foolish again. Rarely had anything made me feel so totally irrelevant. Without being given even a moment's notice, I was informed right into the very core of my being that I had become a stranger to the world and its realities. For the first time in my life I felt old. And even more desperate than when I was confronted by the crippled daughter of my friend Aaroti, Prutha. How come, even when we are exposed all our lives to patent nonsense, we still can't identify what patent nonsense is? Have we become so blind, blasé and blunted that we would call philosophical commentaries in the form of innocent yet loaded fantasies like Alice-in-Wonderland patent nonsense?

Hundreds of thousands of children suffer from acute malnutrition in India alone; thousands of our farmers commit suicides because of droughts and unpaid loans to banks; God alone knows how many millions have died in the Middle East since George Bush attacked Iraq on the false pretence that Saddam Hussein had weapons of mass destruction; every single day the Israelis continue to commit their unspeakable crimes in the Gaza strip and take over Palestinian lands to build Jewish settlements; how many hundreds of thousands are killed and displaced, all in the name and honour of God … the list in never-ending. Ah, and yet with what fortitude and infinite patience we, the more fortunate denizens of this planet, watch this 'patent nonsense'.

Along with patent nonsense, the other phrase that came to be one of my central preoccupations was '*Kya phark padta hai?*' or what difference does it make? Let's look at that proposition a little more closely. At the beginning of 2017, the PM of India along with the chief minister of the state of Maharashtra launched a project to put up the statue of Chhatrapati Shivaji Maharaj on an artificial island in the

Arabian Sea off the coast of Mumbai. The statue will be twice the size of the Statue of Liberty and will cost three thousand five hundred crores, not including cost overruns. What difference will it make, you may well ask, if we got together and opposed this insane project because no one is going to listen to us anyway? Similarly, you may well ask what's the point of opposing the Kundankulam nuclear plant, especially since the current regime has whispered the development mantra in the ears of all of us Indians. What difference will it make if we fight against it since we are bound to fail?

For one thing, no worthwhile task should be begun with a negative mantra, especially when it is chanted by hard-core pessimists like me. Who would have believed that Gandhiji and his freedom fighters would be able to throw out the mighty British Empire on the basis of a non-violent, civil disobedience movement? There's another factor that's just as crucial. Before starting out on any task, our first thought is to check whether we will be successful or not. But this mindset is deadly. Our decision should never be dependent on the binary of success or failure. All that matters is whether what we are seeking is ethically the right thing to do or not, regardless of the success or failure of the endeavour.

While there is endless talk of 'development' in our country, what exactly do we mean by progress? How do we calculate the cost of human life? If human life on this planet has to be saved as our first priority, we must be willing to make the incredibly complex, difficult and demanding changes in our lifestyles to drastically reduce the carbon emissions without any delay.

I'll tell you what difference each and every action of ours makes to mother earth and the future. It's as straightforward as the difference between life and death for mankind. Which is why ethical choices matter so much. If our leaders and those of other nations talk big and have no intention of honouring their words, the burden of coercing them to act for the benefit of mankind rests upon your and my shoulders. It is an incredible responsibility but shirk it and it will be absolutely clear that you and I murdered our children and mother earth.

*What difference does it make?* Just five words. And look how they've encircled the whole of our earth in forty-three years.

At the very end of my afterword to my novel *Cuckold*, I had said, 'As for the rest, storytellers are liars. We all know that.' There's no denying that there are autobiographical elements in *Seven Sixes*. (Show me a novel that doesn't?) But in one particular respect, I was blessed. I had begun to lie unstintingly from my first novel itself. That raises a few questions? Does my mendacity grab the reader? How effective is it? The question is: how good am I as a liar? Can you hear the heartbeat of the men, women and children that I pull out from the magician's bag of tricks, which is of course nothing else but the imagination? Do they blunder and fall and regain their balance like you and me? Like you and me do they also keep doing something even when they know that it's wrong? Do they sometimes reach such a point of despair that they wish to do away with life? Does the reader find an abundance of humanity in their love, rage, hate, pettiness and goodness of heart … this is something only the readers of *Seven Sixes* and my other novels can decide.

In the end all that the author can do is build half the bridge. The other half has to be built by the reader.

Khuda Hafeez.

*A version of this essay was written in Marathi for the fortieth edition of* Saat Sakkam Trechalis. *Translated and adapted by the author*

**Kiran Nagarkar** is one of India's most highly regarded writers. His critically acclaimed novel *Cuckold* won the Sahitya Akademi Award in 2000. Nagarkar received Germany's highest civilian award, the Order of Merit, in 2012. Both the Tata Literature Live! and the Chandigarh Literary Fest felicitated him with Lifetime Achievement awards. His novels have been translated into German, French, Italian and Spanish. *Saat Sakkam Trechalis* won the H.N. Apte Award for best debut novel in 1974.

**Shubha Slee** was born in 1937 and studied at Agra University. She moved to Australia in 1964 and unexpectedly passed away early in 1980.

HARPERPERENNIAL

Harper Perennial presents special editions of its finest books in translation

*Apradhini*
Shivani
Translated from the Hindi by Ira Pande

*Avasthe*
U.R. Ananthamurthy
Translated from the Kannada by Narayan Hegde

*Blue Is Like Blue*
Vinod Kumar Shukla
Translated from the Hindi by Arvind Krishna Mehrotra and Sara Rai

*Diary of a Malayali Madman*
N. Prabhakaran
Translated from the Malayalam by Jayasree Kalathil

*Farewell, Mahatma*
Devibharathi
Translated from the Tamil by N. Kalyan Raman

*The Golden Gandhi Statue from America*
Subimal Misra
Translated from the Bengali by V. Ramaswamy

*A Name for Every Leaf*
Ashok Vajpeyi
Translated from the Hindi by Rahul Soni

*Moustache*
S. Hareesh
Translated from the Malayalam by Jayasree Kalathil

*Seven Sixes Are Forty-Three*
Kiran Nagarkar
Translated from the Marathi by Shubha Slee

*Shameless*
Taslima Nasreen
Translated from the Bengali by Arunava Sinha

HARPERPERENNIAL

*Age of Frenzy*
Mahabaleshwar Sail
Translated from the Konkani by Vidya Pai

*A Life Incomplete*
Nanak Singh
Translated from the Punjabi by Navdeep Suri

*Mohanaswamy*
Vasudhendra
Translated from the Kannada by Rashmi Terdal

*The Music of Solitude*
Krishna Sobti
Translated from the Hindi by Vasudha Dalmia

*No Presents Please*
Jayant Kaikini
Translated from the Kannada by Tejaswini Niranjana

*A Preface to Man*
Subhash Chandran
Translated from the Malayalam by Fathima E.V.

*The Secret Garland*
Andal
Translated from the Tamil by Archana Venkatesan

*Shala*
Milind Bokil
Translated from the Marathi by Vikrant Pande

*The Weary Generations*
Abdullah Hussein
Translated from the Urdu by the author

*Written in Tears*
Arupa Patangia Kalita
Translated from the Assamese by Ranjita Biswas